Doubling Down

CARI Z
L.A. WITT

ISBN: 9781082204999

Copyright Information

Doubling Down
First Edition.
Copyright © 2019 Cari Z & L.A. Witt

Cover Art by Lori Witt
Editors: Leta Blake & Jules Robin

ISBN: 9781082204999

DOUBLING DOWN

CARI Z & L.A. WITT

Chapter One
Leo

"You can trust the US Marshals," they said.

"WITSEC is completely secure," they said. *"And hey, it's better than waiting for trial in a jail cell, right, Mr. Nicolosi?"*

Riiight. Three gunfights, two kidnappings, and one car chase later, the sole thing the Marshals had going for them at this point was my personal shadow, Deputy Marshal Rich Cody. The only other good ones who'd been assigned to my protective detail last week—although, my God, it felt like months ago—were either dead or still in the hospital.

And the bad ones? Hopefully dead or discovered, but in case they weren't, Rich and I were taking no chances. We were on the road—again—heading back to Colorado. In fact, we were *in* Colorado at this point, I was pretty sure. You couldn't see the mountains from Kansas, could you? Or had that been Nebraska? Fuck it—the middle of this country was still mostly a big, bland blur to me.

I'd been driving for around eight hours, and by this point my injured hand had basically cramped into a claw.

If I didn't stop soon, I wouldn't be able to hold onto the wheel. I hated to wake Rich, though. Neither of us had had enough sleep lately, and he was running on even less than I was.

I glanced at him out of the corner of my eye, hunched against the sidewall with the passenger seat reclined back as far as it would go, and wondered for probably the hundredth time what the hell I was still doing with him.

I'd originally come to the Chicago District Attorney with a deal—complete immunity in exchange for information that would take down the Grimaldi crime family. I'd been a soldier for them—not highly regarded, since I was only half Italian and not at all straight, but still useful. Useful until word got out that I was sleeping with the Grimaldi family's eldest son and heir, Tony. The don had ordered a hit on his own child, and the assassins had tried to kill me at the same time.

I'd been lucky, I guess. I'd survived, escaped, and decided that it wasn't enough to just go after Matteo Grimaldi, Tony's younger brother and the person who'd outed us to his father in the first place. I was going to take on all of them. I was going to screw this family into the ground so hard they'd end up six feet under. I had the information to do it, too—I was the brains behind their gambling operations, their investments, their shell companies and hedge funds. I knew where all the financial bodies were buried. I would send them all to prison for the rest of their miserable fucking lives—except for Matteo, who was going to pay *with* his life—and vanish like smoke on a breeze.

At least, that had been the initial plan. One giant clusterfuck of unfortunate events later, Matteo was in federal custody, a bunch of dirty law enforcement was being identified, and the only person I trusted to guard me leading up to the trial was Rich. That was a lot of pressure to put on a man who'd already been to hell and back, and I didn't just mean with me, either. Rich Cody had issues on issues, scars papering over other scars. He should be on a tropical island somewhere right now, drinking fruity drinks and getting his head on straight, not playing bodyguard for the bastard son of a murdered mafioso.

Rich grunted in his sleep and twisted a bit, turning his face toward me. An enormous purple bruise marred the skin over his right cheek—I didn't even remember how he'd gotten that one, but it was one of many. There was a cut at the edge of his hairline and another tiny one bisecting his left eyebrow—flying plasterboard, maybe? He was still stupidly good looking, with short, sandy brown hair, a stubbled jaw that I wanted him to rub against me until it left marks, and sharp hazel eyes that I was just as glad were closed right now. I didn't need Rich to see me stealing glances at him like this even when I wasn't supposed to be driving. I felt like I wanted to duct tape him to my side, while simultaneously wishing he was as far away as possible. You only had to look at us to know that I was trouble to be around.

We'd been lucky, so damn lucky, to survive that last firefight. Be prepared—Boy Scout motto, and Rich's as well. My vest had taken two bullets, one to my shoulder and another just to the right of my spine, and to say they ached would be a gross understatement. I needed a painkiller and a pit stop if I was going to continue driving.

Five miles down the road, the fluorescent lights of a gas station split the seemingly endless horizon. I pulled to a stop in front of a pump and, reluctantly, reached out to wake Rich up.

"Hey." I tapped him on the shoulder and pulled my hand back fast—I never knew with Rich if he was going to come out of a solid sleep lucid or swinging, too full of bad memories to keep them contained.

This time, thankfully, he opened his eyes without throwing any punches first. "Hey. Ow, *fuck*." He straightened out and twisted his head from side to side, groaning. "Jesus Christ."

"Kind of feels like you got into a fight with a wrecking ball and lost, huh?"

He grimaced. "More like I got into a fight with a dozen guys and somehow won."

I pointed at the tiny convenience store attached to the gas station. "I'm getting Advil, a Red Bull, and Doritos. You want anything?"

"The Advil. And water."

I shook my head and undid my seat belt, wincing as I flexed my hand to push the button. "You need to learn to live large, Rich."

He grimaced. "I'm looking forward to being off the grid for a while, honestly. Less living large, more living safe."

He had a point. Which was why he and I were back in Colorado instead of camped in some hotel room in Chicago. The Windy City was where the trial of Matteo Grimaldi would take place, but the DA was more willing to cut me some slack now regarding where I waited things out. I wasn't the star witness against the Grimaldis anymore, since we'd fucking let fucking Matteo fucking live.

"You sure Smitty is going to be okay with this?" I asked.

"I think he feels cheated that we didn't stay long enough for anything to go down last time."

"He's a goddamn idiot."

Rich just grinned. "Yeah, maybe. Go get your Doritos, Leo."

I left the keys in the car as I headed for the store, checking my reflection in the window before I walked in. No stray blood, no hideous contusions I should have been icing—good enough. The door jingled as I walked in, and the bored cashier behind the register glanced my way. "Hey."

"Hey." Nice, simple, one-word interactions. I needed more of those in my life.

I used the bathroom, then splashed enough water on my face to almost drown me. My eyes felt gritty after so long staring at the road, and my hair was so greasy the water didn't even penetrate it. I needed a shower. I needed a bed. I needed decent food and a stable WiFi connection.

I would get everything I needed once we got to Smitty's missile silo. I hoped Rich was right about Smitty. He was a nice guy, for a recluse, but that didn't mean he wanted us invading his space again so soon after we'd left it the first time. I didn't understand how Rich could feel so confident we'd be welcome—he'd said something about Marines and sticking together, but I'd bled for plenty of people who would just as soon stab me in the back these days. I hoped he knew his friend as well as he thought he did.

I browsed the aisles of the store—all two of them— for snacks and meds, grabbed drinks out of the fridge at the back, and paid in cash for all of it plus the gas Rich was pumping into our stolen car.

Really got to trade that, I mused as I rejoined him, tearing open the Doritos and cramming Cool Ranch goodness into my mouth. I held the bag out to Rich as he put the pump away, the car radio on and blaring behind us.

"No thanks." He did grab the water and the bottle of Advil, though, and stopped me when I went to get into the driver's seat. "We're only five hours out. I can drive us the rest of the way there." He glanced down at my bandaged hand and didn't say anything, but then again, he didn't need to.

"Okay." I sat down on the passenger side and chugged half my drink, along with a couple of pills. "Ugh." I glared at the radio. "Why are we listening to NPR? How old are you?" I went to change the station, but Rich caught my hand.

"It's the news roundup. They might mention something about the situation in Chicago."

Oh. Well, okay, that would be interesting. "Hopefully

if they're going to do it, they'll do it soon."

We got back on the road, and I sat through ten minutes of stock market analysis, a litany of bullshit the president was going to try and strongarm into law, a depressing story about North Korea, and finally—

"With the trial of the decade now beginning preliminary hearings in Chicago, federal law enforcement officials are worried that they aren't moving fast enough to secure key players in the Grimaldi crime family, including the patriarch himself, Lorenzo Grimaldi. After an unsuccessful raid on his home earlier today, police are widening the search but say that there's no way of knowing for sure where the mafia don and his men might be hiding. His son Matteo, meanwhile, is in protective custody ahead of a trial that promises to provide a dramatic, and even sensational, look into the world of organized crime. In Cuba this week—"

Rich turned off the radio. "So, he's running. That's not surprising."

"No, it's not." What was surprising was that the feds were behind the ball again when it came to doing anything about it. You'd think they'd have learned when I almost got shot to pieces in the hotel room that *they set up* for me, but no. "You have any idea where he'll go?"

I considered it, ignoring the way my hands were suddenly shaking. Probably just the caffeine hitting my system. "I doubt he'll make it to Europe, or even try. Too much security to get through, and I've frozen all of his bank accounts, so he can't afford to bribe everyone the way he'd need to. Maybe he'll head for Canada. Maybe he'll lay low in Chicago somewhere, although I doubt it."

"You think he'll try to contact Gianna?"

I shrugged. "Hard to say. He never really cared all that much about her, but since she's the only one of his kids who's both alive and not in federal custody…maybe."

Rich drove in silence for a few minutes, then asked, "You think he'll try to come for you?"

Ah. That was the million-dollar question, wasn't it? "Papa Grimaldi is in his seventies now," I said slowly, thinking over the odds. "He was already passing most of the day-to-day operations to Tony before he had him killed. He's tired, he wants to retire. But he's also old school. You mess with him, he makes you dead. You mess with him the way I have?" My mouth twisted in the closest thing I had in me to a smile. "He probably wants me fucking annihilated, and he'll want to see it happen. I give us fifty-fifty odds that he either finds a place to lay low or says 'to hell with it' and tries to track us down."

Rich didn't look my way, but I could tell he was frowning. "Fifty-fifty."

"Yeah."

"Those aren't great odds."

"No. No, they aren't." I held my breath, waiting for him to say *I can't do this*, or *I have family to think of*. Both of those would be completely reasonable excuses for cutting and running. It was too much to expect him to stay with me through this, even though—God damn it, I wanted him to. I selfishly, greedily wanted him to. But now was the right time for him to leave, while he could still be safe.

Instead of letting me down gently, though, he looked over, the tension in his face smoothing into a smile. "Good thing we're headed to Smitty's, then. Nobody's better at beating the odds than him."

Chapter Two
Rich

My old war buddy, Smitty, was nothing if not paranoid. Sometimes I wondered if it was his time in the Corps that had made him that way, or if he'd just been like that from the start. I mean, it takes a certain kind of person to see a heavily fortified missile silo in the middle of nowhere and hang a *Home Sweet Home* sign outside. Out of sight and off the grid suited him just fine.

And with the goddamned mafia breathing down our necks, it suited Leo and me just fine too.

The sun was long gone when, using a burner phone we'd picked up somewhere in Nebraska, I texted Smitty to let him know we were getting close. Whether it was my situation with Leo or some of that warzone past creeping into Smitty's mind, I couldn't say, but he didn't let us drive all the way in this time. Instead, we parked down a service road, well out of sight from the main road. As "main" as any road could be out in the middle of Bumfuck, Nowhere, anyway. Half a mile from there, we found him

15

and his battered old truck sitting on the soft, grassy shoulder.

I pulled up, driver's side door to driver's side door, and rolled down the window. "Don't want something this shiny in your driveway?" I tapped the wheel of the Buick we'd stolen.

"Does it have your name on the title?"

"Uh…"

"That's what I thought." Smitty shook his head. "I don't need the cops sniffing around for a stolen car." He gestured at the passenger seat with the silver hook that had replaced his right hand. "Ditch that thing and get in."

Leo and I exchanged glances. Then I pulled up a few feet, nosed off the road, and killed the engine.

"I don't like this," he said under his breath, as if Smitty might hear us. "We'll be up there with no vehicle of our own."

I looked at him in the pale glow from Smitty's headlights. "Got any better ideas?"

He frowned. After a moment, he sighed, opened the door with a huff, and cursed as he got out. I paused to look skyward and mutter, "Can I please catch a break?" before I too got out.

It wasn't like I didn't understand his reservations or his frustration with basically everything right now. We were both tired of taking extreme precautions, like ditching cars every couple hundred miles and stealing new ones to throw off anyone who might be tailing us. Or using only our meager reserves of cash for food and burner phones because even though my accounts were no longer frozen, it was a safe bet they were being tracked by the Marshals, the Grimaldis, and for all I knew, probably the fucking Reptilians.

It was exhausting, and I was no more impressed than he was about ditching our current car, riding up the mountain with Smitty, and hunkering down with absolutely no wheels of our own.

I wasn't going to put my friend in any more danger than we already were just by showing up at his doorstep, though. Parking another stolen car in his driveway was a liability.

We collected what little we'd brought with us—mostly food and a couple sets of extra clothes—and tossed it in the back of Smitty's truck. Then we climbed into the cab. I took the middle even though Leo probably would have fit more comfortably. He was running on fumes right now, and I had a feeling that making him sit between two elbows might make him snap.

Smitty put the truck in gear and headed back toward the main road. "You two look like hell."

Leo shot him a look. I put a hand on Leo's thigh and squeezed gently. He scowled but then shifted his gaze to the window.

To Smitty I said, "It's been a rough couple of days."

"Yeah? So what's the situation right now?"

I'd only given him the barest story over the phone— we needed to lay low again. He hadn't pushed. No one understood the need for opsec like a Marine, and there was no telling who'd been listening in. There'd been an unspoken agreement that I'd tell him everything I could once we were sure no one was eavesdropping.

Like…now.

Except just thinking about running through everything that was happening made me want to pass out right there in the truck. I was still sore as fuck where a couple of rounds had hit my Kevlar vest. My neck and back hurt from battling it out in Matteo Grimaldi's stronghold, from driving, and from the sporadic hours of sleep I'd grabbed in the passenger seat while Leo had taken the wheel. Everything had gone down over the course of a few days—not even a week—and I was drained like I hadn't been since one of those grueling missions Smitty and I had run back in our combat days.

"Listen." My voice sounded fatigued even to me. "I'll

give you the full sitrep once we're in the silo and Leo and I have had some sleep. Right now, I can't even think straight."

Smitty glanced at me, his one good eye narrowed with *you better not hold out on me, fucker.*

I wouldn't. I trusted him with my life—that was why Leo and I were here for the second time in a handful of days—and I'd tell him everything he needed to know. Just…not right this minute.

The winding road seemed ten times longer than it had been before, and it felt like ages before Smitty finally turned at the hand-painted KEEP THE FUCK OUT sign and started up the steep, dirt-and-gravel driveway. Several long minutes later, he pulled up beside the tiny log cabin and parked.

"All right." He shut off the engine. "We're here."

"Thank God," I muttered. Just being here, within spitting distance of an actual bed that was actually safe, made the exhaustion dig even deeper. At this rate, I was seriously tempted to just lie down on the rug covering the entrance to the missile silo and fall asleep there.

But no, we needed to get inside. I wouldn't feel safe until we were well and truly hidden inside Smitty's fortified mountain fortress.

Smitty got out, but Leo didn't move. I braced myself for some snide comments about… Hell, this was Leo. Stressed-out, hungry, sleep-deprived Leo. He could have a snide comment about anything from our situation to the leaf snagged under the right windshield wiper.

But when I turned, he didn't have a comment waiting for me—he was asleep.

Cautiously, I nudged him with my elbow. "Hey."

No response.

Still careful, I touched his leg and shook gently. "Leo?"

Nothing.

"Hey." I shook a bit harder. "Leo. We're here.

Wake—"

All at once, he gasped and grabbed my wrist, eyes flying open.

"Hey! Hey! It's me." I nodded past him. "We're here."

He looked around, blinking a few times and obviously disoriented. Then his gaze landed on the tiny cabin, and some of the tension in his expression eased. His rigid body relaxed against the seat.

"Come on." I gave his leg a squeeze. "Soon as we're inside, we can crash for real."

"Thank God." He fumbled with the door handle, then apparently remembered he still had on his seat belt, and unclipped that too. He got out, and I followed, and we gathered our things from the back of the truck before following Smitty into the cabin.

Smitty locked the door behind us—had he *added* a couple of locks in the days since I'd been here last?—and then opened the hatch in the floor. "Elevator's working now," he offered once we were through it and into the room below, pointing toward the door opposite the stairs we'd taken last time.

"An elevator?" Leo tried to glare, but he was too tired for it to really come off. "You couldn't have fired it up *last* time we were here?"

"It's not like I use it when I'm alone, and it takes a while to get working." He led us into the dusty-smelling car. "Why waste the energy?"

Leo rolled his eyes, and I put a hand on his back. "Sounds good," I said to Smitty. The ride down was noisy but smooth enough. Once we got to two floors above the lowest level, Smitty led the way out and showed us toward the guest rooms.

"It's up to you who gets what room." He shot me a sly grin. "Or you can share one. Ain't my business."

Leo and I exchanged glances, and I felt myself blush. Clearing my throat, I gestured at the room that had been mine last time. "We'll take that one."

Smitty nodded. "All right. You know where everything is." He clapped my shoulder. "Get some sleep, and then I want that sitrep."

"Got it. Thanks again, man."

"Any time."

Leo and I shuffled into the guest room. I took one look at the bed, and my legs almost dropped out from under me. I desperately needed a shower, but I wasn't even sure I could stay awake that long.

And hell, I wasn't even that gross. We'd both showered in the motel where we'd crashed before hitting the road, and that hadn't been all that long ago.

Fine. I'd sleep now, then shower.

Leo must have had the same idea—by the time I'd stripped down to my shorts, he'd done the same and was pulling back the covers.

Across the queen size bed, our eyes met, and he finally cracked a tired smile. Without speaking, we climbed in and got under the covers. I could count on one hand the number of times we'd shared a bed at this point, but we moved into the middle and cuddled up together—my body molded to Leo's back—as if we'd done this every night for years. He was pressed against some tender spots on my chest, and I was probably hitting a few on him too, but I didn't care, and he didn't seem to, either.

"It's good to be off the road." His words were slurred with fatigue.

"Yeah." I kissed the side of his neck and held him close to me. "Good to be someplace that's actually safe."

He let go of a long sigh and seemed to deflate in my arms. "Yeah. It is." He laced our fingers together and brought mine up to press a soft kiss to my knuckles. "Maybe we can actually sleep."

"Maybe." I ran my thumb alongside his. The warmth of his body against mine tried to wake up my comatose libido, but it wasn't happening. Not now. As much as I wanted him, I just had nothing left. "If I were a little less sore and a little less tired," I murmured into his hair, "we would so be fucking right now."

Leo didn't respond.

He was already asleep.

I woke up a couple of times. My eyes fluttered open and I looked around, realized it was still dark and I was still tired, and fell asleep again.

It wasn't until the third time that it occurred to me that we were a few stories underground. There were no windows—the light in the room was never going to change unless the apocalypse was upon us.

Feeling disoriented and maybe even a bit jetlagged, I blinked a few times. I was on my back now with Leo's head on my shoulder and his arm slung across my stomach. Careful not to disturb him, I reached for the bedside table where I'd left my phone. The movement stretched muscles that didn't want to be stretched, and when Leo sighed and shifted, his elbow grazed one of the angry bruises below my ribs. The sudden jolt of pain made me gasp, which in turn startled Leo awake.

"Shit. What's—what happened?" He sounded foggy and tired.

"Nothing." I patted his arm. "Just bumped one of my bruises."

"Oh fuck!" He jerked away like I'd shoved him. "You okay?"

"It's okay. Relax." I found his shoulder in the darkness and gave it a soft squeeze. "We're both covered in bruises—it's bound to happen."

He exhaled, and even though I couldn't see him, I could feel the tension leaving his body. He eased himself down onto the pillows beside me.

I reached for the bedside table again, felt around, and finally remembered I didn't *have* a phone anymore. Just a burner phone I'd turned off and left in the Buick's glove compartment.

There was an old alarm clock, though, and its glowing blue numbers read 2:22.

I blinked again. It was after two? Really?

And…*which* two?

I had to squint a few times before I finally made out the tiny *PM*.

Holy shit. We'd slept like…eighteen hours? Damn, so much for snapping awake at 0500 like I usually did.

"What time is it?" Leo muttered.

"After two." I gingerly sat up, gritting my teeth as my body protested anything that wasn't sleeping. "In the afternoon."

"Seriously?" Leo laughed softly. "Man, I haven't slept in like this in years. Feels pretty good."

I considered it, then chuckled too. "Yeah. It does feel pretty good." I eased myself back down and draped my arm over him, trying to remember where all his bruises were so I didn't touch them. The worst of them, anyway.

He slid a hand up my forearm. "Is it crazy that I really wish we could stay in bed and fool around, but I'm so sore I'd break your arm if you tried to turn me on?"

I laughed. "I don't think you have to worry about that." I leaned in closer and kissed his stubbled cheek. "Why don't we get a shower, go find something to eat, and recuperate for a while?"

"Sounds perfect." He kissed my lips lightly. Neither of us pushed for anything more. Sex was off the table, and we didn't need to subject each other to morning breath.

Leo was the first to actually get out of bed and—with some creaking and cursing—onto his feet, so he showered first. My own shower brought me far enough back to life that I actually considered going back into the bedroom and seeing if his had made him change his mind about screwing around, but then I reached for a towel and thought better of having sex any time soon. Yeah, I was awake, and no, I didn't feel quite so much like roadkill, but holy shit, I still hurt all over. Sex could wait. Damn it.

I stepped out of the shower, and as I carefully dried off, caught my reflection in the partially steamed-up mirror. I couldn't resist and wiped away the fog so I could get a better look.

Christ, I'd gotten lucky. The worst bruises on my chest and midsection were at that stage where they looked a hell of a lot worse than they were—angry purple with yellowish green halos. The blood had radiated away from the points of impact, making the marks silver-dollar sized instead of forty-five caliber or nine-mill. They looked and felt like hell, but the Kevlar had done its job. I couldn't complain.

I met my own gaze in the mirror. My face wasn't much better than my torso. I couldn't quite place where that smoky-looking bruise on my cheekbone had come from. For all I knew, I'd smacked the window while I was sleeping in the car. I had dark circles under my bloodshot eyes, and another bruise on my jaw warned me against shaving quite yet. I touched it carefully and flinched. Yep, shaving could wait, too.

In the bedroom, Leo was reclining on the bed in a pair of jeans and nothing else. Funny how even riddled with scrapes and bruises, he was hot. He'd been hot from day one, but now he had a bit of that action movie hero thing going on, and I was apparently losing my fucking mind because I was ogling my battered...partner? Friend? I didn't even know what to call him. Technically he was my witness, but things between us definitely weren't just professional anymore.

Especially not when you've been knocked in the head hard enough to be thinking he's hot with a bunch of bruises.

Oblivious to my brain doing weird somersaults, Leo thumbed through a wrinkled magazine he'd probably pulled from the stack on the dresser. *Guns & Ammo*, which somehow didn't surprise me.

"If you see something you like," I said, gesturing at the magazine, "Smitty probably has it or knows where to get it."

Leo laughed dryly. "Eh. I was never a big fan of guns." He tossed the magazine onto my side of the bed and laced his fingers behind his head. "Just wasn't a lot of reading material."

"Yeah, you probably won't find much of that here." I pulled on a clean pair of jeans. "I think he's got some Tom Clancy in the man cave, though."

Leo wrinkled his nose. "I'll pass." With a groan, he rolled to his feet. "He at least has good coffee, right?"

"If he doesn't, he's going to go get some."

"Damn right he is."

Unsurprisingly, Smitty did have some damn good coffee. There was nothing quite like battlefield swill to make a man determined to never drink another bad cup of coffee. Well, that and now that I thought about it, Smitty had spent a few months fucking a barista who worked just outside the base where we were stationed. If memory served, she'd turned him into one hell of a coffee snob. I'd ribbed him about it then. I could have kissed him for it now.

"So." Smitty sipped his own coffee and leaned against the counter. "About that sitrep."

I suppressed some curses. I was well-rested and really wanted to enjoy that feeling for a little while, but the man deserved to know what we were quite possibly bringing to his front door. So, I gave him the rundown of everything that had happened since we'd left the silo last time—the warehouse we'd pretty much blown to pieces, the shootout in Lake Geneva, the crown prince of the Grimaldi family being taken into custody.

"There's really no telling what will happen now," I said. "For all we know, Papa Grimaldi is going to shift gears away from Leo and focus all his energy on taking out Matteo before he testifies against the family."

"But the family is huge and has a lot of soldiers." Across from me, Leo sat back in his chair at Smitty's tiny kitchen table. "And they know I've got access to their finances. I'd be surprised if he didn't have a few dozen people looking for me. Or, well, us."

Smitty grunted before taking another swallow of coffee. "Why wouldn't they just move their money into other accounts? So it's out of your reach?"

Leo smiled evilly. "They can try."

Smitty's good eye widened. I suspected he was wondering how the hell Leo could be so confident, but computers and finances hadn't exactly been Smitty's college majors, so he was probably taking Leo at his word that he knew what he was doing. That was my approach, anyway.

Smitty put his coffee cup down and folded his arms, resting the hook on his opposite elbow. "Okay. And what's the plan now? Just hide out, or…?"

"Mostly," I said. "We, uh, hadn't really gotten further than that. Step one, keep our heads down. Step two…" I shook my head. "Not sure."

"Aside from you checking in with the Marshals and the DA," Leo said. "About me and Matteo appearing in court."

I nodded. "Yeah. I'll reach out soon, and we'll go from there."

Smitty stared at the floor for a long moment before he finally spoke. "You know, the odds of those fuckers finding you here are slim to none, but it might not be a bad idea to play this like the odds aren't in your favor."

Leo shifted his weight. "How do you figure?"

"We stock up on essentials," Smitty said. "Make sure we've got food, water, and ammunition." He paused, glancing first at Leo, and then looking pointedly at me. "And we bring in some backup."

"Backup?" Leo sputtered, eyes suddenly wide. "*Oh*, no. We're not bringing anyone else into—"

"Actually," I said, "Smitty might be right."

Leo gaped at me. "Are you insane?"

"Probably, but the thing is, we're basically in a corner. If anyone does catch up with us, our backs are against the wall." I shrugged. "It might not hurt to have some allies, you know?"

"Like who?" Leo nearly squeaked the words. "You want to call in the fucking Marshals or something?"

"No." I glanced at Smitty. "But the rest of our boys from the Corps would be here in a heartbeat if we asked."

Leo stared at both of us in horror. "Yeah, and up until a few days ago, you implicitly trusted the rest of the Marshals, too."

I fought the urge to roll my eyes. That would only piss him off. "These aren't just people wearing the same badge as me, okay? These are guys I've fought next to. I *know* them."

"And how do you know none of them have been compromised?" He showed his palms. "I get that they're your friends and war buddies. I get it. I do." Lowering his hands, he looked me right in the eye. "But the Marshals—and the Grimaldis who've infiltrated the Marshals—probably know about them too. How can you be sure none of them have been, I don't know, blackmailed? Threatened? You don't think one of these boys will turn on you if *the fucking mafia* threatens to murder their families or something?"

I swallowed. He had a point, and I couldn't argue with him. "I can't be sure," I said, barely whispering. "But I also can't be sure we can do this alone, and our Marine buddies are the only people I can think of who I'd bet my life on."

"Yeah, well, I'd rather not bet my life that they'd pick you over their wives or *kids*."

Smitty and I glanced at each other. He shifted his weight and looked at Leo. "I'd rather not bet mine on the three of us against whatever a mob family sends our way. Those odds are a hell of a lot less promising than the odds of us still being able to trust our boys."

Leo glared at him, then at me. "I assume we're doing this whether I agree with it or not?"

"Do you have any better ideas?" I asked.

He eyed me, then sighed. "No. I just… I don't trust anyone. Nobody except you." He flicked his gaze toward Smitty. "No offense."

"None taken," Smitty said with a shrug.

I reached across the small table and put a hand on Leo's arm. "It's a risk. I totally acknowledge that. But given the choice between trusting people I've been in the trenches with and hoping we can hold our ground against Grimaldi soldiers?"

He scowled, the crevices between his eyebrows deepening. For a moment, he watched my hand resting on his arm. Then, finally, pushed out a resigned sigh. "Okay. Call in the cavalry."

CARI Z & L.A. WITT

Chapter Three
Leo

I didn't bother to listen in as Rich and Smitty went about calling up the Boy Scout Brigade. I was tense enough as it was—I didn't need to compound it by witnessing them blow our secrets to hell and back because they were dumb enough to trust a bunch of guys I'd never even met before.

It wasn't fair, and I knew that. I wasn't in the mood to be fucking fair, though. Nothing in life was fair—people you loved died, people you trusted betrayed you, and at the end of the day, the only person you could rely on was yourself. I needed to remember that, especially when all these guys showed up and started bro-ing out with Rich.

Okay, maybe...*maybe* I was just a tiny, little bit jealous. Rich had lived an entire life that I knew next to nothing about, one with friends who would apparently risk their lives for each other. That was a level of commitment I couldn't even fathom—not beyond, well, *Rich* at any rate. And maybe Gianna, at this point. She'd come through for me on the hard stuff, helped me put her baby brother away and turn her father into a pariah. She'd loved Tony as much as I had, and her family's betrayal of him had been the last straw.

So, fine, Rich trusted whoever was coming to back us up. Great. I'd already established that Rich was a trusting soul, way too much for his own good. Smitty—well, he was more cautious, hence the whole "living in an abandoned silo in the middle of the forest" thing, but for these guys, apparently his caution took a backseat.

Me, though? I didn't trust a single one of these strangers. I wouldn't bring it up with Rich again—I didn't have to, he knew how I felt—but I figured it was also a good idea to hold back that I was planning on stashing every weapon I could spare in places only I knew about, just in case.

That was for after Rich and Smitty left to get supplies, though. For now, I propped my feet up on the coffee table in what passed for the living room, polished off the dregs of my cappuccino—and Smitty had been holding out on me last time, because he had some serious skills—grabbed the nearest book and started to pretend to read it. At least it wasn't Tom Clancy; this was a history of the bombing of Dresden in World War II. Nice, light reading. Jesus Christ.

"Hey."

I looked up as Rich and Smitty entered the center of the silo. Smitty had thrown a flannel monstrosity over his battered green t-shirt, his version of "dressing things up," I guessed. Rich had combed his hair into something more controlled than the bedhead he'd woken up with, and that was about the extent of how far his personal grooming could go, given the bruises. I liked the stubble, though. If his face hadn't been purple beneath it, I would have shown him exactly how much I liked it.

"Hey," I replied. "Going into town?"

"Yeah. It'll only take a few hours. Are you good here?"

"Totally."

"You sure?"

I rolled my eyes. "I mean, I might have a desperate pining for Walmart deep in my heart, but I'll control it if it means hanging out in air-conditioned comfort while you guys shop for Pop-Tarts and Cheez Whiz."

"Hey, don't knock Cheez Whiz," Smitty said. "That shit is delicious."

"I…don't even know how to respond to that."

"It's best not to," Rich said. "Once you get him going about processed foods, it's hard to make him stop."

Smitty pointed his prosthetic at Rich's chest. "Yeah, you laugh, but if the world went to hell tomorrow, I'd be the one eating Moon Pies five years from now while all the rest of you are just dreaming of sugar."

I sloppily saluted him. "Touché. And yeah, I'm fine, go for it. I'll be—" An uncomfortable thought occurred to me. "Wait. Are you expecting any of your buddies to show up before you get back? How will I know friend from foe?"

"The closest guy is still a full day's drive out," Smitty said. "You're good. But for future reference, there's a special knock."

Of course there is. "Well, you can show it to me when you get back. Bye-bye, boys. Have fun storming the castle."

Rich huffed a little laugh as he bent over to kiss me. It felt—oddly domestic, getting a kiss from him before he went shopping, like we were a normal couple instead of a US Marshal and his charge waiting it out before trial. I liked it, simmering sense of danger and all. I wrapped a hand around the back of Rich's neck and deepened the kiss, tasting sweet coffee and warmth and *damn*, now that I had some caffeine in me maybe I could—

"All right, cool it down, Romeos."

Oh yeah. Smitty. I let go of Rich, and felt more than a little smug as he opened decidedly glassy eyes, and had to clear his throat before he straightened up. "Drive fast," I advised.

Rich grinned. "I think I can handle that."

"Who's the guy with the only car that isn't hot?" Smitty reminded him as he walked toward the exit. "*I'm* going to be doing the damn driving here. Pair of—"

Whatever else he was going to say got cut off by the door, which was fine with me. I planned on making the most of the time to myself.

For such a paranoid guy, it was a little surprising that Smitty didn't have security cameras set up inside the silo. *Outside*, there were a ton of them, plus motion detectors, heat sensors—a squirrel couldn't take a shit within a mile of this place without Smitty knowing about it, the perv. But inside, there was nothing. I guess he figured if you made it in, he knew he wasn't going to need to kill you. That, or he'd hidden them so well that I'd never find them.

It didn't matter. I was still going to hide my extra guns. I had a whole damn duffel bag of them, courtesy of my Uncle Angelus's protégé, Kara. She and I didn't see eye-to-eye on many things, but at least she knew how to pack for maximum damage.

I went back to the room Rich and I were sharing, opened up the duffel, and started going through its contents. I counted seven handguns, three of which Rich and I had used before, so I set them aside. The remaining four were two Smith and Wesson nine-mils, a Springfield XD-S that looked like it had seen better days, and a gaudy as fuck Sig Sauer that could have been a My Little Pony accessory. Seriously, who wanted an iridescent rainbow barrel on their gun? No wonder she'd given this one away.

Whatever, this was what I had to work with. I checked to make sure they were all loaded, grabbed the duct tape, and went looking for decent hiding spots.

There was an art to ferreting away weapons. They had to be places that a normal person wouldn't look but weren't too hard to access. A secret gun wouldn't do me a lot of good if I had to run across the fucking silo to retrieve it. My usual hiding places, though—taped under the couch, for example—probably wouldn't fly here, because I wasn't dealing with normal people. These guys were Marines, and knowing Rich and Smitty the way I did, probably not entirely stable. They'd be paranoid too, so if I wanted to keep my weapons to myself, I needed to work a little harder this time.

The first one was easy, though—I taped one of the Smith and Wessons to the leg of my bedframe, close enough that I could grab it while I was lying down. If someone came into this room who wasn't Rich, then fuck subtle. I wanted fast.

The next ones, though... I wandered around for a while, through the vast center of the silo and into the side rooms on the main floor. Kitchen, bathroom, pantry—a huge damn pantry, and yep, there were the vaunted Moon Pies. Smitty hadn't been kidding. Actually...this looked like his prepper pantry, so not a place he'd raid for food unless he had to. Perfect. I reached up to the top shelf, pulled down a box of Grape Nuts—I guess they were good apocalypse food, because how would you even tell if they went stale—opened it up and tucked the second Smith and Wesson inside. I put it back and marked its place—third from the right—and nodded. One more down, two to go.

The kitchen wasn't a safe bet. There would be too many people in and out of it, opening drawers and snooping around just because they could. Same with the bathroom—no inside of the toilet tank for me. That left the enormous central living room, which was both big and bare, or something on another level. I chose one of each.

There would be people hanging out in the living room, sure, but there were no drawers to open, no doors to unlock. If I could just find the right place... I moved from furniture to furniture, checking them for just the right spot. The couch was out—too many butts would be on this; I'd never get away with putting something in the cushion. The chairs were better, harder, but still... I checked out the coffee table, which was nice and broad and low, but knowing my luck, these idiots would decide to play a game of paintball and upend the thing to give themselves cover. Nope, not going here.

The lamps, though... Those were ugly as fuck, twisty chrome columns with huge bases that were just begging to be used. If they were hollow underneath... I turned the first one over, took a look, and started laughing.

"Son of a bitch." There was a weapon there already— not a gun, but a big fucking Ka-Bar knife. Because Smitty. Of course.

Fine, I'd use the other one then. If it could fit one of those enormous knives on the bottom of it, it could fit my little Springfield.

The matching lamp—and I was almost sure now that Smitty had bought them because of their tactical capabilities, not their aesthetic qualities—was empty on the bottom, so I filled the space with my gun. Nice. Now all I had left to hide was the rainbow magic bullshit firearm. Seriously, if unicorns existed and packed heat, this would be their weapon of choice.

I walked up to the second level, which was mostly spartan bedrooms or completely empty rooms—and one room with a pool table and a mini-fridge, which I passed on. I didn't want another place where I'd have to worry about a lot of people seeing what I was doing. I needed covert and quiet.

I walked around the level, glancing into rooms. Any place someone might take to sleep in was out. The empty rooms didn't give me a whole bunch of cover, though. I could move something into one of them to *provide* cover, but if Smitty took a look and got suspicious, then that wouldn't end well. Maybe this one was—

Huh. Actually, this one kind of worked. It had a couch in it—old and ratty, with fraying edges, but not dusty. There was a recliner too. I could modify that to hide my gun in a heartbeat. I stepped inside the room, then blinked as the art on the wall came into view.

I mean, *art* was kind of a stretch. It was one of those LED-lit pictures that made it look as though the waterfall it depicted was actually moving. It was—honestly, it looked like it should be trying to sell me a cheap bottle of rum. What the hell was this doing in here? And why did the room smell kind of like stale cat pi—

"Meep."

"Fuck!" I jumped and turned simultaneously, my hand trembling on the trigger of the Sig as a black and white cat crawled out from under the couch and jumped up onto its arm. It sat down and purred, blissfully ignorant of the fact that I'd almost taken one of its nine lives. "Who the hell are you?"

"Meep," the cat said helpfully and licked a paw.

I hung my head for a second, getting my equilibrium back, then sat down next to it on the couch. It butted its head against my shoulder, shamelessly seeking affection. I gave it a scratch, then reached for its collar. "Inigo." Huh. At least Smitty had good taste when it came to naming cats.

"Don't scare me like that," I told Inigo. "I might do something rash, and then your daddy would kill me."

"Meow."

"Changing it up a little, I like that." I sighed. "If I hide a gun in here, you have to promise not to tell anyone. Or play with it, got it?"

"Meeee...eep."

"I'll take that as a yes." And now that I'd officially lost my mind over a cat, I needed to hide the damn gun and get out of here before the scent of well-used kitty litter clung to me.

On the other hand, it was kind of nice to know that there was at least one other living thing in this place I wouldn't have to worry about double-crossing Rich and me. Faint comfort, but I'd take it where I could get it.

Chapter Four
Rich

It was kind of weird going into Costco with my mind in survivalist mode. We weren't just stocking up on munchies for a Super Bowl party or snacks to stash with our gear before we deployed. There was no telling how long we'd have to hole up in the missile silo, whether it was just the three of us or with our buddies from the Corps. Whatever we bought today could quite possibly be all we had for the foreseeable future.

So basically this was a normal grocery shopping trip for Smitty. I guess there are worse things than having a paranoid off-the-grid survivalist in your top five "*who to call when the sky starts falling*" list. Especially when it came time to stock up and hunker down.

We each grabbed a shopping cart and started through the giant store. Paper products. Toiletries. Snacks. *So* many snacks. Detergents for anything that required detergents. Coffee in unimaginably huge containers. Smitty relieved the meat section of several large packages of frozen beef and chicken. I side-eyed a pack of assorted condiments in enormous containers, wondering if that would be more than we needed, but then Smitty grabbed two packs of them, so I guess that answered that. And who the hell needed a two-pack of sixty-something ounces of spaghetti sauce? We did, apparently. Wait, no, make that two.

"Uh," I said as he wedged the jars into a pocket of space in my cart, "do I even want to see the pallet of noodles we're going to get to go along with that?'

Smitty gestured over his shoulder. "Blue boxes. Grab three."

I looked past him. Yep—long blue boxes of spaghetti noodles. I dutifully grabbed three and didn't even joke about whether we were getting meatballs or parmesan to go with them. I was afraid to ask.

As we continued through the store, I walked past a display of Red Vines in giant plastic buckets, then backtracked and grabbed one. It would probably only last Leo a day or two, given how fast he could get through a package of them. On second thought, I'd picked up another one.

Smitty arched his eyebrow as I balanced the buckets precariously on top of everything else we'd picked up. "Since when do you have a sweet tooth?"

"These are for Leo."

Smitty glanced at the bucket, then at me, and he chuckled.

"What?"

"Nothing, nothing."

"Smitty…"

He shook his head as he pushed his heavy cart alongside mine. "I just think it's kind of cute how you're here to get shit for World War III, and you still remember to buy your boy's favorite candy." He clapped my arm. "Never thought you had a romantic side, Chainsmoker."

My cheeks were on *fire*. "It's not… I'm not…" I sputtered. "It's only fair that if we get snacks, he gets snacks."

Smitty chuckled. "Whatever you say, Casanova."

"Fuck you."

Another laugh. As he continued down the aisle, casually perusing a display of cashews that were sold by the metric ton, he said, "The pharmacy has the jumbo packs of condoms, by the way."

A lady with a couple of kids nearby shot us a dirty look. I replied with an apologetic one. To Smitty, I said, "Dude. Really?"

"What?" He shrugged and grabbed one of the buckets of cashews. "We're here to get necessities, right? You might as well pick up a few packs so at least neither of you gets bitchy from not getting laid."

The lady made a disgusted noise and herded her kids away. I might have laughed if I hadn't been so mortified. Had Smitty always been this unfiltered?

My mind went back to a night in an undisclosed location where he'd casually asked one of our boys to check the lump on his ball sac.

"Is that a pimple or cancer? Cause I can't fucking tell."

It hadn't been cancer, and yeah, he had always been this unfiltered.

And it was me, him, and Leo. In a missile silo. For the foreseeable future. With all kinds of hell waiting to rain down on us if we poked our heads out.

Well, I could say this—things were not going to be boring.

We continued through the store, picking up industrial-sized everything until I was pretty sure we'd destroy the shocks on his truck. Assuming I had enough cash to cover it all.

About the time I thought we were done, he stopped and hoisted a couple of bags of cat food into the cart, along with some buckets of litter.

"Come on, man," I said. "We don't need to go that hardcore survivalist, do we?"

"This isn't for us, dipshit." He balanced a litter bucket precariously on top of his cart. "It's for my cat."

"Wait, you have a cat?"

He rolled his eye. "Well, I can see why you're a Marshal and not a detective."

"Hey, fuck you. I've been kind of preoccupied. When the hell did you get a cat?"

"Dude, he was there the last time you visited."

"No, he wasn't."

"Yeah he was. I mean, not just when you came with Leo. Back when you and all the guys came out, what, three years ago?"

I furrowed my brow. "I don't remember a cat."

"Do you remember *anything* from that weekend?"

I set my shoulders back and glared at him. "I plead the Fifth on the grounds that answering that question may incriminate me."

Smitty just snickered. "And yes, he was here last time too. You just didn't see him because when he's hunting a mouse, *nobody* sees him. Not even me."

"Wait, you have mice?"

"Not anymore. He caught the fucker."

"Well. That's good."

We continued shopping, and mercifully, we were done not long after that. Smitty covered half the bill, so it didn't cost as much as I'd anticipated, and we loaded everything into the bed of his truck. Then we headed home.

Though we'd snarked at each other all through our shopping trip, Smitty was unusually quiet on the way back to his mountain hideout. Being quiet wasn't out of the ordinary for him, but the silence between us right now felt…weird.

It took about twenty minutes for that weirdness to get unbearable, and though I wasn't sure I wanted to know, I said, "Something on your mind?"

He glanced at me, then faced the road again. "I need you to be straight with me, Smoker."

I briefly considered a retort about how I was the last person who was going to be straight with anyone, but the seriousness of his tone made me bite back that comment. "Okay?"

He tapped his thumb on the wheel. "Leo. Are you sure you're being objective about this guy?"

"What do you mean?"

Smitty exhaled hard. "Come on, man. You're banging him. Don't tell me that doesn't—"

"Yes, I am, but that doesn't mean I trusted him from day one. I trust him because he's saved my ass more than once. And he almost got himself killed in the process."

"Right," Smitty said with a slow nod. "But he still needed you alive. What happens if you can't help him anymore? Or you turn into a liability for him?"

I shifted uncomfortably. "He knew I was a liability the first time he saw me have a flashback."

That earned me a startled glance. "He saw you do that?"

"Yeah. While we were still getting out of Chicago after shit went south." I pressed my elbow under the window and kneaded the back of my stiff neck. "And again in our hotel. I freaked out from a nightmare and punched him before I even woke up."

Smitty whistled. "And he still fucks you."

Heat rushed into my face. "Yes, Smitty. He still fucks me. Not that we've had a lot of opportunity or energy for that."

Smitty again went quiet, but after a few mileposts had whipped past, he spoke. "You don't think that's why he's sticking around, do you? Because you two are screwing?"

I laughed before I could stop myself. "Yeah, no. I'm pretty sure a couple of frantic fucks wouldn't be enough to keep Leo from protecting his own hide and bolting." My own words sobered me. I gazed out the windshield and sighed. "Look, I don't know what there is between us. I really don't. We've been relying on each other ever since everything blew up in Chicago. He's had ample opportunity to take off, and if he decides he's better off without me, he'll run. If he decides he can't trust our buddies from the Corps, he'll run. I can't stop him." I kept working at the tense muscles in my neck. "But can I trust him? At least enough to not sabotage things and screw us over? Yes. Absolutely."

My friend stared at the road ahead for a long time, then nodded slowly. "All right. If he's got your endorsement, that's good enough for me." He paused. "But mark my words, Rich—if I have reason to believe your objectivity is compromised because of your feelings for him, and I think he's going to put you, me, or our boys in danger? He's gone. Understand me?"

I swallowed. Knowing Smitty, that could mean anything from kicking Leo out of the missile silo to… Well, I didn't want to think of what he might be capable of. Smitty wasn't cruel. He wasn't a cold-blooded killer. But I'd been to war with him. I'd seen him shoot without flinching to save one of his men. If he thought Leo was a threat, he would neutralize that threat. End of story.

Smitty glanced at me again. "Understand, Smoker?"

Moistening my lips, I nodded. "Yeah. Got it."

And suddenly I needed to get back to the silo.

I needed to get back to Leo.

By the time Smitty and I had stowed everything we'd bought, I still hadn't seen heads or tails of Leo. Cold fear prickled along my spine. Had he taken off? Bolted out into the great wide open with no way for me to find him? He'd been ready to do that after everything had gone down in Lake Geneva. Had I left him alone long enough for him to work up the courage and run? Shit, what if he took the car we'd stashed in the woods a ways down the mountain?

But when I walked into the room we were sharing, a couple of plastic bags of toiletries hanging off my forearm, I found him.

He was sprawled on his stomach, hair tousled and face buried in the pillows. Leaning against him, bent in half with its hind legs splayed, a black and white cat licked its butthole.

I chuckled as I shut the door. Apparently Leo had made a friend while Smitty and I were gone.

As I started across the room toward the bathroom, the cat looked up and meowed.

"Hello to you too." I leaned over to scratch behind its ears, and as I did, the bags dangling from my arm rustled.

Leo grumbled, then lifted his head. "Rich?"

"Yeah. It's me. Don't roll over—you'll squish the cat."

He pushed himself up a little and craned his neck. Then, chuckling, he turned toward me and dropped onto his stomach again. "When did you get back?"

"Little while ago. Smitty and I just finished unloading everything."

"Oh. Shit." He rubbed a hand over his unshaven face and sighed. "I'm sorry. I would've helped."

"It's okay. If you needed sleep, you needed sleep."

He grunted softly, then eyed the bags. "Are those…" He squinted. "Is that an industrial sized box of condoms?"

"Uh…" I glanced down, and sure enough, the plastic was just transparent enough to let the distinctive Trojan logo peek through. "Maybe?"

Leo cut his eyes toward me, a grin forming on his lips. "You get the fifty-gallon drum of lube while you were at it?"

I laughed. "No, but I don't think we'll run out any time soon." I shuffled the bags around a little. "I got you a couple buckets of Red Vines too."

His dark eyebrows shot up. "You did?"

"Yeah. You like them, don't you?"

"I do." His full lips pulled into a sleepy smile. "Just surprised you remembered."

I smiled back but didn't say anything. I wasn't sure what to say. God, he looked so sweet like this—a little tired, a little disheveled, gazing up at me with those beautiful dark eyes. The thoughts I'd had in the truck made me sick with guilt right then. It was easy to let doubts creep in when we were apart, but somehow whenever I looked at him, it made perfect sense to trust him. To just take for granted that yes, he was going to have my back just like I would absolutely have his.

I understood why Smitty distrusted him. Smitty distrusted everyone until he had a reason not to, and I got that. If he'd seen how many times Leo had put his neck on the line to save mine, he'd trust him in a heartbeat too.

"Are you sure you're being objective about this guy?"

Oh, I absolutely wasn't, but not in the way Smitty thought.

"Hey. Earth to Rich." Leo sat up, grinning playfully. "Don't zone out on me."

I shook myself. "Sorry."

He didn't push. Instead, he reached up and tugged one of the bags. I thought he was trying to take it off my arm, but instead, he used it to reel me closer. Then he moved up to my sleeve and pulled me down onto the mattress.

"It's going to take us ages to get through all those condoms," he purred. "Maybe we should get started on them."

Whatever I thought to say vanished when his lips met mine. I absently let the bags slide off my arm and onto the floor, breaking the kiss just long enough to unsnag one that had caught on my watch. Once they'd all fallen away and my hands were completely free, I wrapped an arm around Leo, slid my hand up into his hair, and let him draw me all the way down.

There was an indignant meow followed by an equally

indignant thump, so the cat had jumped to the floor. Good—now we could take up the whole bed without worrying we might squash him.

We shifted around until we were both on our sides. Leo's warm hand slid under my shirt and up my back, and I cradled the back of his head, his hair soft and cool between my fingers. We made out lazily, our hips moving *just* enough to let our clothed erections rub together. Not hurried, not enough to get either of us off, but enough to make it clear we both meant business despite all the bumps and bruises.

So why the fuck couldn't I lose myself in it the way I wanted to? Opportunities like this had been few and far between for us. I didn't want to waste one by worrying myself sick, but the wheels that had been turning in my head since the drive home were squealing now. Even as we kissed and touched, I couldn't make myself believe he was really here. Or rather, that he would stay here. Yeah, he was in my arms right now, but more and more I was aware that Leo was a flight risk. I trusted him not to put me in danger, but could I trust him not to run?

Are you in this for the long haul?

Leo broke away and looked in my eyes. "What's wrong?"

There was no point in pretending everything was fine. He was good at picking up people's tells, and God knew he'd figured out plenty of mine. And if he'd *felt* me start withdrawing, well, it wasn't like I could gaslight him and pretend he'd imagined it.

"Just…" I broke eye contact, which was a challenge when we were this close. "I'm worried, you know?"

Leo stroked my unbruised cheek. "About what?"

"Everything? How this is going to play out? What happens when it's all over?"

"Assuming we aren't dead when it's all over?"

I met his gaze again, and couldn't tell if the comment had been a dark attempt at humor or some cynical resignation. If he was certain we were going to die before all was said and done, or if he was just as uncertain as I was about the future. Suddenly overcome with the need to reassure him that I was in it till the end, I cupped his face in both hands. "Whatever happens, I'm either going to see this through until it's over, or go down swinging."

"You better not go down," he said with both fierce determination and a note of fear so raw it was almost…innocent? Childlike? "I didn't come this far to come out alone on the other side."

I believed him. It was that simple. Despite everything Smitty and I had talked about on the road and all the doubts left hanging in my mind, all it took was that declaration to send my doubts scattering like startled pigeons. Maybe that made me gullible and too trusting, but I believed Leo. If I'd wanted him a minute ago, I fucking *needed* him now.

I pulled him into a kiss, and Leo returned it just as hungrily.

That unhurried kissing and touching from earlier was a distant memory. Clothes came off so fast they might as well have gone up in flames. We both still had plenty of healing bruises from our recent ordeals, but I barely noticed whenever he grazed mine, and he didn't exactly recoil when I touched his. Pain was bearable. Being separated from him by even an inch wasn't.

"God, I want you," I groaned between kisses.

He mumbled something. Then, "We should break open that industrial size condom box."

I raked my hand through his hair. "Yeah, we should."

"Mmm." Leo pushed me onto my back and straddled me, his powerful thighs hot against my hips. "Don't move—I want you just like this."

A full-body shudder made my breath catch. Just thinking about fucking him had me shaking with need. "Not… Not moving."

He grinned, kissed me once more, then leaned away to

get one of those huge boxes I'd brought home. Something rustled. Then Leo was sitting over me again, and wasn't that a glorious sight? Leo's sculpted body sitting up over me, all the scars and fading bruises like a roadmap to remind me this was Leo and nobody else, as he tore the foil with his teeth.

Neither of us spoke as he put the condom on my cock. He'd retrieved the lube, too, and stroked that on, and then we were kissing again, groping and holding each other and making out while the need to be inside him almost drove me out of my head. Somehow, we got some lube onto my hand, and he lifted his hips so I could reach between us, and… Holy fuck. I'd really gone my whole life without Leo riding my fingers and moaning into my kiss? Without his hips rocking on top of me as if we were already fucking, my fingers stretching his tight hole while his tongue demanded access to my mouth? Oh, but I was doing it now, and the only way it could be better was—

"Fuck me," he growled. "Right now."

I slid my fingers free. We were both so frantic we were shaking, but between us, we managed to guide my cock to him. Holding my breath, I stayed still and let Leo set the pace. He took me faster than I would have expected, biting his lip and groaning as he sank down onto my cock. With every stroke he eased himself down a little more, and it took every bit of restraint I possessed not to thrust up into him. Even when he'd taken me all the way, I held back, waiting for him to find his rhythm before I complemented it.

Dizzy with arousal, I stared up at him. None of this should have made sense. We had no business screwing each other blind in a missile silo guest room while we hid from people who wanted us dead. And I was distantly aware of how fired I would be if the Marshals ever found out I'd been balls deep in this man, but I didn't care. Maybe this was just that need for intimacy that had driven me to sleep with another Marine between missions. Maybe we were just horny and needed something that felt good after getting battered against the rocks for so long. Or, hell, maybe we were just spelling out in ways we couldn't speak that no matter how badly the world was burning down around us, we needed each other, and we had each other's backs.

It didn't matter why, and it didn't matter what would happen if anyone found out. Let them fire me, just don't let it happen until Leo and I were the spent, sweaty wrecks we needed to be right then.

Leo shuddered, letting his head fall forward. His hands slid up my chest to my shoulders, and the heel of his hand landed right on a bruise, but I didn't care. He gripped my shoulders as he rode me faster. I gripped his thighs and thrust up into him. The bed protested, and my muscles ached, and neither of us quite kept a steady rhythm, but God, he felt so good, and he sounded so fucking sexy as he swore and moaned.

Abruptly he let go of one shoulder and started pumping his cock, and it only took three strokes before he released a helpless, strangled cry and unloaded on my stomach. I arched under him and moaned and let his orgasm carry me into my own climax, and I almost sobbed as I came.

With a sigh, he slumped over me. He lifted his hips enough to let me slide free, then came all the way down, and we just lay there.

"I needed that," he said into my neck.

I had no idea if he meant the sex or the non-verbal reassurance that we weren't letting each other go. Either way, I said, "Me too."

Arms around him, panting hard as we trembled together, I closed my eyes.

More than ever, I wanted us to see this through.

Because I wanted to know what we could be when we weren't dodging bullets.

Chapter Five
Leo

Sex was awesome. Sex with Rich was better than awesome—it took me out of my mind and helped me forget everything that made me anxious, angry, and frustrated, at least for a while. It was enough to let me fall asleep without dreams or nightmares for once, helped by the warm weight of Rich's arm across my waist. If you'd asked me two weeks ago whether I thought it would be possible to be not only comfortable, but *happy* in the sleeping grip of a lawman with a martyr complex and serious PTSD, I would have laughed my face off. Now, though, his grip kept me grounded. I don't think I could have slept much otherwise, never mind this hard.

We'd slept in again yesterday morning and crashed early last night. I doubted Smitty had actually bought our story about being tired from everything, and unless our room was soundproof, our alibi was shot. I really didn't care. The last thirty-six hours or so had been some downtime and together time that Rich and I had desperately needed, and I wasn't apologizing to anyone for it. Not even our host, who could never resist smirking at us.

Waking up this morning wasn't the most comfortable thing—we hadn't bothered to clean up last night, and I'd gone past sticky into tacky territory, headed toward dried glue if I didn't get a shower fast. Rich was still asleep—thank God, because he needed the rest even more than I did. With a light kiss to his forehead followed by an eyeroll at my own dumb squishiness, I crawled out of bed, grabbed my clothes bag, and headed into the bathroom.

Fifteen minutes of hot water, soap, and a clean shave later, and I felt readier to face the day. Not entirely ready, though—I needed coffee. And maybe an ibuprofen. It had been a *long* time since I'd taken someone as big as Rich, never mind three times in thirty-six hours, plus I'd kind of rushed getting him into me that first night. I didn't regret it—it had been amazing, stretch and all—but I did want to be able to sit down without Smitty smirking at me. And he would smirk. In my head I could already see it on his smug, bearded face.

I dressed in a plain black T-shirt and jeans, sneakers, and a hoodie—it was kind of chilly in the silo, even in the summer—and crept out of the bedroom to head for the kitchen. I'd get Smitty to whip up a frothy coffee masterpiece, or I'd make it plain if he wasn't in there.

It turned out he was in there. He wasn't alone, either. I walked into a scene that made my shoulders tense and my jaw tighten. It wasn't just that one new guy had shown up—no, because that would have been too easy to handle. There were two new people with him in the kitchen, sitting around the table, drinking coffee and eating scrambled eggs and bacon with our host. They turned to look at me as I froze in the doorway like a deer in headlights.

I'd thought Rich was big. Hell, I'd thought *Smitty* was big, and he was, in a scurvy, messy, modern-day pirate way. Smitty was scary, but he was a known quantity, and with just one hand he could only pull a single weapon on me at a time. The guy sitting directly across from him at the little table was…immense. Clothed in black cargo pants and a green Henley, he was built like a big blond human brick, and looked like he had about the same amount of body fat. The weirdest thing about him was his face—it was round, almost moon-shaped, and oddly boyish on top of such a gigantic body. He smiled, stood up, and offered me his spade-sized right hand.

"Hey, you must be Leo. I'm Andy Kaczorowski. Nice to meet you."

I stared at his hand for a second too long before finally remembering to take it. "Hi. Yeah, um…you too."

Smitty's shoulders were shaking with silent laughter, and I resisted the urge to cuss him out for springing these guys on me. *What, you'd rather he stuck his head into your bedroom while you were wrapped up in Rich to let you know their war buddies were arriving?* Honestly, kind of, but it was too late to do anything about it now.

"Great." Andy let go of my hand—he wasn't a competitive squeezer, thankfully, or I wouldn't have had a hand by the end of that shake—put his own in his pockets and looked at me with open curiosity. "So. You're the guy who's got the entire service all shaken up. No, I'm not a marshal," he added, probably catching my *oh shit* expression, "but I've got some other friends who are. Over a dozen people have been suspended pending investigation, thanks to you, not to mention the ones who were outright arrested."

"I'm glad to hear it," I said frankly.

To my surprise, he chuckled. "I bet you are. So am I. People like that have no business being in charge of vulnerable witnesses."

"Aw, Bleeder, you're such a softie." Smitty got up and went over to the coffee machine, prepping it to make something fancy that better be for me.

I blinked. "Bleeder?"

Andy made a face. "Because I'm such a bleeding heart."

"And because he almost passed out from a nosebleed once," the other guy at the table said. He turned in his chair to face me more fully but didn't bother to get up. "Good thing he had a tampon on him."

"Dude, I don't know why you knock them, they're so useful. They're lightweight, sterile, you can pack 'em into bullet wounds, unravel them into bandages, use them to filter particulate matter out of water—"

"You're an embarrassment to manliness."

Andy shrugged. "Maybe, but I'm not gonna be the person who loses a guy in the field because he didn't come prepared." He immediately flushed. "Shit—that wasn't directed at you, Dallas, you know that. Right?"

The guy—Dallas, apparently—folded his hands over his lean stomach. He was shorter than Andy by probably five or six inches, and under his weight by at least fifty pounds, but of the two of them, he was the one I wouldn't have wanted to cross. He had sun-bronzed skin, close-shaved dark hair, and a face reminiscent of a viper—wide cheekbones, flat mouth, unblinking eyes. He might have been good-looking if he smiled, but it looked like he didn't even know how to make that expression. He also hadn't bothered to check his gun at the door like the rest of us—a Colt 1911 sat in a holster at his hip. "I know it wasn't. I don't take things like that personally. Not like Chainsmoker does."

Andy smiled again. "Yeah, and you guys call *me* the bleeding heart." He glanced my way again. "Smoker was always giving his shit away in the villages we went through. You couldn't keep that guy's med kit full, and any packages he got from his mom he parsed out to the local kids. Like chocolate chip cookies. Homemade, and not even stale after all that time in transit." He shook his head mournfully. "I offered him an entire bottle of Tabasco sauce for just one of them, and he still wouldn't take the trade."

"He's a giver," Dallas said, still staring at me. "He gives and gives."

Oh, fuck everyone, and fuck this guy in particular. I wasn't going to play nice with someone who obviously thought I was no better than something he'd scraped off the bottom of his shoe. I smiled lasciviously. "He certainly gave it to me plenty last night, if you know what I mean."

Andy looked shocked. "What, really? Wait, since when is Smoker even gay?"

Smitty rolled his eyes. "Since forever, dipshit. He just doesn't advertise where he sticks his dick like the rest of you." He came over and set the lattes on the counter, knocking his foot against Dallas's leg on the way. "You think he'll wake up any time soon?"

"As soon as he gets a whiff of this, he will," Smitty said. I turned and left, and just barely made out a hiss of, "Motherfuckit, Dallas, I didn't ask you here to act like a little bitch."

No, but he was going to be a little bitch anyway. This was just the beginning, I could already tell. Growing up surrounded by mafiosos full of piss and vinegar, it didn't take long for the ability to read a room to become a survival skill. Any time a group of people got together, there were going to be some weird dynamics.

At first glance, Andy seemed like a placater, a peacemaker. There was probably some heat in there somewhere, but he was more of a gentle campfire than a raging inferno.

Smitty—Smitty was probably a little island unto himself, most times. He moved in and out of conversations with the ease of someone who didn't cling. He was self-reliant, first and foremost, and he was doing this to help a friend, not to score brownie points with his buds or find an excuse to host a reunion. Smitty I could deal with.

Dallas, though…

CARI Z & L.A. WITT

Every group had that guy, right? The one who was just a little sharper around the edges than everyone else, who took things just a little too seriously. The one who, in short, was a little *extra* in all the scariest ways. In this group—so far, at least—Dallas was that guy. I bet he slept with an AR-15. He would be the hardest person to please, the toughest nut to crack, but frankly I just didn't have the energy for it. I was trying to stay alive, not win a beauty pageant.

Although given the competition so far, I would totally win. Rich would come in second. We were hot. It was simple fact.

I got back to our room, sat on the edge of the bed and waved the mug beneath his nose. He stirred, pressed his face a little harder into the sheet and stretched one hand out for me. I smiled despite myself, and set my own mug down on the floor.

"Hey," I said, catching his hand. "Wakey-wakey."

One eyelid cracked open. "Is that for me?" he asked hoarsely, lifting his head up a little. His bruise looked better today.

"Yeah, but only if you get up. I'm not going out there by myself again unless I have to."

He groped for the mug. "Why not?"

"Because two of your buddies are here, and one of them's a royal asshole."

Rich paused, then sat up and drained half of his latte in one long go. "Dallas, then? Or is it Curtis?"

"You were right the first time," I told him. "And if Curtis is as much of a douche as this guy is, you might have to keep them in separate rooms."

Rich shook his head. "Curtis is usually okay. He just might be a little touchy coming off a divorce. Dallas..." He sighed. "He's a good guy, Leo. He really is. He just has some trust issues."

"Well, he needs to fucking handle them instead of foisting his 'issues' off on me," I replied. "Why did he

54

come at all if he isn't even willing to give me a chance?"

"Because he's paranoid about us dying," Rich said baldly. "When we were deployed, we got into some bad situations a few times. Dallas almost singlehandedly fought us out of two of them. The third time our unit got split up, and—" He stopped for a second, his mouth working but no sound coming out. He was holding his mug so hard I thought he might shatter it. I reached out and carefully worked at his hand until he let go, took it and put it down on the floor next to mine.

"His life sucks and he's worried about you," I summarized. "Okay, I get that." I'd known a few guys like that, guys who didn't really give a rat's ass about themselves but would rip apart anyone who threatened their friends. Hell, I'd *been* a guy like that when it came to Tony. Who gave a fuck about me when he was there? Not even me, that was for sure. But I'd changed my tune when Rich barreled into my life. It was scary as hell, and a big part of me still thought I should just make a break for it on my own and leave him alone but safe. He didn't want that, though, and it wasn't just my decision to make.

That was true here, too. "I get that," I repeated. "And I agree with him when it comes to making sure you're okay. But I'm not going to let him treat me like a fucking Typhoid Mary until the trial, or for however long it takes us to make sure the Grimaldis aren't coming after me. This isn't his place. I didn't ask him to stick his neck out for me, and I don't have to listen to him insinuate that I'm using you, like he even has a fucking clue what we've been through together. These guys are your brothers-in-arms, great, but they're not *us*. And they don't get a say in what we do or what we are."

I felt a little wrung out after my impromptu speech, almost shaky, and I stared at Rich and waited to see how he would react with more than a little trepidation. I didn't want to make it a "me versus them" thing, but—

"Leo, Jesus. Calm down." Rich smiled and took my

hand. "I'm close to them, it's true. We were in the field together for some long stretches, and we bonded out there. But that time... It's important, but it's not right now. *You're* my right now. You're my present and my future, and you're important, too. Dallas can think whatever he wants, but if he starts telling me that you're bad for me, or that you're using me, I'll tell him to fuck off."

That was exactly what I wanted to hear. I relaxed a little bit. "Yeah?"

"Yeah. Although honestly, I don't think you'll be the focus of Dallas's ire for much longer." Rich got out of bed, nude and completely unconcerned about it, and walked over to his duffle bag to hunt up some clean clothes of his own. "As soon as JD gets here, he's going to be completely diverted."

"Who's JD?" I asked absently, not even trying to hide the way I was staring at Rich's ass. Fuck, it would feel so good to bury my cock in there. Or my tongue. Or my fingers...

"JD is James Daimler, also known as Jack Daniels, and he thinks he's a comedian. He was the ultimate prankster while we were deployed. Funny as hell, but he also cut things a little too close to the bone sometimes. He's almost given Dallas several heart attacks. They're less friends, more..."

"Frenemies?" I suggested.

"Something like that." He straightened up and turned around, and oh...damn. "Who's the other guy?"

"Huh?"

"Leo." Rich waited for me to make eye contact and grinned. "The other guy in the silo? Who is it?"

"Oh, um... Andy K-something. Bleeder."

Rich grinned. "Nice, he got here early. Probably traveled up with Dallas—they only live fifty miles apart, near the Oklahoma panhandle. You'll like him; he's a nice guy."

"Yeah, he seems it. He has a weird thing for tampons, though."

"Hey, don't knock tampons. They're useful."

I grinned. "So I've been told."

"Yeah, well you haven't lived until you're hunkered down behind your Hummer bleeding from a shrapnel wound and your medic comes over brandishing a tampon, then shoves it into the gash and tapes you shut." He shrugged. "It worked great, though."

"Andy was your unit's medic?" I could see that. There was something very Care Bear about the guy. Plus, he was big enough to carry a wounded Marine all by himself.

"He was. He's a nurse in a VA hospital now, I think. Seriously, he's a nice guy."

"Glad to hear it." I got to my feet, closed the distance between us and wrapped my arms around Rich's waist, pulling his body tight against mine. He started to harden immediately. "I can be a nice guy too, you know."

Rich's eyes glittered. "Hmm, maybe you can."

"I can. I'll prove it to you."

"How?"

"Why don't we start with me eating you out in the shower and go from there?"

Rich groaned, then leaned in and kissed me hard. He pulled back just far enough to let us both breathe and said, "Sounds like a plan."

Damn straight it did.

Chapter Six
Rich

I didn't know why I was nervous about seeing my old war buddies again. I wasn't on bad terms with any of them. Well, none of the boys who were here yet, anyway. JD had never quite forgiven me for getting out three months before we were supposed to deploy again; Lucky had never been able to look me in the eye after he'd caught me with Valentine's dick up my ass, and Sarge... Well, let's just say we never slept on the same side of a tent or sat at the same end of a table. We could work together, and we'd put up with each other when the whole crew was relaxing, but there was no love lost between us. Quite frankly, I was amazed he was coming. I'd fully expected him to tell Smitty that I could go fuck myself, but no, he was on his way.

Awesome. I was grateful as hell for everyone who was willing to help me and Leo, but I wasn't going to pretend I relished the idea of being in the same room—or missile silo—as Sarge.

But he wasn't here yet, and I could handle Dallas and

Bleeder, so yeah, why the fuck was my stomach in knots as I wandered from our room to the kitchen?

When I stepped into the room, we all stopped.

Dallas.

Smitty.

Bleeder.

Me.

Smitty was against the counter with a coffee cup in his hand. Bleeder was lounging in a chair at the kitchen table. Dallas had been about to take a sip of coffee but lowered the mug. I stood in the doorway. Eyes moved, but nothing else did. No one made a sound.

And to my surprise, I started getting choked up. It had been a while since I'd seen my Marines, and knowing they were here to put their asses on the line to help me… Shit. It shouldn't have surprised me that these men—the guys I'd fought with in the goddamned desert—would have my back, and maybe it didn't, but it sure as shit hit a soft spot in me.

Bleeder was first to break the standoff. He got up and spread his arms wide. "Smoker! Jesus Christ, how long has it been, asshole?"

I laughed and let myself be pulled into a bear hug. Bleeder always had given the best hugs.

As he let me go, he eyed me. "By the way, when the fuck did you start being gay?"

I blinked, then realized Smitty or Leo must have said something. "What?" I grinned, gesturing the way I'd come in. "Have you seen the guy I'm blowing? Who wouldn't be gay?"

Bleeder rolled his eyes and clapped my shoulder, almost knocking me sideways. "Jackass."

I just chuckled. The tension in the room had broken, and Dallas got up to give me a half-handshake, half-hug. Then he sat down again with a groan.

"Man, you sound like you're getting old," Smitty said.

"Shut up. I can hear your back popping from halfway

down the mountain."

"That's different. Those are war wounds."

"Pfft. Whatever helps you sleep at night." Dallas resumed drinking his coffee. "So where's Leo?"

I gestured over my shoulder. "He's plotting and scheming with Smitty's cat." I looked at Smitty. "They've made friends, so don't expect to see either of them any time soon."

Dallas smirked. "So what you're saying is, your dude ditched you for some pussy?"

"Long as he's not ditching me for your ass."

"His loss," Dallas said with a shrug and took another swallow of coffee.

For as worked up as I'd inexplicably been, the banter had come easy. I fell in with my boys like we'd never been apart. And hell, I hadn't realized anyone in the unit didn't know I was gay. I'd thought it was a pretty open secret, especially after me and Valentine, but apparently not. Didn't seem to bother anyone, though. We all shot the shit while we drank coffee and I ate breakfast, and it felt like it had back in our fighting days.

Which was good, because these were fighting days again.

The thought sobered me. This wasn't just a visit to Smitty's silo so we could drink ourselves stupid, play indoor paintball, and hope no one fell over the railing. We were here to hold down a fort against a real enemy with real bullets.

"So, um." I cleared my throat. "I'm guessing you two brought along some firepower?"

Dallas and Bleeder both laughed.

"You make it sound like Smitty doesn't already have enough to hold off an army," Bleeder said.

"I did before you two came out here for a hunting trip," Smitty muttered into his coffee cup.

"Oh please." Bleeder rolled his eyes. "We didn't use that much."

The look Smitty shot him told me that, yes, they had used that much, and I'd spent enough time on the range with these assholes to believe Smitty in a heartbeat. Ammo was the only thing they went through faster than beer and hot wings.

Dallas chuckled, but when he looked at me, he'd sobered again. "We brought everything that wasn't nailed down and fit into my car."

"Couple of ghillie suits too, just in case we need 'em," Bleeder added.

Part of me kind of wanted to laugh, mostly because I desperately wanted to believe that ghillie suits were overkill. Kind of like how I wanted to believe that hiding in the mountains in a goddamned missile silo was overkill. But it wasn't. If the Grimaldis closed in on Smitty's place, ghillie suits might not even be enough.

Fuck, I was in over my head.

Trying like hell to look casual, I leaned back against the counter and rested my hands on the cool edge. "All right. Between all of us and everyone who's still coming, we've probably got firepower covered. Today, I need to go out and make a call."

Smitty's eyebrow arched. "You think that's safe?"

"I don't think anything is safe, but I need to check in with my handler and find out what's going on with the trial. And if there's any news on Daddy Grimaldi."

"I'm going with you." Dallas's chair scraped on the floor as he stood, and the rock-hard look he shot me said this wasn't negotiable. "We can take my truck."

I wanted to argue, but I knew better. When Dallas made up his mind, that was that. Smitty and I were about ninety-nine percent sure that played a role in the absence of a wedding band on Dallas's hand—his soon-to-be-ex-wife had apparently gotten fed up with "*my way or the highway.*"

So I didn't argue. Wouldn't hurt to have backup anyway, just in case something happened. Not that I expected anything to happen, since the Grimaldis had no way of knowing we were in Colorado, never mind *where* in Colorado. Not yet, anyway. They had resources at their disposal that I wasn't about to underestimate, and it was only a matter of time before they found us. Probably not much time, either—not with the trial coming up fast.

Couldn't be too careful.

"Fine," I said. "But I'm driving."

"Whatever. Just don't scratch her."

Dallas and Bleeder went outside to finish unloading everything they'd brought with them, and I went to let Leo know I'd be gone for a few hours. Not that he seemed like he'd miss me. He'd curled on up on our bed with Inigo, and he'd discovered some weathered paperbacks in Smitty's collection—something besides Tom Clancy, apparently—so he was perfectly content to hole up while I was out.

"The rest of the guys probably won't be in until tomorrow or the next day, but some of them *could* show tonight," I said. "I should be back by then, though. I'd just as soon you had a buffer when you met them."

Alarm widened his dark eyes. "A buffer? Why?"

"Well, they're…" I shook my head. "JD and Lucky are all right. Lucky might get weird once he figures out we're sleeping together."

"Homophobe?"

"I guess. He's never said anything outright, but he busted me and another one of our guys screwing while we were deployed, and he just…never quite looked either of us in the eye after that."

Leo chuckled wickedly. "Trust you to traumatize someone with your dick."

I snorted. "To be fair, I was the one getting someone else's dick, so…"

Leo sobered, and a shiver went through him. "Oh, so you *do* switch."

"Maybe." I flashed him a toothy grin as I leaned down

CARI Z & L.A. WITT

for a kiss. "If you behave."

"Mmm." He squeezed the front of my pants and murmured against my lips, "Behave badly? Or…?"

I groaned, then gently nudged his hand away. "Asshole. Now I'm going to be at half-mast until I get back."

Leo, being an asshole, just winked.

"Anyway." I straightened. "I'm not really worried about JD or Lucky. Sarge…that might get a little awkward."

The amusement fled Leo's expression. "How so?"

"We've just always had kind of an odd dynamic. Don't particularly like each other. Never have."

Leo inclined his head. "But he's coming to this little party?"

"Yeah. That's the thing—everyone in the unit has always had each other's backs. I'd trust the motherfucker with my life any day of the week, but don't ask us to room together."

"Ah, one of those." Leo's features relaxed. "Sounds like half the people I grew up with."

I wrinkled my nose. "Sarge and I aren't mafiosi."

"No, you just play them on TV, right?"

"Something like that." I bent for another kiss. "Okay. I gotta go. Dallas is coming with me, and Bleeder and Smitty will stay here. I'll see you when I get back."

"Okay." He cupped my cheek and held my gaze. "Be careful, okay?"

"Always am."

"Be *more* careful."

Dallas didn't wait long to start grilling me. The house covering the silo's entrance hadn't even disappeared in the rearview before he said, "So, this guy. He your witness or your boy?"

I stared straight ahead as I drove down the mountain. "Any reason he can't be both?"

"Don't they have rules about that?"

"There were rules about me and Valentine too."

"Fair." He fell silent for a moment. "I mean, whatever you guys do, it's your business. If he's got your seal of approval, then he's got mine too."

"Oh." I negotiated the tight hairpin near the end of Smitty's driveway, and as the road straightened out again, I finally glanced at him. "You really approve of him?"

"Sure." Dallas shrugged. "You're not stupid. Never have been. If you say this guy's worth protecting, then I'm gonna take you at your word."

Well that was…unusual. "This from he who trusts literally no one."

"I didn't say I trusted him. I don't. Won't pretend I do. But I'll stay here and stick it out to make sure he doesn't get killed."

We'd reached the bottom of the hill and turned from the rough road onto the pavement. As I continued on smoother ground, I said, "So you don't have to like him, but you'll keep him safe."

"Wouldn't be here if I wouldn't. I don't have to trust him. I trust you, and if you think he's all right, then I'm not going to question you. Doesn't mean I have to trust him myself."

That was about the most Dallas thing Dallas had ever said. "Well, it'll be good to have you onboard so I can keep him in one piece."

"That's why I'm here."

"I know. Thanks." I paused. "And for the record, it's my job to protect him whether I like it or not, so—"

"Gonna go out on a limb and say you're kind of going

above and beyond the call of duty with this one."

I shifted in the driver's seat. "A little, yeah. But everything about this case has been kind of above and beyond anyway. The guys who want him dead massacred my entire team the day I met him."

Dallas whistled. "No shit?"

"No shit. And it's basically been me and him against the world ever since. I haven't really had time to stop and think about whether I'd do this for anyone else."

"The hell you have."

I shot him another look. "Huh?"

Dallas snorted and elbowed me. "I mean, don't get me wrong—I know you'd go to the ends of the earth to protect someone no matter what. But don't act like you're just doing your job. Not with this one."

"How do you figure?"

"Because I know you, asshole. And I know you wouldn't call in the cavalry for just anybody." He chuckled. "That, and I've never known you to fuck guys you don't like."

My face burned. He had me there.

Conversation stayed lighter after that. I appreciated his candor; he didn't have to like or directly trust Leo, but I trusted *him* to have Leo's back just as much as I trusted him to have mine. I'd been in enough firefights with the man to know he wasn't blowing smoke, either. To this day, he and Lucky hated each other, but Dallas had literally taken a bullet for the man. He didn't have to be the most trusting man on the planet. I was just damn glad he was on my team.

I drove us out into the middle of nowhere just like I had the day I'd gone to call my dad while Leo and I were first on the run. The déjà vu out here was eerie. As we descended into the lowlands, crossing into some flatter plains ringed by distant mountains and dramatic rock formations, I could literally feel the sick dread that had hit me the moment I'd heard someone shoot my dad on the other end of the line. Maybe for my next call, I'd go find someplace else because this area gave me the creeps.

I found a place to pull over, and Dallas stayed in the car while I stepped out. There wasn't much signal out here, but thanks to a booster, I managed to get two bars, and I made the call.

Vanessa Martin, my handler, picked up on the first ring, and when she realized who it was, she quickly said, "Oh my God. I've been trying to reach you."

"Yeah? What's going on?"

"A lot. How secure is this line?"

"It's a burner phone that's going to get crunched under my tires when we're done."

"Okay. Good." A door closed in the background. Then a chair creaked, and Vanessa started talking fast. "Listen, I've been in touch with Chicago PD, and they've got some undercovers working within the ranks of the Grimaldis. Have for a while."

"Thank God for that."

"Yeah, especially since they're the ones who've alerted us that at least a dozen Grimaldi soldiers have left town."

My heart stopped. "Left town?"

"Yes. Thing is, Lorenzo Grimaldi was arrested two days ago, and the whole family is pissed."

"Oh, shit." Bringing in the Grimaldi patriarch was a good thing, but it wasn't going to endear Leo or me to the family. "Anyone making any noise about coming after us?"

"Everyone's being tight-lipped, but the undercovers said the consensus is the men have gone hunting."

"Oh, fuck. Please tell me the mafia is more outdoorsy than I thought."

"Afraid not."

I swallowed. "Any indication that they know where we are?"

"None that's gotten back to me, but I wouldn't take any chances." She paused. "You're someplace safe and remote, right?"

I looked back at the distant mountains as if I could see the entrance to Smitty's missile silo from here. "Yeah. We're good. There's a safehouse in North Dakota, and we're—"

"I don't want to know," she said quickly. "This line is secure, but you just never know."

"All right, all right. We're safe, though. I promise."

"Good. I'm keeping an ear to the ground, and we're monitoring the Grimaldis from every angle we can, but…" Vanessa sighed. "Just keep yourself and that witness safe, Cody."

"I'm doing the best I can."

We hung up, and I scanned the wide-open plains and the distant plateaus and mountains. There wasn't a single soul in sight, but I felt exposed and vulnerable. All it would take was one well-trained sniper with a high-powered rifle and a spotter, and they could drop me where I stood. I wanted to believe the mafia didn't have that kind of firepower, but I was taking nothing for granted.

I tucked the phone under the front tire of Dallas's car, then got into the driver's seat. I rolled forward, back, forward again, and when I was satisfied the phone was duly destroyed, I headed back toward the highway.

Most people would have asked how the call had gone or what we needed to do next. Dallas knew me, though. There were things you learned about people in foxholes, and one of them was to read the subtleties of body language. I didn't know how subtle I was being, but I didn't imagine anything would get past him.

He cut right to the chase: "Incoming?"

Nodding, I released a long breath and accelerated. "We need to get back to the silo."

Chapter Seven
Leo

Bad things happened when Rich left the silo to make phone calls. The last time he'd gone off to talk to someone like this, he'd come back looking like death warmed over because he'd heard his father get shot over the phone. This time wasn't quite as bad, but he sure as hell wasn't happy.

"What is it?" I asked as soon as I saw him.

He shook his head. "Let me just tell everyone all at once."

"Fuck that." Dallas had already gone back toward the kitchen, so that asshole could be the one to tell the other guys what had happened to put such a spooked expression on Rich's face. "This is about the two of us more than it's about any of them, and I have a right to hear it from you first." I took his hand, and after a moment he squeezed mine in return. "Now *talk* to me, Rich."

He sighed and gave me a *you asked for it* kind of look. "Lorenzo Grimaldi is in custody, and a bunch of his men have taken off from Chicago. Nobody knows where they're headed, but it looks like they're on a mission."

"Wha—what the hell?" I had to force myself to speak. I couldn't clam up now; if I did, I might not be able to get started again. "I thought they were all supposed to be on lockdown, or followed, or some kind of—how did they—"

"There wasn't enough direct evidence to indict everyone, Leo, you know that." Rich ran his free hand through his hair—that was his stress tell, clear as day. It was one of the reasons he was a shitty poker player. "Plenty of the lower-level soldiers stayed on the streets, and now a dozen of them are missing. Word is they're hunting someone down."

I nodded slowly. "And you think that someone is us."

"Who else could it be?"

"Gianna springs to mind." Gianna was Papa Grimaldi's middle child and his only daughter. She had known about my secret affair with her brother Tony and had only told us to be happy and careful, in that order. *Shoulda ranked those the other way around.* She'd been the one to give up Matteo's location to us, allowing us to track him down and convince him—nicely, since I'd left him with all his limbs—to turn tail on his father.

Gianna had also betrayed her father, and in a way, her betrayal probably burned worse than the youngest son's. Matteo had at least been physically coerced into acting against the family, while Gianna had flouted mafia convention by not only going against her father's orders, but actively working to help take him down. She was getting the plea deal of a lifetime out of this whole thing, too—Matteo would still go to jail in the end, even after acting as the star witness in the trial against his dad. Gianna and her family were escaping clean.

Or maybe they weren't.

Fuck it. She had a husband. She had *kids*. I had to warn her. The Marshals might have shared this info with

Rich, but I seriously doubted they would think to share it with the Don's daughter. "I need to call her."

"Not until tomorrow."

Tomorrow might be too goddamn late. "Rich—"

"No." He sounded very final. "We can't make any calls from this location. It's not safe. Tomorrow I can drive you out onto the plains, and you can contact her from there. It's too late to go now. We'd get stuck driving around in the dark."

"God forbid we get stuck in the dark," I snarked, dropping his hand. He took mine back and tugged me a little closer, expression somber.

"When we're possibly being hunted by maybe a dozen guys who'd all love to stick a knife in your back or lodge a bullet in your brain, yeah, Leo. We stay out of the dark. We play it as safe as possible, because I'm not losing you. Not now."

Not ever. He didn't have to say it, but I could see it in his face, hear it in his voice. He hadn't spoken the words yet, but I was pretty sure that Rich loved me. He was the kind of guy to fall fast and hard when it was right, and this thing between us—it *was* right. It was crazy but right, and he loved me and didn't even know it yet.

I, on the other hand, knew exactly how I felt about him, which was going to make lying to him a real pain in the ass. "Okay," I said, closing the distance and looping my arms around his neck. "Okay. No calls until tomorrow."

A little of the tension went out of Rich's shoulders. "Thank you."

"It's fine." I tried to smile. It was hard, and it probably looked wobbly, but not for the reason he thought. "It's going to be fine."

"Hey, assholes!" Dallas called from the other side of the silo. "You want to eat, come and get it now before Bleeder finishes everything off."

"I've got a high metabolism!" I heard Andy—I just

71

couldn't think of him as Bleeder—protest.

"And I've got a limited bank account and no desire to go back to damn Costco anytime soon, so get your mitts off the pasta bowl," Smitty said.

"Just like old times," Rich muttered, and I chuckled and leaned my head against his shoulder for a moment.

I'm sorry, baby. "Make sure he leaves some pasta for me," I said before kissing his collarbone and straightening up. "I need to go clean up. I need a...a second."

Rich looked at me searchingly. "Take all the time you want," he said finally, then moved around me and headed for his friends.

I went straight for our bedroom and rummaged through my duffel, looking for the burner phones. We had three, all of them brand new, so surely it would be safe if I just—

"Fuck." No fucking bars. This was what I got for relying on the cheapo networks. I bet they didn't have cell towers anywhere near Smitty's mountain hideaway. But *Smitty* could make calls here. That meant his phone would work. Probably any of the major brands would.

And who did I know who was carrying cellphones with big-name providers? Not just Smitty, but Andy and Dallas too.

Okay, fine. I had to get access to one of their phones. It would have to be discreet, too—I could tell that Rich was on edge now, wondering about me. I needed him more firmly on my side than ever, so I couldn't just ask to play games on one of the other guys' phones. I'd have to get access to one without its owner knowing it, which meant I'd have to guess their passcode too.

I groaned under my breath. Damn it, this was going to be tricky. I'd done it before—guessing passcodes actually wasn't too hard, but you had to know the person to make it work. Four numbers to get in—it was way too many to guess. I needed answers. I'd also need a chance to slip their phone back to them after I got it, but that would come.

It looked like I was going to have to arrange another poker game. With three guys, it would take some time to get anywhere, but people always wanted to play for answers, even more so when it was people who already knew each other.

Now...how to make it happen? Smitty would be the stumbling block—I'd won against him before at cards, and he didn't trust me any better now than he did then, but maybe I could use that against him.

Loose plan made, I headed back to the kitchen. Everyone was either sitting or standing, a bowl in one hand and a fork in the other, or in Dallas's case, holding a beer. Nothing about it should have been remarkable, and yet I had to pause in the doorway because something was setting off my alarm bells. What was wrong with this picture?

I got it after a second. They were all too close to each other, cozied up in one half of the kitchen and well within an arms' length of the next person in line, even though they'd probably be more physically comfortable if they had a little more space. I couldn't think of anyone other than Rich I wanted that close to me, not even my uncle, not even Gianna. Admittedly, my uncle was an infamous hitman, and Gianna would have slapped me for presuming to get so close to her, but still. It was uncomfortable just watching it.

"You coming in to get some food or hanging over by the door like a naughty puppy?" Smitty asked, one eyebrow raising impatiently.

I leered at him. "I don't know. Will you swat me with a rolled-up newspaper if I stay where I am?"

"What kind of kinky shit is your guy into, Smoker?" Dallas asked.

I smiled and cocked a hip. "Wouldn't you like to know?" It didn't take a lot of effort for me to put on a "sleazy rent boy" persona. "I'll give you some hints if you're really interested. First, let me tell you about the

73

wonderful world of handcuffs and the ability to fold yourself in half. I'm talking head down, ass up, all bent over and ready to—"

"Leo." Rich sounded pained. I took pity on him and picked up an empty bowl, then filled it with clearly-overcooked pasta. Plus some premade, sugar-filled spaghetti sauce. God damn these Marines and their inability to tell the difference between good food and shitty make-do food.

"I had a girlfriend once who could put both her feet behind her head," Andy said, a far-away look in his eyes. "Sex with her was awesome. Until she got a cramp, and then I had to get out of there fast as possible or I'd get kicked in the head when her legs sprang back down."

"You have the weirdest girlfriends," Smitty told him. "Was this the circus performer?"

"No, Shelly was a yoga instructor. Leila was the circus performer. Her stage name was Python." Andy chuckled. "Oh man, that was fun. It was, like, a year of my life I'll never get back thanks to her crazy, but she could be really fun."

We were off to a good start already. "Are you seeing anyone now?" I asked, forcing down a bite of tomato-flavored mush. Anything relating to partners might correspond to passwords.

"Nah, not for a while." He shrugged. "I'm sick of the bar scene, and don't even get me started on Tinder. I will not be swiping right or left for anybody, that's just rude."

"I like it. It cuts through the bullshit." Dallas took another swig of his beer. "You look for someone who wants to fuck and see if they want to fuck you. End of story."

Andy made a face. "Man, that's just sad. There's nothing meaningful about that kind of thing at all."

"Who wants something meaningful?"

"Everybody! Who wouldn't want to find the person—or people, 'cause I'm not judging, poly is a thing—anyway, who wouldn't want to find someone else to be happy with? I mean, Sarge found Jennifer, Rich found Leo, Smitty found his cat…"

"No pussy jokes," Smitty warned. Rich laughed, and even Dallas cracked a smile. It faded a second later, though.

"I like to keep it simple, that's all. I don't need the extra fucking hassle."

Andy looked unimpressed. "Oh yeah, you talk a good game, but I bet it's all hearts and roses in your profile." He lunged for Dallas's back pocket and jerked his phone out before Dallas could do more than spit beer onto the floor.

"What the hell?" Dallas demanded, wiping his mouth with the back of his hand. "Give me my phone!"

Andy already had it open and was running through apps. "Should have changed the password, everybody knows your favorite type of gun," he said absently. "Here we go…"

I could have kissed him. Dallas still had the 1911 on him—it seemed like the equivalent of his security blanket. I wondered if he even took it off when he was meeting up with the ladies he'd swiped right for. Now all I had to do was get it from him.

"'Looking for a night or more with the right lady,'" Andy read. "'Drinks are a must, and it won't be wine. Don't ask me to dance, but do ask me if I can hold you up against a wall for fifteen minutes.' Dude, never mind, you're a dog."

Dallas snatched the phone away and shoved it back in his pocket. The snarl on his face very clearly said "*don't fuck with me.*"

Naturally, Rich started to fuck with him. "Fifteen minutes, huh? Is that an average or a minimum?"

"Smoker—"

"Do you do that in the shower? Because that's really not safe for either of you," Andy added. "I've handled scenes where people have fallen while fucking in showers, and they're always a huge mess. Have you ever seen a broken penis? Because I still have nightmares about that one."

Dallas pressed a hand to his face. "Bleeder, honestly, it's not—"

"And what have you got against wine?" Smitty demanded. "Wine is classy."

Dallas was starting to look desperate. "Can we change the subject already?"

"Sure." I put down my bowl and reached for the drawer where I knew Smitty kept the cards. "How about a round of blackjack?"

It was kind of funny having the guy I knew liked me the least be the first to leap at my suggestion. We moved to the living room, where I could use the coffee table to deal, and I decided right from the get-go not to make this fair. I needed to separate out Dallas, to get him to stick with me while the others got bored. I needed to make him lose.

That, I could do. I didn't even have to be sneaky about it. I took a quick peak at the deck while I set up, then got down to business. "What do you want to bet that I can make any one of you win that I want?"

"Bullshit," Dallas said.

"No, he's serious." Smitty wasn't bothering to play, sticking with a book on the couch instead. Inigo was with him, purring up a storm in his lap. I wasn't jealous. Much.

"What, like palming cards?" Andy asked interestedly.

"I don't even need to palm cards when I'm the dealer," I told him. "I just need to know how to control the deck. Watch." I dealt out a card to each of us, then a second. I had seventeen, the highest sum on the table. "Now I've forced you all to hit."

"So what? Seventeen probably isn't enough for you to win with," Dallas pointed out.

"Yeah, but I don't want to win. I want *Rich* to win." I batted my eyelashes at him, and he laughed. "So…" I dealt out a third card to each of them. Dallas ended up with twenty-three, Andy with eighteen, and Rich?

A perfect twenty-one.

Andy's eyes were wide. "Okay, how did you do that?"

"Reserve card at the top of the deck. I dealt the card beneath it each time until I used it to tip the balance the way I wanted."

"I didn't even notice!"

"Good," I told him. "Then I haven't completely lost my mojo. I learned these tricks from a bunch of mobsters, but if they ever caught someone else cheating like this, usually that somebody ended up dead."

"Can you make any number you want?"

"Only if I know the deck well enough." Which I did.

I spent the next hour cheating at blackjack, letting Rich win, then Andy, even myself a few times. Not Dallas, though. Never Dallas. He stuck it out like I knew he would, stubborn to the point of idiocy.

After the umpteenth game, I put the cards down and flexed my fingers with a grimace. "Man, that gets old fast. My hands hurt like hell."

"Just desserts." Dallas glared at his latest round of cards like they'd personally betrayed him. "I still don't—"

"You big baby." Andy clapped him on the shoulder, then rose. "C'mon. Let's go get some more beer and snacks, and then we can watch him kick your ass some more."

Dallas huffed, but tossed his cards down and stood. "Fine."

My gaze went straight to the table, and the phone he'd left sitting beside his cards. Now was my chance.

Stretching, I stood too. "I think I'll go up and get some fresh air."

That earned me a glare from Dallas. "No, you won't."

"Yeah, I will."

He shook his head. "It isn't safe."

"Pfft. Even if the Grimaldi soldiers hopped on a plane

this afternoon, rented a car at the airport and headed straight for this place, they still wouldn't be here until the morning," I argued. "I've been cooped up in here all day, and I need some fresh air. In fact, I need a goddamned smoke. I won't be long."

Dallas stared at me, unblinking. *Snake*, I thought again. I almost wanted to blow in his face just to make him take a break from eyeballing me.

"Let him go," Rich muttered. "Trust me—if he actually feels the need to smoke, he'll be a lot easier to deal with once he's had one." That was fair. I'd only smoked once or twice since Rich and I had met, and it was only when I was absolutely at the end of my rope. Rich looked up at me. "And he's not going anywhere." He raised his eyebrows as if to ask, *right?*

"Are you kidding?" I huffed a laugh. "Forget mafia goons. There's probably… I don't know. Bears out there."

"You'd probably like a bear," he said with a wry grin.

That prompted groans from both Andy and Dallas, who shook their heads and headed for the kitchen. Rich just smirked.

"Ass," I said, chuckling.

He started organizing the cards to shuffle them, and shrugged with fake innocence. "Am I wrong?"

"You're not a bear, jackass." I leaned down to kiss him and felt a little guilty about using his momentary distraction to palm Dallas's phone. I really didn't feel like smoking, and couldn't even remember if I'd brought any cigarettes with me. In the interest of maintaining my cover story, though, I went into our shared room and dug around in my bag. Sure enough, I found the wrinkled pack and neon green lighter I'd been carrying for God knew how long.

Then I took the elevator up to the top floor. From there, I exited the dank little cabin and emerged into the clearing at the top of Smitty's property. The floodlights were off, and only a hint of light from the cabin illuminated the shiny edges of the small fleet of vehicles parked outside.

I looked up at the stars, transfixed. The sky was completely clear, and there was no light pollution out here to dim the sight of them. It was gorgeous, and even though I'd come up top as a ruse, I really did feel better in the fresh air. I closed my eyes and breathed in deep for a second.

After I'd lit a cigarette I didn't actually want, I moved a few paces away from the cabin and took out Dallas's phone. The screen was blindingly bright out here—I needed to work fast in case someone followed me.

The passcode got me in, and though the cell signal was weak out here, there *was* signal. I got into Dallas's text messages and, using a remembered number, sent a coded text to Gianna. Much like Rich and his dad had an elaborate system of codes to communicate sensitive information on unsecured lines, Gianna had had one with Tony, and they'd let me in on it in the months before Tony had been killed. The message I sent her now would be meaningless to anyone who intercepted it, but would tell her in no uncertain terms: *It's Leo. Keep your head down, shit's about to hit the fan, don't respond to this message.*

Then I deleted the message from Dallas's phone, shut it off, and wiped the screen and case with my T-shirt just because I was too paranoid to leave fingerprints.

Now that the message was sent, I was jittery with adrenaline, both from the information I'd sent her and from completing my risky objective in the first place. All that remained now was to get the phone back into Dallas's hands. By now he may or may not have noticed it was missing. All I'd have to do was go back down and casually "find" it on the floor under the couch or something, and all would be well.

First, though, I was going to finish this cigarette, because now I really did need the damn nicotine.

I stared out into the darkness. It was strange up here,

so remote from everything else. I'd never been more than a few minutes from people before—Chicago wasn't just a city. It was a sprawl, parts of it masquerading as suburb and country, but all of it connected by shitty, crowded highways less than a mile from wherever you found yourself. Here, though, the only people within probably twenty miles were in the silo. It felt incredibly isolated, like a real wilderness.

Behind me, the cabin door opened. I jumped but tried not to let it show, and casually blew out some smoke. Knowing Rich, he wanted a moment alone, and I sure as hell wasn't going to say no to—

"Let me know when you're done enjoying nature." Not Rich. *Dallas*. Ugh.

Buzzkill. "Why do you care?"

"Because I'm up here until you're good and ready to come back down." He sounded *so* thrilled.

"If you don't want to be up here, feel free to go inside," I suggested, hoping he wouldn't take me up on my offer. "Or wait here while I stretch my legs and have another smoke." *Please.*

"Nope." He walked over to me. "Smoker would lose his shit if something happened to your dumb ass, and now that I'm up here, he'd blame me if something did happen. So, you're not getting rid of me."

"I won't tell him you came up here." I took a drag off the nearly finished cigarette, and turned to Dallas in the dim light. "What he doesn't know won't hurt him."

Dallas did blink this time, looking at me a little strangely. "You don't really understand Rich very well, do you?"

I bristled. "What the hell is that supposed to mean?"

"It means that lying to him, even in a little way, even if you think it's for his own good? It hurts him when he finds out, bugs the hell out of him. The only time I've ever seen him really angry with one of our guys was when he caught them in a lie. For someone who claims to be into him, I'm surprised you don't get that yet."

Well, fuck. That didn't make me feel any better about my current situation. I was committed now, though. The message had been sent, and Gianna would be smart and—.

A woman's scream ripped through the night, close enough to us that I literally jumped. "What the fuck!"

Dallas instantly moved in front of me, a weirdly protective gesture that I appreciated more than he knew. What the hell, there was a girl getting *murdered* up here?

The scream came again, and I tensed even as Dallas seemed to relax. "Just a mountain lion," he said.

"Bullshit."

"That's their mating call." Dallas looked around like he could see in the dark. "It must be close."

"Wonderful," I snarked.

He glared at me. "So you going to have another cigarette or what?"

As if on cue, the scream came again, closer this time. It was immediately followed by another one a bit farther down the side of the mountain.

"Oh shit." There were two mountain lions less than a hundred feet away from us, in the dark, in the mood to get it on. "Y'know, I think I've had enough nicotine *and* the great outdoors now. Let's go back inside."

"Yeah," Dallas agreed. For all his apparent cool, he had one hand on the butt of his gun. It wasn't just me who was nervous. "Let's do that."

We turned and headed back for the shack, him leading the way. I crowded him, like I was too skittish to tolerate any distance between me and the man with the gun and returned his phone to him even as he shot me an annoyed look over his shoulder. "Learn to walk, dipshit."

"Learn to walk *faster* so we don't end up as appetizers for Inigo's big-ass cousins."

"Bitch, bitch, bitch." He did pick up the pace, though, and we made it back to the elevator just in time to hear another chorus of screams, even closer than before.

I was definitely done with nature for a while.

Chapter Eight
Rich

"I don't like your boyfriend."

Dallas's icy words pulled my attention away from the bowl I'd been scrubbing. He stood in the kitchen doorway, arms folded across his chest and a sour expression on his face.

"Um." I quirked my eyebrows, then returned my attention to the bowl. "Thanks for sharing?"

"I mean it, Smoker."

I studied him. "Why the one-eighty? When we were in the truck, you said you trusted my judgment. Now this? I mean, what? He beats you at cards, and suddenly—"

"Come on, you know me better than that," he snapped. He came closer and pressed a hip against the counter. Dropping his voice, he added, "Something's shady about him."

I rolled my eyes and cocked my head. "Really? A deck-stacking gangster hacker strikes you as shady? Wow. You have really honed those observation skills in the last—"

"Cut the crap," he growled. "I'm not joking. I trust your judgment, but the longer I'm around that guy?" He stabbed a finger at the doorway, as if that would indicate Leo. "The more I gotta wonder why in the *fuck* we're putting our necks on the line for that asshole. What's so—"

"You're welcome to leave, Dallas." I put the bowl down and stepped up in his face. "You know where the fucking door is. If you don't trust him, and by extension, me, then hit the road. Get the fuck out and let the rest of us deal with it. Because if you're not going to have his back as much as you have everyone else's, then I'd rather not—"

"Whoa. Whoa. Slow the fuck down." He narrowed his eyes. "Don't you ever fucking imply I won't have one of my boys' backs."

"Right now, 'your boys' includes Leo," I threw back. "And before he beat your ass at cards, you were willing—"

"Damn it, Smoker. Would you just shut up and *listen*?"

I clenched my jaw and folded my arms, but didn't speak.

He exhaled, still glaring at me. Voice a little calmer and quieter now, he went on. "I mean it—I trust you. And if you think this guy needs protecting, I'll protect him. That's not a question. The question is whether *he's* a danger to *us*."

I blinked.

"He's mixed up with the mob, which I don't like, but he's also… I don't know, man. Every time he's in the room I get a vibe off him like he's trying to pull one over on us or give us the slip somehow. Like we're on the up and up with him, but he's got half the deck up his sleeve, and I don't mean when we're actually playing cards." Dallas shook his head. "It doesn't sit right."

I pursed my lips and stared at the weathered linoleum between our feet.

"I'm not trying to be an asshole here," he continued.

"I just don't want a repeat of when Smitty got hurt."

A shudder ran through me at the memory. A kid in Afghanistan had begged us for help, said he could lead us to a cell of insurgents who were raining terror on his family's village. We'd known better, and we'd been cautious, but he'd been battered and bloody, eyes filled with fear that I'd never imagined a human being could truly fake, and he'd won us over. It was Smitty who'd caught the scent that something was off, and he'd busted the kid planting an IED that would have killed or maimed all of us if he hadn't sounded the alarm. Instead, it had killed the kid and cost Smitty an arm and an eye.

Leave it to Dallas to invoke that fucking awful memory. Like I wasn't already feeling some serious pressure to make sure my boys and I could trust Leo. I did trust him. I'd been in the proverbial trenches with him, and he'd saved my ass more than once. Even if it had been because I was useful to him, he'd still done it, and I was still useful to him now. So were the guys with us in the silo.

I sagged against the counter and sighed. "Okay. I get it. But I do trust him. Every time he's tried to give me the slip so far, it's been to protect me."

Dallas's eyebrow arched. "Yeah, that sounds romantic as shit, but do you buy it? Do you *really* buy it?"

I did up until you started questioning everything.

Squaring my shoulders, I met his eyes again. "Yes. I do. Because he's had ample opportunity to bolt, whether it was for my own good or for his, and he hasn't. He's scared, he's vulnerable, and he's got the wrath of a mob family coming down on him. Don't tell me you wouldn't act a bit weird and slippery if you were in his shoes and surrounded by heavily armed strangers who think you're—"

"If I were in his shoes, I wouldn't have tangled my criminal ass up with the mob."

"Uh-huh. Let's hear you say that once you actually

know his story. And anyway, your concerns are duly noted, but I trust him. If he fucks up, it's on me."

Please, Leo—don't fuck up.

I hated myself for worrying he would. And deep down, I really didn't think he would. I was scared too, and fear bred paranoia. *Should* I trust Leo? *Would* my boys have our backs? I also knew I'd stopped being objective about Leo a long time ago. *What, like a week ago? Holy shit, has this all happened in less than ten days?* That was arguably why I needed the guys here more than anything—because someone needed to be objective about the situation, and it sure as shit wouldn't be me.

Deputy Marshal of the Year, right here.

I opened my mouth to reassure Dallas that we'd be fine as long as we all stuck together, but two figures rushed past the open doorway. Dallas and I exchanged alarmed looks, then poked our heads out.

It was Bleeder and Smitty, and they were moving fast, clomping up the metal steps toward the missile silo's entrance.

We jogged after them.

"What's going on?" I asked.

Just before they disappeared through the door, Bleeder threw over his shoulder, "JD and Sarge are here."

I groaned. "Oh, fuck my life."

"Hey now." Dallas clapped my shoulder, shoving me forward in the process. "He may not like you, but he's here to help."

"Greeaaat." I rolled my eyes and followed the boys outside. I was thrilled we had more backup—the more Marines involved, the better—but I couldn't say I was looking forward to seeing Sarge.

Smitty turned on the floodlights, and we all filed out of the little house on top of the silo as a huge pickup rumbled in and dwarfed all the other vehicles. I had to chuckle. During our active duty days, we'd all relentlessly teased JD that his penchant for huge trucks meant he was compensating for something. He had a good sense of humor about it, though. In fact, this shiny blue beast sported a license plate that read CMPNS8R.

The jacked-up Ford's engine shut off, and the woods were once again still. The doors swung open. JD hopped to the ground in his usual cowboy boots and hat. Some things definitely didn't change.

Sarge used the running board instead of jumping. No one gave him shit about a dainty exit—he'd had his knee and ankle reconstructed so many times, we'd have kicked his ass if he'd tried to be all manly about getting out of the truck.

JD and Smitty shared a quick embrace, and JD asked, "When are you gonna put in that pool? I'm telling you, all this empty space and no pool is a wasted opportunity."

"You gonna show up and clean out all the pine needles and dead critters?" Smitty grumbled as he let him go.

"That's what filters are for," Sarge said.

"Uh-huh. Fine. I'll put in a pool, and you boys better be here for a Polar Bear swim in fucking April because this is the mountains of goddamned Colorado, you morons."

"No, thanks," Sarge grunted. Then he turned to me, eyes narrow. "So where's this asshole we're supposed to be watching?"

"Hello to you too," I muttered back.

His features hardened. "Whatever. I'm here to do a job, not play nice. So where is he?"

"Wondering if they train politeness out of you in bootcamp." Leo's voice made me jump. "Or if it's a prerequisite for enlisting."

Sarge glared at him. "You must be the asshole hacker."

"Can't say I've ever hacked an asshole." Leo came closer, smiling that sweet smile he always gave when he was fucking with someone. "But I'm sure I could if someone gave me a chance."

JD snorted. "Oh, I like this guy already." He extended a hand to Leo. "Name's James, but everyone calls me JD."

"Leo." Leo shook the offered hand, then slid his gaze back toward Sarge. "So you're the chipper one in the group? The one who keeps morale up?"

Sarge eyed him, then me, his expression screaming, "*are you* shitting *me right now, Smoker?*"

I shifted my weight and wrapped a protective arm around Leo's shoulders. "Listen, we really appreciate you and everyone else coming out. We need all the help we can get if we're going to stay ahead of—"

"Yeah, I heard," Sarge said coldly. "Fine mess you pulled your idiot ass into."

Leo tensed beside me.

"You don't have to stay if you don't want to," I said through my teeth. "If your head's not in the game, feel free to—"

"Oh, my head's in the game." He gestured at JD, Dallas, and Smitty. "I'm not going to let any of them take a bullet because you stuck your dick where it didn't belong." Before I could snap back with something, he said, "So what are we up against, anyway? You said there's a mob family involved? How big? How much firepower?"

"Enough that it made sense to call in the Marines," Leo said flatly.

"Uh-huh." Sarge trained that icy gaze on Leo. "How much did you fuck up for them to paint a target on your back?"

Leo didn't even flinch. "Well, it started with putting *my* dick where *it* didn't belong and escalated to getting a member of the royal family killed and another one tossed in prison. So you could say I'm not very popular in their circles."

Sarge grunted, and he inhaled like he was about to fire back something characteristically snide. Fortunately, Smitty picked that moment to clear his throat in that way that reminded everyone his house wasn't the place for their pissing matches. "Hey, so, let's get you boys settled in and go crack open some beers."

And like magic, Sarge softened. "You had me at beer." He and JD took their weathered green rucksacks out of the truck bed, and we all headed back inside.

"He's a charmer," Leo whispered to me on the way in.

"Oh yeah." We started down the stairs since the elevator was too full. "Just wait until he settles in and stops being polite."

Leo's eyes widened in horror. "That's him being polite?"

"Mmhmm."

"Oh. Yay. This is going to be *fun*."

"I don't trust him." Leo sat on the edge of the bed we'd been sharing, and emphatically snapped off a chunk of a Red Vine with his teeth.

Great. Dallas and Sarge didn't trust Leo. Leo didn't trust...someone.

"Him?" I sat beside him. "Which one?"

"You know which one." He waved his hand, almost smacking me with the licorice. "What the fuck is Sarge's problem, anyway? He doesn't even like *you*."

"That's kind of the crux of it, to be honest. He doesn't like me. I don't like him. Never have."

Leo bit off some more candy and chewed slowly as he stared at me like he was expecting me to elaborate.

I sighed, leaning back on my hands. "If you want some dramatic origin story, you're going to be disappointed. We just don't like each other."

"So why the fuck is he here?"

"Because the team needs him."

Leo didn't look convinced. At all.

"I don't know what you want me to tell you." I shrugged, then lay back on the bed, folding my hands on my stomach. "Sarge and I never liked each other, but we always had each other's backs in the field. If he came all this way, then he'll have your back and mine now."

Leo eased himself down beside me. I decided he'd been spending too much time around that cat—he was starting to move like him too. He stretched out on his side, and while his expression stayed placid, I swore if he'd had a tail, he'd have been twitching it with annoyance.

"Look," he said after a moment. "I know these are your buddies and you trust them. And I mean, I'm not military, but I get what it means to bond with someone on a battlefield."

From anyone else, I might have taken that as patronizing, but given the things Leo had been through in his life? Yeah, I could believe it.

"I don't want to fuck up what you've got with these guys," he went on. "But I've got a gut feeling that I don't like."

I slid my hand over the top of his. "Is it a gut feeling specific to these guys? Or one that comes from being hunted by a powerful mob family?"

"Probably both." He turned his hand over and curled his fingers between mine. "You said I should trust my instincts, right?"

I nodded.

"Okay. Well. My instincts are telling me something isn't right."

"With…?"

Leo stared at our hands, chewing his lip. "How much did your guys know about our situation before they got here?"

"Only the basics. That I needed help protecting a witness and that the mob was involved."

He dug his teeth harder into his lip. Much more of that and he was going to draw blood.

I squeezed his hand. "Talk to me, Leo."

He blew out a breath, then finally met my eyes. "My gut is telling me not to trust Sarge. The other guys..." He shrugged. "They seem all right. But there's something about Sarge, and it's not just the fact that you and he obviously don't like each other. I can't even tell you what it is. Just that...something doesn't sit right."

"Do you think he won't protect you?"

"I think it's a few steps worse than that." He searched my eyes like he was trying to preemptively gauge my reaction. "Like he's not here to *help*."

I blinked. "You... Are you saying you think he's here to sabotage us?"

"I have no evidence whatsoever. Just instincts and vibes and gut feelings." His expression turned pleading. "But something feels *wrong*."

Nodding slowly, I ran my thumb along the back of his hand. Leo had every right to be paranoid, and Sarge had been a dick from the moment they'd met. In this kind of situation, it was hard to tell the difference between not liking someone and thinking they were dangerous. I sure as shit couldn't tell them apart, especially since everyone— liked or otherwise—had the very real potential to *be* dangerous.

I wanted to believe the men I'd served with in combat could be trusted because they'd always been trusted. Even the one I didn't like was still a solid, loyal Marine. So maybe I wasn't being any more objective about Sarge than Leo was. Maybe his paranoia was keyed up while mine was toned down. Maybe the truth was somewhere in the middle. I had no idea.

But I believed that, as much as we could be under the circumstances, we were safe right now.

I freed my hand, rolled onto my side to face him, and draped my arm over him. "You know *I've* got your back no matter what, right?"

That brought a tired smile to his lips. "If I had any doubts about that, I wouldn't be here."

"Good." I kissed him lightly. "I'll keep an eye on the guys, and you should too. Anything hinky, we talk between us before we mention it to anyone else."

Leo nodded. "Okay. I can do that."

"Okay." I stroked his cheek. "It's been a long day. You want to just call it a night?"

Some more life appeared in his eyes, and he slid closer to me. "The day hasn't been *that* long. Get over here."

Chapter Nine
Leo

There was nothing like a morning-after surrounded by guys who hated your guts. Oh yeah. Nothing aided the digestion of generic sugary cereal like eating it in the presence of Mr. Doom and Gloom and his merry band of brothers. And why the hell Smitty couldn't have sprung for the name brand Sugar Puffs when he drank nothing but Ethiopian Yirgacheffe, I had no idea.

I knew guys like Sarge. They were the enforcers, the middle managers who kept the entire mafia working. They didn't make quite enough to live the high life, but they weren't down there scrambling in the dirt with the rest of the foot soldiers either. They kept order, discipline, and if they were skimming off the take, they had to be *smooth* about it. And Sarge, for all his cold stares and stolid silence, seemed like the kind of guy who could be smooth if he needed to be. He also seemed like the kind of guy who could use the money a man like Papa Grimaldi could provide.

Who was I kidding, though? Any one of these guys could have used that sort of money. These were former soldiers—excuse me, *Marines*—and none of them had gone from that to being a stock broker or a CEO. Hell, I didn't even really *know* how Smitty made money apart from his disability check. Dallas worked in the gun section of a sporting store—go figure—while Andy was a nurse at the VA. Sarge, from what I'd been able to glean, ran a small construction company with his brother, and JD *worked* construction but was considering going to law school. From what I'd gathered so far, the most he'd gotten out of the process was a bunch of bad jokes.

How did something like "I'll juris *your* prudence!" get laughs? And yet it did. People were weird.

Still, as long as he was cutting the tension with his bad jokes, I wasn't in as much danger of spontaneous combustion thanks to Sarge and Dallas's combined glares. Thank fuck Smitty didn't give a shit and Andy was a teddy bear, because Rich needed someone on his side who wasn't me.

Of course, all these guys were on his side. That was why they were here. They weren't all on *my* side, though, and I didn't really care, but I knew it was stressing Rich out. So it was on me to buddy up to some of them, whoever I could, because it would make him happy.

Christ. I was doing things I hated because it would make Rich happy. I was so fucking gone on him it was scary.

It wasn't even worth trying with Sarge or Dallas, and I might want to ease Rich's mind but I didn't want to put myself through that wringer for nothing. Smitty, I'd done as much with as I could—as much as I thought he'd let me. We'd come to a détente, and that was all I wanted out of the guy. That and more time with his cat, who apparently was a bit of an attention whore and would sit on just about *anybody*'s lap. Right now he was on Sarge's, and he was petting his with one hand and sipping his coffee with the other, all while maintaining a glare that should have struck me blind.

That left Andy and JD. JD bounced around the kitchen like a squirrel on crack, flitting from person to person and chatting like he was being paid to do it. Andy was leaning next to the sink, polishing off an apple as he watched. I used the pretense of washing my bowl to say, quietly, "Is he always this perky?"

Andy turned to me with a smile. "Who, JD? Yeah, always. Him and Sarge were the only early risers in our squad. Sarge did it because it was habit, he said, but JD—it's like his body could only stand to be still for so long, you know? He was the youngest guy in our whole unit. His parents actually had to sign a letter allowing him to join the Marines."

"Sounds tiring," I offered as I headed for the door. He took the hint and followed me. We went into the rec room, where Andy dropped onto one of the couches.

"JD's not so bad," he said, stretching his tree trunk arms up over his head until something in his ribcage popped loudly enough to make me wince. "Ah, there we go." He rolled his neck, cracking it even louder, then relaxed and, surprisingly, went for the deck of cards I'd left on the low table in the center of the room. "We needed a guy like him around," he continued, pulling the cards out and cutting them, over and over, his movements slow and a little awkward. "Someone to help us remember how to have fun out there. If it was all Sarges and Dallases, or Mister Responsibilities like Smitty and Smoker, I don't think we'd have laughed even once a week." He paused, then looked up at me suddenly. "Hey, um…can I ask a favor?"

A favor? From me? This was bound to be good. "Sure," I said, sitting down next to him.

"Can you teach me a card trick?"

That…wasn't what I was expecting. "Uh, why?"

CARI Z & L.A. WITT

"So, every other Saturday I volunteer at the local Children's Hospital. For years I brought my dog Freddie and the kids loved him, but Freddie's really too old to work hospitals anymore, and without him, I kinda…don't know what to do to entertain them."

Oh my good God. And I thought Rich was ridiculous. "You want to learn card tricks to perform for sick kids."

He looked a little anxious. "I mean, not if they're really hard." He held up his huge hands. "I can insert an IV in under five seconds, but for anything else I tend to be a little clumsy."

"Uh-huh." I held out my hands for the cards. "Well, lucky for you, having big hands will actually make some of these tricks easier." I did a quick riffle shuffle, then laid the cards out in a smoothly-overlapping line on the table. "Let's start with a ribbon spread." It wasn't a trick, just a flourish, but I'd always loved seeing it as a kid.

I taught him how to lay the cards out evenly, then induce the chain-reaction that would turn them all over from back to front. Rich came out of the kitchen as breakfast dispersed and sat down next to me, making the couch a little tight, but I just squeezed in closer to him and gave Andy pointers.

It was hard to focus with Rich right there, still fresh and a little damp from his shower that morning, the scent of coffee on his breath and the warmth of his body a firm, inviting presence against mine. I wanted to shut my eyes and turn my head and hide my face against his shoulder, or maybe lick him from collarbone to jaw—tough call. I held back, though, and let myself be satisfied with what I had. For now.

After another few minutes, JD flopped down across from us onto the chair. "Are you teaching him to cheat at cards?" he asked, loud and grinning, his cowboy hat angled forward so that I had to lean a little to see his eyes. "Can you teach me too?"

Not if you want to avoid getting punched in the face, I can't.

96

With a guy like JD, I already knew how things would go—he'd learn one trick and then pull it out like it was a diamond, showing it off even when it did him no good. This kind of indiscretion almost always ended with a punch in the face, if not something more damaging. "I'm showing him a few little magic tricks," I said pleasantly. "For the kids."

"Shit, are you still using up your weekends at that hospital?" JD shook his head. "You're not even dating that nurse there anymore, man! Isn't it awkward, having to be around her?"

"Why would it be awkward?" Andy stared down at the cards as he worked the ribbon spread again. He was starting to get the hang of it. "Melanie and I are still friends."

"That's just weird, Bleeder."

"You're weird," he said, but he was smiling. "Seriously, you've never stayed friends with an ex after you broke up?"

"Are you kidding me? No way! If I didn't have kids with her, I'd never talk to my ex-wife again." JD made a grumpy, bitter noise and added, "I mean, it's not like you break up with a person because you *like* them, right? You wanna get rid of them, wanna move on."

"Or you end up having different goals but still enjoy and respect them as a person and can be totally civil to them."

JD chuckled. "Jesus, you sound like Sarge."

"And you sound like Dallas," Andy replied. "Who do you think is the better role model when it comes to life skills?"

"Um…neither? That's allowed, right?" He looked over at Rich. "Seriously, man, what do *you* do when you break up with someone? Do you stay 'buddies' and drunk text them like a loser, or do you cut them off and get on with your life?"

Rich shrugged. "I've never had a bad breakup. I might

CARI Z & L.A. WITT

not be friends with my exes, but it's not like I go out of my way to avoid them either."

"What about with Leo?"

Ah, prurient curiosity raised its head at last. "What *about* with me?" I intercepted the question like it had been meant for me—because it had. I could tell JD was curious, but for all his cracky squirrel behavior, he wasn't quite comfortable enough to come right out and talk to me without a segue.

"Well, I mean—say if you two were to break up. Would you stay in touch?"

"I guess it depends on why," I said. "For example, if I ended things because I was getting thrown in prison for the rest of my life and didn't want to drag Rich down, then I expect I'd still hear from him because he's a kind human being who wouldn't want me to be friendless on the inside. If he ended things because I'd done something so morally repugnant to him that prison was too good for me, then no, I'm sure he wouldn't keep in touch."

JD tilted his hat up, exposing the furrowed quirk of his brow. "Damn, that's kind of dark. Those are your only two options?"

"They're the first ones that sprang to mind." All of a sudden, I was sick of this. Everybody in this damn silo wanted to pick our relationship apart, dissect it and see what it was made out of in all its gory glory. I couldn't really blame them, but my patience for it had worn thinner than I'd thought. "I'm going to go have a cigarette. Andy, keep working on that spread, you've almost got it."

He beamed at me. "Thanks."

Thank God for this guy. His disinterest was like cold water on a burn. I turned to Rich. "Want to come keep me company?"

"Yeah." He stood up and we walked over to the elevator together. I didn't bother getting my cigarettes because I really didn't feel like smoking—I just needed a few minutes up there and away from here.

Neither of us spoke until we were actually outside. It was a beautiful summer day, not too hot because of the high elevation, just comfortable. The air smelled like pine trees, a mix of pollen and sap and slowly rotting needles.

After a while, Rich touched my shoulder. "Are you okay?"

"As okay as I can be." He got it. Especially with all the tension since the boys started arriving—he had to know how I felt about the people around us, Sarge especially. And after last night, he knew that no matter how skittish I might be acting now, it wasn't about him. "Just...it's strange."

"They're a strange group of guys."

I snorted. "No fucking kidding. How the hell did you manage so many disparate personalities in the middle of a battlefield?"

He shrugged. "How does any commander do it?"

"In the mob? Fear," I said bluntly. "You follow orders or you get killed. That's not an option for Marines, I imagine."

"A lot of it's habit." Rich tucked his hands into his pockets and leaned against the shed's doorway. "That's what basic training is all about. You don't just train your body, you train your mind. Obedience becomes ingrained."

I suppressed a shudder at the thought of it.

"Respect for your commanders helps," Rich went on. "And I know you don't trust Sarge, but—for us, back there, he was the best kind of guy to have in charge. He was steady and strong and not afraid to get his hands dirty. He was determined to bring us back alive."

"And he did," I said quietly. Rich might have nightmares and terrible PTSD that made some days a challenge, but he was here. Between that and the alternative, there was no competition.

"Yeah, he did." Rich glanced at me. "Do you really want to smoke?"

"No. Why?"

"Because there's something else we could be doing with your mouth."

"Ah, right." I nodded sagely. "Blowjobs."

Rich coughed out a laugh. "Jesus, not—*kissing*, you asshole. I meant kissing."

"You're such a sweet talker," I said. "I mean, I guess kissing is okay too." Despite my words, I was already leaning in to start making out, but before I could grab Rich, he held up a hand.

"Wait."

"Wait for wh—"

"*Shh.*" He tapped his ear.

I shut up and a moment later, I heard it too. It was the sound of a car struggling up Smitty's road.

"Are we expecting anyone else?" I asked quietly.

"No," Rich said grimly. "Not for a few days yet. Get Smitty, tell the guys to be on alert. I'll wait up here."

"Rich, that's not—"

"I'll stay in the shed and lock the door." The flimsy, plywood door. "Go, fast. It might be nothing."

Or it might be a car full of mobsters waiting to gun him down. I grimaced but ran for the elevator.

A little over sixty seconds later, I was amazed anew at the efficiency of these people. They were armed, staged, and ready to move before I'd even finished telling Smitty what was going on. Definitely more discipline than the mafia.

"You stay down here," Smitty told me as he headed for the elevator.

"Nope."

"Leo—"

"Rich is up there, so that's where I'm going."

"Where's your gun?" Dallas protested.

"On my ankle." Hell, if everyone else was going to be carrying as they walked around the place, then I was too. "And if this is the Grimaldis, then I should be there unless there's some sort of surveillance system that lets me watch and communicate from down here."

"Or maybe you should get your ass into your room and lock it so you stay out of the damn wa—"

"Never mind, he's coming." Smitty hauled me into the elevator behind him.

"*Smitty*—"

"Stay sharp." The door closed, sealing us in and everyone else out, and he folded his arms, then looked at me. "There *is* a surveillance system," he said after a second.

"I figured."

"But it's in my bedroom."

"Nice and private."

"I do like my privacy." He rubbed his only hand down his face and I sort of felt sorry for him. He obviously wasn't used to having this much company, and it was wearing on him. "I'll rewire it somewhere more public." The elevator stopped. "You stay in here," he told me quietly. "Head down if there's any trouble." The elevator opened just as I opened my mouth to protest, and there was Rich in the shed, waiting for us.

"Not Grimaldis." He nodded toward the cabin's entrance, which someone was banging on loudly from the outside. "He says he's a neighbor?"

"Huh." That was the most surprised I'd ever heard Smitty. "I'll see what he wants. You two—"

"We've got your six." Rich pulled me over to the side and whispered, "You should have stayed downstairs."

"While you were up here? No way." Ahead of us, Smitty opened the door a crack. Rich swallowed whatever he was going to say next in favor of listening.

"Big Mike. What brings you my way?"

"Smitty, hey." I couldn't see Big Mike, but he sounded jovial—almost too much so. "It's been a long time! How've you been?"

"Fine." Smitty's voice was completely flat. "What do

you want?"

"Nothing much. Just noticed a lot of traffic heading your way and got curious, wanted to make sure you were okay." He paused, probably to gesture at the vehicles parked outside the shed. "Anything going on I should know about?"

"Nope."

"Uh…huh. Look, son, if you're in some sort of trouble, you should let me help. I was sheriff of the neighboring county before I retired, I could lend you a hand. Got all kinds of things at my disposal that could be useful to you."

"Really."

"Yeah. How about, ah, how about we have a beer and you can tell me—"

"Maybe later, Mike." Smitty shut the door. A moment later, Big Mike called out, "Some other time, then! Glad you're okay in there, son." A minute after that, a car started up. Once the engine petered out, Smitty turned to us with a frown.

"You have a nosey neighbor," I said to him. "Does he always bug you like this?"

"No." Smitty's lips pressed tight together. "Never. Big Mike is the nearest person for miles, but we don't share an access road. There's no reason he should have seen any of you driving up here, especially not as spread out as you arrived. And his home doesn't sit on high ground, so looking in with binoculars wouldn't cut it."

Despite the heat of the shed, I felt a little chilled. "What does that mean?"

"It means he's been spying on us, probably with a drone. And I doubt he was doing it because he's bored."

I could read between the lines. He was either being paid or forced to do it, then. And the only people ballsy enough to approach a retired sheriff that way…

Were probably the Grimaldis.

"Great." Now it was *my* voice that was flat. "They've found us, then."

Chapter Ten
Rich

"Why the fuck is your hillbilly neighbor watching us with drones?" Sarge growled.

"And how does he know there's any reason to watch us?" JD was unusually still and sober...but not. Instead of bouncy and hyper, he was twitchy and nervous, and that did nothing to calm me down. Oblivious to me, he asked Smitty, "Does this yoyo just watch you all the time for the hell of it?"

Smitty released a world-weary sigh, rubbing his hand over his face as he pressed back against the counter. We were all crowded into the silo's kitchen, and it seemed way too small with everyone in here. Not just claustrophobic, either—like if someone stormed the silo, we had our backs to the wall. Of course we were heavily armed—everyone had handguns, rifles leaned against chairs and counters, and there was more ammo than food in here right now, which said a lot.

Smitty lowered his hand and scanned the room with

his good eye. "I've never seen a drone over the silo, and Mike's never given me any reason to think he's keeping an eye on me. And his shit about never seeing so many people here? That's shit. He's seen you boys here a hundred times." He gestured upward as if to indicate where he and his neighbor had had their chat. "He seemed edgy, too. Nervous. To be honest, he kinda reminded me of some of those insurgents who'd act like our buddy just so they could stick a bomb in our shit."

A shudder went through every Marine in the room. Leo was standing beside me against the wall opposite the door, and he pressed into my side. I wrapped my arm tighter around his shoulders.

"So somebody knows something." Sarge cut his eyes toward Leo but only for a second. "This can't be a coincidence."

All heads turned toward Leo. Wait. No. Toward *me*.

I shifted nervously. "The Marshals don't even know we're here. No one does."

"Someone apparently does," Sarge growled. "I don't buy for a fucking second that Smitty's neighbor is suddenly curious for no reason." He turned to Smitty. "How far away does he live, anyway?"

"The property line is about five klicks east of the silo," Smitty said. "His cabin is a good five more from there."

"Does he know what kind of facility you've got here?" Bleeder asked.

Smitty shook his head. "No. He knows about the cabin, but that's it."

"But he knows you have half a dozen Marines hanging out here on a regular basis?" Leo asked. "Where does he think you're putting them? Bunk beds?"

Sarge glared, but everyone else chuckled quietly.

"He thinks we all camp in the woods." Smitty shrugged. "As many times as he's heard us all drinking and hollering out here, I'm pretty sure he believes it."

Sarge bristled. "Or he believed it until he sent a drone

up here."

That sobered Smitty. All of us, really.

"Okay, look," Dallas said. "We're not going to figure out why he's watching us by arguing here in the kitchen. I say our top priority is securing the perimeter of the property." He turned to JD. "You think we can jury rig some signal jammers to fuck with the drone?"

JD shrugged. "If Smitty doesn't mind me dismantling some of his electronics."

Smitty's shoulders sagged. He pointed his hook at JD. "You fuck with my coffeemaker, I will end you."

"I won't touch the coffeemaker. Jesus." JD shifted. "But the video game consoles and TV might need replacing after this."

Smitty swore under his breath. "Fine. Fine. Whatever you gotta do."

"How much surveillance gear do you have?" Sarge asked. "Anything?"

"I got cameras and motion sensors. Took a lot of it down because there was nothing to see, but it's all downstairs."

"We'll need all of it," Sarge said. "We need to set up surveillance on the road, at all edges of the property line, and on the driveway. We got enough for that?"

"If we don't," I said, "one of us can go into town. Might not hurt anyway, just to see if anyone is following or watching us."

Sarge's lips pursed, but then he nodded. "Good idea." He turned to Smitty again. "You got a map of the property?"

If there was one thing a bunch of Marines could be trusted to do besides drink and shoot, it was to be prepared. And if we couldn't be fully prepared, we could sure as fuck improvise.

Dallas and JD had gone into town to raid the electronics stores, and Sarge and Bleeder had driven out just to see if anyone followed them. By the time they'd all come back, there hadn't been a peep from anyone. No drones. No cars. No hunters "accidentally" strolling through Smitty's woods.

For the rest of the afternoon and evening, the silo's rec room smelled like solder, burnt electronics, pine trees, and hot glue. JD had—at the cost of an Xbox, a pile of cheap cell phones, and an old VCR—finished building the contraption that would allegedly confuse the shit out of any drones. The rest of us had busied ourselves camouflaging cameras.

"This feels like arts and crafts day at the Marine retirement home," Leo had mused as he'd hot-glued some camo netting to a black tripod.

The guys had chuckled.

"Hey, if it's arts and crafts day," Bleeder had said while carefully arranging some fern fronds around another camera's lens, "there better be some goddamned glitter."

"Damn it, Bleeder." Smitty'd tossed a pinecone at his head. "Don't you dare bring glitter into my silo. That shit gets everywhere."

Dallas snorted. "What? You don't want your place infected with craft herpes?"

"Keep it up, smartass." Smitty shook his head and continued painting a camouflage pattern on the leg of a tripod. "Soon as you're asleep, I'll hot glue your dick to your leg."

Leo had a point—if arts and craft day was a thing at the retirement home for Marines, this was exactly how it would play out.

Arts and crafts were over, though. After some shut-eye, we'd spent yesterday testing equipment and putting up cameras on the north and west sides of the property. This morning, we were back at it. Dressed in head-to-toe green digicam, we divided and conquered an hour before sunrise. Sarge and JD slipped into the woods with a map of the adjacent properties and JD's jamming device. Bleeder kept watch at the entrance of the silo while Smitty monitored the cameras from inside and Dallas took a sentry position at the top of the drive. Curtis and Lucky would have been handy as hell right now, but they were still en route.

As for Leo and me, we hauled some heavy camouflage packs down the side of the mountain to install a few cameras and motion sensors along the edge of the property line that ran parallel to the road. There was already some gear down this way, but the new equipment would essentially upgrade what Smitty had installed. Anything so much as twitched out here, whether it was a mule deer or a car full of Grimaldi goons, we'd know about it.

I had an M-4 slung over my shoulder and kept it against my chest, barrel down and finger outside the trigger guard, as we walked. Leo wasn't carrying a long gun, but he had a pistol on his hip and another on his ankle. It seemed like overkill, considering we were just wandering through the woods of Smitty's property, but with no idea what we were up against, the group had unanimously agreed that when it came to defense, overkill was the bare minimum.

Neither of us said much as we picked our way down the steep hillside through the gray dawn light. We'd both been quiet this morning. Everyone had. Part of it was because it was early as fuck, but mostly, everyone was getting nervous and paranoid; the air in the underground building had been thrumming with it in the thirty-six hours since Smitty's neighbor had come around.

Once we'd reached the bottom, and we were well and truly alone, Leo asked a near-whisper, "What do you really think about the neighbor?"

I shook my head as I motioned for him to turn around. He did, and I started rifling around in his pack for the first of the sensors. "I don't know. Something's weird, though."

"No shit." Leo exhaled, but he didn't press. I knew what he was thinking. He didn't fully trust my guys, and now there was a good possibility some Grimaldi tentacles had reached us here. As spooked as I was right now, even I didn't know who to trust. I'd trusted these guys with my life a million times over, but what if one of them could be bribed? Or blackmailed? Or otherwise threatened?

I shivered and zipped Leo's pack again. "Let's just get all this gear in place."

He didn't argue, and I didn't like that. I could live with him not trusting my guys. But did he still trust me?

I turned to him, camouflaged camera and battery pack still in hand. The sun was coming up, the daylight thin and bleak, and he was searching our surroundings as vigilantly as a trained soldier. His expression was hard to read, which was nothing new for Leo.

"Hey." I touched his waist. "You're still with me, right?"

He looked up at me, and a faint smile broke through. "Why wouldn't I be?"

"I don't know." I brushed a few strands of hair off his forehead and tucked them under his cover. "Just...everyone's getting twitchy and paranoid."

"We're in the middle of nowhere and the mafia probably found us. Of course we're twitchy and paranoid." He slid a hand up the front of my buttoned blouse and curved it behind my neck. "But if I wasn't still with you, I wouldn't be out here in the woods with you and that." He tapped a fingernail on the rifle slung over my shoulder. "And I sure as hell wouldn't have slept next to you."

I couldn't help shivering. We'd done more than sleep last night. It hadn't seemed like the time—did it ever, when it came to us?—but we'd needed the break from all the insanity and fear, and sex was the best escape either of us could think of. I wondered if Leo and I would ever know a time when sex happened just because we wanted it to, not because we were seizing a frantic opportunity that could very well be our last.

We both cleared our throats and broke eye contact.

"We should get these set up," he said.

"Yeah. We—" I stiffened.

A low hum tickled the edges of my senses. I lifted my gaze, searching the slowly brightening sky and the spaces between evergreen branches for the telltale movement of a drone. The hum came closer, though, and resolved itself into the distinct sound of a car engine.

Beside me, Leo had straightened too, and we both stood stone still, searching and listening like alarmed prairie dogs.

The distant engine whined with exertion. Not just from climbing the steep mountain—it was climbing *fast*. Then tires squealed.

I touched the button on my earpiece, "Incoming vehicle. High rate of speed."

"How far?" Sarge asked.

"Not sure. It's coming up from the south and—"

The first volley of gunfire sent Leo and me to the deck. We flattened ourselves on the ground, and I only gave myself a split second to wince at the rifle biting into my ribs before I was on the radio again.

"We've got gunfire!" I pushed myself up and readied the rifle. With the scope, I surveyed the road, but I couldn't see well enough from here.

"Smoker, what's going on?" Sarge's voice was tinny in my ear.

"Don't know. Stand by." I started to rise and said to Leo, "Stay down." I patted between his shoulders, partly to touch him and partly to encourage him to keep his head down, and started running toward the road in a low crouch.

"Where the fuck are you going?" he called after me.

"Stay *down*," I snapped over my shoulder. I moved toward the road as fast as I could, trying to both use the environment as cover and not trip over it.

Engines and squealing tires. Louder now. Headlights came around a curve.

I dropped to my belly. Using my elbows as a bipod, I steadied the rifle and peered through the scope.

A car was coming in hot, and seconds behind it was another. When gunfire rang out again, the muzzle flashes were visible from the pursuing vehicle. The first car swerved, though I couldn't tell if the driver had lost control or if it was an evasive maneuver.

The second car sped up and slammed into the back of the first. This time the first had definitely lost control and started to fishtail. Shit. There was no telling who any of these people were, whose side they were on, or if they had anything to do with us at all.

The first car spun and went off the side of the road. I squeezed off a few shots at the second car. Not enough to take out tires or the engine, carefully aiming so I didn't hit any occupants, but enough to make sure they knew someone was shooting at them.

I definitely had their attention—the car screeched to a halt. Pistols waved out windows as if they were looking for where the shots had come from. I fired again, deliberately missing one of the hands by just a few inches. The hand jerked back into the car. I shot at the pavement near the tires. Then at the fender.

The driver threw the car into reverse, and with some squealing tires and the whine of an engine, executed a U-turn on the narrow road and retreated. I kept firing after them to make sure they didn't rethink their escape.

Once they were gone, the day was still and quiet again except for the distant engine. I lifted my head and searched for the second car.

It had gone into a deep ditch, steam rising from beneath the hood and a rear wheel still spinning in the air. I got up and jogged the rest of the way to the road. The other car was out of earshot now. Or maybe I just couldn't hear it over the idling engine of the crashed vehicle.

Rifle at the ready, I approached slowly. No one moved. No one made a sound.

When I reached the lip of the ditch, I craned my neck and peered in through a large bullet hole in the rear window. Someone was in the driver's seat, slumped part way over the console. A woman, I thought. Carefully, I continued around the car, which was a challenge given its odd angle in the ditch. No one in the backseat. No one in the passenger seat.

The rifle was too cumbersome to maneuver, so I slid it around onto my back and drew a pistol from my hip instead. Then, with my free hand, I pulled open the driver's side door.

The driver was alive and conscious, but bloody. She rubbed the side of her head with a shaky hand, and groaned as she tried to right herself.

I glanced around, making sure I was still alone, then touched her arm. "Hey."

She whipped around, and something hard connected with my jaw, turning my vision white and sending me stumbling back.

I grabbed the car door for balance before I tumbled all the way down into the ditch. As it was, I landed on my back, once again on top of the damn rifle. "What the—"

In a heartbeat, she was over me, pistol trained on me. "Don't fucking move!" she snarled. "Put your gun down!"

Moving slowly, I put the pistol on the uneven ground beside me, then brought my hands up behind my head.

"Smoker?" Sarge said in my ear. "What's going on, man? We're on our way, but we're still a ways out. What's your twenty?"

I couldn't respond. Not without giving myself away.

The woman glared down at me, dark eyes full of suspicion. She opened her mouth to speak, but then—

"Gianna?" Leo's voice raised the hairs on my neck. I craned my neck to see him jogging across the street and holstering his weapon. "Holy shit. Are you okay?" His eyes darted to me, and he stumbled. "What are you doing? Let him go!"

"Let him..." She glared at me again, then looked at him, puzzled. "He's with you?"

"Yes!" Leo gestured for her to lower the gun, and she did. I released my breath.

She tucked her pistol into her waistband, then offered me a hand. I hesitated but took it, and between her and the car door, managed to get to my feet on the steeply angled ground.

Once I was up, we dusted ourselves off. Gianna brushed some glass off her leather jacket and shook some out of her long black hair. There were some cuts on the side of her face and head that looked scary, but I'd spent enough time in the field to recognize them for what they were—superficial wounds that liked to bleed *a lot*.

"Are you okay?" Leo asked again.

"Yeah," Gianna and I both said.

She tugged at the shoulder of her jacket and scowled. "Sons of bitches."

"What?" But then I saw it—a hole in the leather and a bloody wound underneath. "Shit, do you—"

"Fuckers ruined my jacket," she snarled.

"Uh. What about your shoulder?"

"Just grazed me." She shrugged gingerly. "I'm fine."

Yeah, she did seem reasonably okay, though she'd need someone to check her out. I debated if I should take her into town to a hospital, or call Bleeder.

She gingerly rolled her shoulders and her neck, then looked at Leo. "I'm so glad I found you. Dad's got men looking for you everywhere. There are more coming, too." She paused, brow furrowing, and turned to me. Her gaze slid toward the rifle on my back.

I flicked my eyes back and forth between the two of them. "Uh, someone want to fill me in?"

Leo swallowed. A mix of emotions flashed through his eyes. He was nervous, definitely. Wary. Maybe downright scared. He lowered his gaze and gestured at her. "Rich, this is Gianna Grimaldi."

"Gianna...Grimaldi?" I sputtered. "As in..."

"Yes." Leo looked me in the eyes again. "And we should get her inside and have someone check out her injuries instead of standing here talking about it."

I clenched my teeth. I wanted to tear into him—into both of them—right here, right now, but we were sitting ducks out in the open like this.

I touched the button on my radio. "Guys, we've got a situation."

I stood in the kitchen doorway, a small icepack pressed against the spot on my jaw where Gianna had pistol-whipped me. Silently, I watched Bleeder suturing the wound on Gianna's shoulder. She had her elbow pressed to the table and an icepack against her head. She barely flinched each time the needle broke her skin, but she looked miserable.

JD appeared beside me. We exchanged glances. I turned to Bleeder, decided he had things under control in here, and followed JD out into the middle of the silo. There was a bit more breathing room out here. The cylindrical silo extended a few stories above and below me, a pine needle-littered window on top and darkness at the bottom, ringed by steel grate decks and crisscrossed by a couple of bridges. Leaning against the railing, I rubbed my eyes and sighed.

"We've got her car hidden in the woods," JD said quietly. "There was no way it would make it up Smitty's driveway, so that was the best we could do for now."

"Anyone check for a LoJack or anything?"

"Yeah. There were no trackers on it. Looks like it's stolen."

I laughed dryly, dropping my hand to the railing. "Of course it is."

He nodded toward the kitchen. "How is she?"

"Bleeder thinks she has a mild concussion, probably from the crash, but she'll be fine. Bullet grazed her arm, so he's sewing that up now. Then he just has to pick all the glass out of her skin and hair."

JD's lips pulled tight. "Who the fuck is she, anyway?"

I glared at the kitchen doorway but didn't answer.

Right then, Dallas appeared. "Hey guys. Sarge wants everyone in the rec room."

Without a word, we followed him. Everyone except Bleeder and Gianna were in here, including Leo, and my guys were a mess of confusion, shouting over each other.

"Who the hell is she?"

"How did she find us?"

"Who in God's name was in the other car?"

"What the fuck is going on?"

"Guys," I barked. "*Guys!*"

They all fell silent. All stared at me.

Slowly, I turned my head toward the one person who hadn't said anything.

Narrowing my eyes at Leo, I growled, "Start talking. How the fuck did Gianna Grimaldi know where we are?"

Chapter Eleven
Leo

Mother. Fucker.

I had never heard that tone of voice from Rich. *Never.* Not when I was giving him shit as we drove across the country in a stolen car, not when he'd had to pull me off of Matteo Grimaldi to stop me from killing him, not even when we'd had to plan a rescue of his parents before his father bled to death. He sounded...like he thought I was the enemy, which was uncomfortable on a visceral level.

"What makes you think I know?"

"Don't bullshit me," Rich snapped. He wasn't even using my name anymore, shit. This was *not* good. "You're the only reason she'd have to come here in the first place, and I know you wanted to contact her. Fuck, you *did* find a way to contact her, didn't you?"

I opened my mouth, ready with a lie, then shut it.

The only time I've ever seen him really angry with one of our guys was when he caught them in a lie.

Fuck that fucking Dallas for putting that thought in

my head. "Yeah, I did," I said, and a chorus of groans, shouts, and insults started to fly.

"Shit for brains—"

"—think this is, a goddamn summer camp?"

"—operational security at risk, and considering the only reason we're out here in the first place is to save your scrawny ass, maybe you've just proved you're not worth it."

I hated the way that Sarge's curt announcement put a pained look on Rich's face, but I hated the way he didn't speak up to immediately countermand the suggestion even more. "I did text her, but I guarantee you that's not what led these guys here."

"How the hell can you be sure of that?" JD demanded. Gone was the bouncy, squirrelly energy—in its place was a stone-cold Marine who looked like he was itching to point his gun at someone and start pulling the trigger. If I didn't tread carefully, that someone might be me.

"They don't have the resources."

He scoffed. "They've got US Marshals on their side! FBI agents, cops, judges—"

"Do you know anything about my case? Anything at all?" I countered. "Do you have any idea how big the fucking hole I've blown in the law enforcement establishment is? Do you know how many of those people are in holding as we speak? Do you really think there's *any* chance that one of them is stupid enough to try and requisition the equipment it would take to track a single text made to a burner phone that I seriously doubt Gianna is dumb enough to let anyone know about, and then follow it back here? And then on top of that, you think they managed to do it in under twenty-four hours?"

"People do dumb shit sometimes. Just look at you," Dallas said.

"Yeah, and other people should change the fucking passcodes on their phone so dumb shits like me can't use them to make texts," I shot back.

Sarge smacked Dallas upside the head. "Jesus Christ, is he serious right now? You let him get your phone?"

"I didn't let him get anything, I—" His eyes narrowed. "You distracted me with those mountain lions!"

"Oh yeah," I said, heavy on the sarcasm because fuck it, who cared if I pissed any of these assholes off at this point? The only person I cared about right here was Rich, and he wasn't talking. "I orchestrated the passionate lovemaking of two enormous apex predators in the dead of night, all so I could steal your phone. I'm good, don't get me wrong, but I'm not a freaking wizard."

"That's not the point! You—you—"

"It doesn't matter what you say at this point," JD broke in. "You can't prove it *wasn't* that text that brought this shit down on us."

Oh boy, and now it was like having an argument with a dude who'd taken a single philosophy class in college and thought he knew how to win an argument with anyone. I expected him to whip out the "how do you even know anything is really real" argument next. "And you can't prove that it was. Touché, we're at an impasse."

"What else could it be?"

"I don't fucking know. I didn't tell Gianna how to find us. I told her to be careful so they didn't find *her*." I put up my hands. "That's it. How they found us beyond that? *I don't know.* Maybe they tracked down one of you guys. And hell, this is a freaking *missile silo*, you don't think someone's keeping tabs on it even though it's been decommissioned?"

Sarge started to speak, but Smitty cut in.

"Enough," he said, and I shut up and listened. In the end, this was his place. Sarge might be his former commanding officer, and these guys might be his brothers-in-arms, but the silo was his refuge. He had the final say about anything that went on here. "How they figured out where you are is irrelevant."

"I don't think so."

Smitty looked at Rich with concern. I was barely able to keep my jaw from dropping to the floor.

"You lied about one thing," Rich went on, quiet and calm enough to give me chills. "Have you lied about anything else?"

"Rich..." I spread my hands, helpless against his disgust. "You know I haven't."

"I don't know that at all."

It was ridiculous, how much hearing that hurt. I would nail myself to a cross for this man if he let me, if I thought it would help me get back into his good graces, but he didn't care about self-flagellation. Rich was a good man, and he wanted to be on the right side. I had to reassure him that I was on it, too.

I didn't know how to, though. My mouth worked but nothing came out. I could be glib with everyone else here, talk circles around them, pick their pockets and cheat them at cards and steal their phones and not feel the slightest twinge, but Rich was my undoing. He had been from the moment I met him, and he'd gone and saved my stupid life.

"Maybe I can help clear some things up," a new, decidedly feminine voice purred from the direction of the kitchen. Gianna walked toward us, her perforated jacket draped over her good arm. Her bullet wound was bandaged, and she seemed to be walking fine despite the concussion—in glittering Balenciaga knife heels, no less. Andy trailed her like a puppy, with the slightly glazed look that almost all heterosexual men got in her presence. Gianna was a queen, and she didn't hesitate to make sure people knew it.

"I trust you've all heard who I am at this point. My brother is in prison, my father is *going* to be in prison very shortly, and I'm on the same list of traitors marked for death as Leo." She reached out and took my hand, and I swayed a little toward her, magnetized already. She smelled like Guerlain—something smoky and dark, the kind of scent only a woman confident in her own power would dare to put on in the first place. "I did come here because of him, that's true. But I wasn't followed." She tilted her gaze toward the skylight, a wry smile gracing her lips as she pointed her index finger straight up. "In fact, *I* followed *them*."

Sarge was the first to speak out. "Explain that."

"It's simple. I've been laying low in Chicago ever since my brother was taken into custody. My first priority was getting my husband and children out of the country and to safety—once that was done, I needed to concentrate on myself."

"Why not go with them?" Dallas demanded. "If you wanted to be safe, why not stick together?"

"Oh, dear," Gianna said with a sigh. "You poor thing. You don't understand how this works at all, do you?"

"What the *fuck* is that supposed to mean?"

"It means that Gianna has been marked for death by her father, the same as me," I said. "But Papa Grimaldi is old school. If it was easy to scoop up her husband and children, he'd kill them just to teach her a lesson first. She's his focus, though. Staying away from her family is probably enough to keep them safe, as long as the trial happens on schedule."

"Throwing away his whole family, piece by piece." Gianna looked at me sadly. "There was no way back for him after Tony. He just didn't realize it at the time."

Smitty cleared his throat. "Getting back to how you knew where Leo was…"

She shrugged. "When I noticed half the people looking for me were suddenly leaving town, I got suspicious. Also, Leo left me backdoor access to some bank accounts that aren't frozen, so I watched until I started seeing plane tickets being purchased at the last second. That, coupled with Leo's text warning me about people who might be converging on *me* was enough for me to infer that they were, in fact, coming for him. So, I followed the money and followed them."

"And they didn't…notice?"

"Not until the end." Gianna grinned fiercely. "And then I think they noticed quite a bit." She paused, sobering. "You should also be aware that there was a not-insignificant chunk of money moved recently as well to an offshore account. It moved literally minutes before the accounts started being used to book travel and before my father's men started leaving town."

Sarge huffed with palpable impatience. "And? Why should we fucking care if the—"

"Because it's probably a bribe," I said, sounding a bit winded even to myself as the truth sank in. "Someone tipped them off about where we are. The Grimaldis paid them. And then they came after us."

I wished I could have found some satisfaction in the startled look on that fucker's face, but I was still reeling from what may as well have been a black-and-white notarized confirmation that someone had been paid to give us away.

"Why come here?" That was Rich, finally speaking again, and he was asking Gianna. He was still quiet, but he'd lost some of the implacable, unreadable calm that was so weird to see. "Why follow your enemies like that? Why not take the chance to run?"

"Run where?" Gianna met his eyes coolly. Gianna had taken after her mother, from what I'd heard—cold and calculating, not hotheaded like her father and brother. She evaluated all her options before making a move, but when she committed, she salted the fields behind her so there was no turning back. "My father wants to make a statement out of me. I, in turn, must make my own statement if I'm going to be safe. I don't have the means to hire a private army of my own, but I figured if the feds were going to go all out protecting anyone, it would be Leo."

"You're just here to hide behind us, then." Sarge

sounded as dry as a desert.

Gianna laughed, her rich contralto echoing off the concrete walls. "Do I look like the kind of woman who hides behind a man?" she demanded. "I'm here to *use* you, certainly. But I'll fight with you as well. I'd think another marksman on your side would be appreciated, given the trouble that's brewing out there."

"How much trouble?" I asked.

"Fifteen soldiers, one capo. It's Dorian."

"Fucking fuck."

She patted my shoulder. "I know."

Rich sighed and closed his eyes for a second, pinching the bridge of his nose. "Let's sit down," he suggested after a second. "I think it's going to take some time to work this out, and I'd rather not keep you on your feet any longer than necessary after a car crash."

"Such a gentleman," Gianna teased, but very gently. She led the way to the couch and I, just like Andy, followed.

Half an hour later, Gianna and I were alone in the room that Rich and I shared. The one we were still sharing, as far as I knew, but that might change. I didn't know. I couldn't get a read on him right now, and he wasn't helping.

Gianna had taken a shower and accepted one of Smitty's ratty terrycloth robes with an aplomb that impressed me. For a woman used to silk, she was surprisingly okay with the downgrade. She sat beside me on the bed, fanning her dark hair out over her shoulder. Her legs were crossed, feet poking out from beneath her calves. Her toenails had been painted in a rainbow of colors, green on some, blue on others, and dots of pink and purple everywhere. She noticed my gaze and smiled. "Lianne wanted to exchange pedicures. She picked the colors, of course."

Lianne was her youngest, a little girl who'd just turned five, if I remembered right. This time last year I'd been at her birthday party, hosted by Tony, helping run herd on a score of the adorable little maniacs as they flitted from bouncy castle to fairy picnic to laser tag. She'd asked for it, so her Uncle Tony had delivered.

Fuck. Think about something else.

"I was worried about you," I offered.

"I know you were. Why else risk your own safety by sending that text?" She patted the ends of her hair with the towel she was holding. "Especially in this kind of company."

"They're not so bad." Except for the fact that, in all likelihood, one of the Grimaldi's men had used one of them to figure out where we were. If they knew about Rich and Smitty's connection, then saw a bunch of Marines he used to associate with suddenly mobilizing at the same time and likely heading in this direction, it would have made sense to assume we were here.

"You're a fox, Leo, surrounded by a pack of wolves. Different types of predators, different kinds of strength. I know you trust your marshal, but when you're outnumbered like this, it pays to have backup."

I snorted. "Are you a fox too, then?"

Gianna grinned at me. "Hell no. I'm a hyena. Matriarchal, and way bolder than you or them. I do what needs to be done and don't look back." She put the towel aside and touched my hand. "I'm serious about being a help to you here. Tell me what I can do."

"There's nothing to be done, right now." Rich and his friends were reassessing every weak spot—again—and arguing about homemade IEDs, last I checked. I didn't have anything to contribute, and it wouldn't have mattered if I did anyway. Rich wasn't talking to me. And I deserved that, but it still hurt like a gut shot.

"Then tell me what's making you most afraid."

"I'm not afraid," I said reflexively. Gianna rolled her eyes.

"That's absolute crap, and you know it. You're so afraid right now you can barely even look at me, and I'm the only one here who's completely on *your* side. How bad would your avoidance be if it was your marshal in here, instead of me?"

I stared up at the ceiling. "I don't want to talk about him."

"Why not?"

Oh God, were we really going to do this? Bare our souls to each other like we'd ever been more than slightly distant friends? It wasn't like I didn't love Gianna—she was the sort of woman who inspired awe—but she'd been Tony's family, not mine. I loved her for her support of her brother and myself, and I loved her for sticking with me when everything else was going to hell. I did *not* love that she was here. "You were supposed to be safe, not driving to the mountains of Colorado like a maniac and getting shot at."

"I know, I know. You wanted to knock me off your list."

I frowned at her. "What are you talking about?"

"Your list, your mental checklist." She stretched out a foot and nudged my thigh with it. "I've known you since you were a kid, remember? You used to write them down. I pulled one out of the trash once. *How To Beat Tommy Lucci Without Getting Caught.* You had bullet points, sub headings—I was impressed."

I thought back to the list she was referring to. "I was ten when I wrote that."

"Yeah, and by the time I found it, Tommy Lucci had gone to the hospital with a broken collarbone after his bike jettisoned its front tire while he was chasing you on it." She smiled. "The little shit deserved it."

"Why did you come here?" I asked quietly. "Don't give me the answer you gave those guys, I want the real reason. Why?"

Gianna smiled again, but it was a tight, brittle thing. "Freddie wants a divorce."

"Oh, no." Frederick Mackintosh was a stockbroker, and just the kind of slippery bastard I hated—he was mostly friendly, but when he hurt you he made sure you felt it. He and Gianna had met in college. They'd been married for fifteen years now. "I'm sorry."

"One too many attempts on his life, I guess." She braided her fingers together. "He wants full custody of the children. I told him to go to hell, but he's got a good lawyer. I have to clean things up if I'm going to be seen as a fit guardian for my own kids, and that means making sure that no one's left to come after me once dear old Dad is rotting in prison with Matteo."

"And if Freddie's lawyer finds out you played an active role in taking out your father's soldiers? What then?"

"Then I'm no worse off than I was a day ago, hiding in a hole in Chicago, and will be afforded considerably more respect by the people who count. Anyway," she tossed her hair back over her shoulder, "there's no sense in asking what-if. I'm here now, and this has been coming with Freddie for a while. It's better to get all my mid-life crises over at once, I figure."

"Right, sure. You lose your business, your assets get frozen, half your family is hauled off to prison and their assassins have you in their sights, and your dumbass husband wants a divorce. Sounds to me like you definitely deserve a Lamborghini."

Gianna wrinkled her nose. "Ugh, don't even go there. All of Freddie's insipid money manager friends have those cars. I can't walk past them without wanting to scratch their paint. A Maserati for me, please." She gripped my hand. "And I found those 'emergency funds' you set up for me as well, Leo. Thank you for that."

"It's the least I could do." After being the major architect of the destruction of her glamorous, carefully-maintained life, I felt responsible for helping her rebuild it. A hidden and well-stocked account that only she and I could access seemed like the absolute minimum.

"So…Rich."

I jerked my hand away. "I said I don't want to talk about him."

"Well, I do. He's interesting to me."

"Why?"

"Because you're in love with him, that's why."

I shook my head, the hopeless feeling I'd been fighting off welling in me again. "What does that matter? He's furious at me."

"It matters for a lot of reasons, but primarily because it probably means he loves you too. You're not the type to pine hopelessly after a guy. And if he loves you, you need to make him see that you're worthy of it by not hiding in here like a scared little mouse."

Oh, screw you. "I'm…acclimating you. We're acclimating."

"I'm just fine, thanks," she said, raising one eyebrow. "But your best defense is out there surrounded by his packmates, some of whom are going to be filling his ears with poison about you. Are you going to let that happen, or are you going to fight back?"

She had a point. But still… "I feel…overwhelmed. I feel like just being near him right now must seem like an insult, because I lied to him."

Gianna sighed. "Love is work, Leo. Freddie and I forgot that. We let the hard work lapse, and now he's trying to take my children away. If you want him? In whatever way you might be able to have him after this?" She pointed one of her perfectly manicured fingers at the door. "Then you'd better go get him."

Chapter Twelve
Rich

I couldn't remember ever feeling this much tension with my Marines. Sitting around Smitty's game room, exchanging unreadable looks, we may as well have been an alley full of cats waiting for one to hiss so we could all start spitting and yowling again.

At least the arguing had stopped for the moment. We'd come back from checking the property's perimeter, and for the last hour, we'd been balls deep in one of the biggest shouting matches we'd ever had as a team. Everyone was freaked out over the Grimaldis knowing where we were, pissed off that Leo had made contact with Gianna, and livid over now having Gianna—an unknown we all instinctively distrusted—in the silo with us. And there was that tiny detail about the money someone had moved in what appeared to be paying off a bribe, because *that* didn't make us all paranoid. Maybe it was unrelated to our situation. There was no way to tell at this point, and none of us liked unknowns. We were cornered, outnumbered, possibly outgunned (though with this bunch, that would be a hell of a feat), and really, really fucking tired of surprises.

Predictably, the end result was some incredibly cranky Marines.

We'd run out of steam a few minutes ago. My throat was raw from trying to shout over Sarge before JD and Dallas had stepped in between us. Then JD and Sarge had gone at it, and Smitty and Dallas had gotten involved, and then I'd jumped back in, and… At some point, everyone had stepped back and let the dust settle. This wasn't over by any means, but maybe we'd gotten enough out of our system that we could start talking strategy.

It was Bleeder who finally broke the standoff, his voice calm as he said, "Guys, I think we're missing a pretty big point here."

Everyone turned to him, and his eyes flicked from one of us to the next.

"Yeah?" Sarge's patience was hanging by a thread. "What point is that?"

Bleeder inhaled slowly. "Gianna's story lines up with Leo's. Maybe they had a cover story. I don't know. But we need to consider that they didn't, and that they're not lying." He put up a hand before I'd even realized Sarge was about to cut him off. "I'm not done."

Sarge closed his mouth, and his jaw worked as he waited for Bleeder to go on.

"*If*," Bleeder went on, "those two are telling the truth, then how the fuck did the Grimaldis find us?"

"Exactly the point," Sarge snapped. "They couldn't have found us, so—"

"But they did," Smitty said. "Don't get me wrong—I ain't ready to let Leo off the hook, but we need to consider all angles. And until we're absolutely sure Leo gave us away by contacting Gianna, we need to consider that Gianna did find us by following Grimaldi's men. If she did, then that means Grimaldi's men knew where to find us."

"And that they still do," I said. "Whether they *paid* someone for that information or not, they obviously *have* it now."

Sarge glared at me as if I were a traitor for even hinting that I might be going along with this theory. "This is stupid. Of course Leo and Gianna concocted their cover story when they talked. They both admitted he contacted her, so why the fuck wouldn't they—"

"Why the fuck *would* they?" I growled. "Look, I'm as pissed as all of you about this, but the one thing Leo wants to do is survive. I've run from the fucking Grimaldis with him, and when it comes to evasion and survival, he's not stupid and he's not reckless."

Sarge laughed humorlessly.

I ignored him. "He knows how to cover his tracks, and he's even more paranoid than I am. Hell, he was the one who wouldn't let me contact my dad while we were on the run. Not until we had a burner phone and were out in the middle of Bumfuck, Nowhere." I paused, then quietly added, "He'd have made a damn good Marine if he could handle taking orders."

The other guys cautiously chuckled, but Sarge didn't. His glare hardened. "He'd have made a damn *dead* Marine if he was this careless with opsec."

"Except how do we know it was his opsec fuck-up that led Grimaldi to us?" Dallas had been so quiet, his voice actually startled me. "I'm with Bleeder, man—we *have* to consider that Grimaldi knew where we were *before* Leo made contact with Gianna. I'm not saying we drop the possibility that Leo's text tipped them off, but we've got to cover our bases. Which means we need to figure out every possible way Grimaldi could have tracked us down."

Suddenly all eyes were on me. I shifted nervously. "What?"

Sarge lifted his chin. "Are you absolutely sure the Marshals don't know—"

"I haven't told anyone." I showed my palms. "Leo and

I checked every vehicle and device we touched to make sure there was no way to track us, and every time I've made contact with my handler, it's been from out in the middle of nowhere on a burner phone. I even told her we were in North fucking Dakota." I paused. "That… That might actually be something I need to do, now that I think about it. Like it or not, we may need some backup from the Marshals.'"

"Oh hell no," Smitty grumbled. "We are not inviting them to this party."

"We might not have a choice," JD said. "We might need all the help we can get."

"I can at least make contact and see what she's heard in Chicago," I said. "Doesn't mean I'll have her send in the cavalry."

Smitty and Sarge both scowled but said nothing.

JD shifted uncomfortably. "Leo keeps insisting that the Grimaldis are lacking in resources right now, but I don't think we should take that for granted. If the Marshals can back us up…"

"Let's not jump that gun quite yet," Sarge said. "Smoker, you get as far from here as you can and make contact." He jabbed a finger at me. "And make sure you're not followed."

My mind said *no shit, asshole*, but my mouth wisely went with, "Will do."

Sarge turned to the other guys. "Smitty, I think you might want to have a talk with your neighbor. Find out why he's suddenly so interested in what's going on over here. Maybe you and Bleeder pay him a visit, yeah?"

Bleeder and Smitty exchanged uneasy looks but nodded.

"We've still got a little daylight left." Smitty jerked his head toward the door. "Let's set up roving watches."

Bleeder got up. "All right. Let's go."

As they headed out, Sarge turned to the rest of us. "Dallas, assume watch midway down Smitty's driveway.

Stay covered and out of sight. We'll rotate watches every two hours. JD will relieve you. I'll relieve JD, and we'll figure out the rest of the rotation once Smitty, Smoker, and Bleeder come back."

Dallas gave a sharp nod and left, probably to arm up for his watch. He was still in camo pants and a drab green T-shirt, so he'd just need to throw on a blouse and cover and he'd be good.

JD looked at me and Sarge. "So what do we do about Leo?"

"We don't do anything about Leo," I said before Sarge could answer. "I'll handle him."

Neither man seemed thrilled with that idea, but they didn't push. They turned to each other, hammering out some details about watch rotations and perimeter checks.

I should have been listening so I'd know what was up too, but I kept going back to my own declaration that I would handle Leo. I was going to do that…how? I was still pissed and had no idea if I could or should trust him after this.

He was my witness, though. Whether I liked it or not, protecting him was my job. Even if he may have compromised our safehouse. And fucked up my Marines' trust in me.

Well, I'd deal with all that. All I knew right now was that no matter where things went from here between me and Leo, I wasn't backing down from my responsibility to protect him. Not even if I wanted to choke him myself. That meant I needed to keep him close to me. My guys had had mixed feelings about him from the start, and now they were suspicious of him. I wanted to believe they'd still have his back because they were doing this for me, but these were men who'd lost friends in warzones. At the end of the day, they'd have each other's backs—including mine—before Leo's.

Something clenched in my gut. I fully expected their loyalty to be with their fellow Marines, but desperation could drive people to do a lot of shit. One of our men had lost his security clearance and been discharged after his house was foreclosed. Another had had to fight to retain his clearance after a nasty divorce had wreaked havoc on his credit rating. Being seriously desperate for money made a person's moral compass spin like a pinwheel. They could be bribed. Effectively bought by the highest bidder, no matter what that bidder wanted. The military didn't trust them with high-level assets or intel.

Curtis, one of the boys who was still en route, had just been through a hell of a divorce. Sarge, JD, and Dallas had all divorced within the last few years too. Among the team, there'd been some lost jobs and desperate financial times. The VA had fucked around with JD over some back surgery, ultimately leaving him with the bill. We couldn't technically be denied jobs because of PTSD, but Bleeder and Sarge had both struggled to get and stay hired. And hell, I'd hidden my PTSD from the Marshals because I was afraid I wouldn't get hired, so I knew as well as anyone that it could keep certain jobs out of reach.

So it was entirely possible that, among the Marines here at the silo, someone could be in dire enough financial straits to accept a bribe from the Grimaldis. And with that money the Grimaldis had allegedly transferred before they'd left Chicago…

I swallowed bile. That wasn't something I wanted to think about any more than I wanted to think that Leo might have compromised us. But one way or another, the Grimaldis had found us, and we couldn't discount any possible explanation.

Sarge dismissed us, but as he started to go, I stopped him with a hand on his arm. "Hold on."

"Hmm?" He glanced at JD, who eyed us uncertainly. With a curt nod, Sarge dismissed him, and a second later, we were alone in the game room. Sarge met my gaze. "What's up?"

I chewed my lip, glancing at the door JD had closed

behind him. "I think… I think there's one other possibility we might need to consider."

His eyebrows rose.

I gulped. "I don't like the idea. I don't want it to be true. But…" I shifted nervously. "I think we need to consider that someone on the team might have—"

Sarge grabbed the front of my unbuttoned blouse and slammed me up against the wall hard enough to take my breath away. "Don't you fucking go there."

"Sarge," I sputtered. "I'm not saying I don't trust—"

"Pull your *shit* together, Marine," he spat. "We're all risking our necks for you and your crook-ass boyfriend. Don't you fucking think for a second that anyone on our team is selling you out."

"For fuck's sake, I don't think that!" I shoved him back, though he kept a grip on my blouse, so we both stumbled a few steps before he let me go. "I sure as shit don't want to think it." I jerked my blouse to straighten it. "I said we have to consider it."

"No, the fuck we don't." He stabbed that finger at me again. "Bring it up one more time, and you and your boy are on your own. Don't think I won't have our boys packed up and out of here in ten minutes flat."

I put up my hands. I knew when there was no longer any point in arguing with him, so I didn't. Especially since, as defensive as he was at the mere suggestion we could have a mole on our team, I had to wonder if I'd just figured out who that mole was.

Sarge stormed out and slammed the door behind him.

Alone, I sagged against the wall he'd thrown me against a moment ago, and muttered, "Fuck." Maybe I should have kept that card to myself. Or at least thought a little harder about who to show it to. If we had a mole, and Sarge was it, then who was to say he wouldn't turn the rest of the team on me? Just letting them know I had suspicions about any of them—even vague ones that didn't have any particular name attached—could make us unravel when we needed each other the most.

I pushed myself off the wall and shuffled out of the game room and into the middle of the silo. At least I had some time to myself, and I'd have even more once I hit the road to make my call. Admittedly, it was a relief to be away from the boys for a while. I didn't blame everyone for being tense and heated. Stress did that, and being cooped up underground like this gave the distinct feeling of being fish in a barrel—fish just waiting for Chicago gangsters to come along and shoot us—and if that wasn't stressful, I didn't know what the fuck was.

"Rich?" Leo's voice stopped me dead in my tracks.

I turned and gritted my teeth as he met my gaze from a few feet away. He looked as exhausted and wrung out as I felt.

He took a few tentative steps closer, the sound of his boots on the metal grate beneath our feet echoing through the core of the silent, empty missile silo. "Can we talk?"

I didn't have the energy to hash things out with him right now, but could this really wait? I needed to know the truth about how Gianna found us, and I needed to know if I could trust the man who slept beside me. Or if I wanted him to *keep* sleeping beside me after all this.

"Okay. Sure." I gestured toward the room we'd been sharing. "Let's talk."

In silence, we went into the room. Something—the click of the door shutting behind us, the realization that we were finally alone, *something*—made me snap, and I spun around to face him.

"I need you to tell me straight. No bullshit. How did Gianna find us?"

Leo flinched, and he didn't meet my gaze, but he also didn't get defensive like I thought he would. "I wasn't lying and neither was she. When I texted her, she put two and two together, and she followed them here." He finally looked at me, fatigue radiating off him. "Yes, I made contact when you told me not to, and I'm *sorry* for that.

But she was in danger, and I had—"

"And she seems like the kind of woman who can take care of herself. Besides, how can you be sure she's not the reason *we're* all in even *more* danger?"

He rolled his eyes and threw up his hands. "I don't know what else to tell you, Rich. I texted her. I told her to be careful because if they were coming after me, they'd also be coming after her. She took it from there. End of story."

"Do you honestly think she needed to be warned? She seems pretty damn smart, so I find it hard to believe she needed—"

"Would you have warned your dad if you knew Grimaldi's goons were on their way to shoot him?"

I stared at Leo, stunned that he'd gone there.

"Of course you would have." His tone was softer now. "Your dad's trained and he's smart, but come on. If you could have given him some kind of warning that they were coming, don't act like you wouldn't have."

I pursed my lips. He...did have a point.

"And anyway, I owed her one," Leo ground out. "She warned Tony and me about the hit on us, and she told you and me where to find her brother. You and I both owe her, and you better believe I wasn't going to just leave her to the wolves. Not when she's one of the only two people left on earth I actually care about." As soon as he said it, his teeth snapped shut. Cheeks coloring, he broke eye contact again.

I swallowed. "Leo..."

"I care about you, okay?" he whispered. "If you'd been the one on the other end of that text, I'd have sent it too." With some work, he looked in my eyes. "I don't want to lose anyone else. Not you, and not her."

"I don't want to lose you, and that isn't just a professional commitment. I didn't bring all my buddies out here for fun—I don't know what we're up against, and I want our best odds of defending ourselves. Defending *you*." Turning away, I threw up a hand. "But I can't do that if I'm getting blindsided by shit like this."

"What did you want me to do? Tell you before I texted her?"

"Or just not text her."

"No." The word came out firmly, but not sharply.

Facing him again, I narrowed my eyes. "Leo, any outside communication could compromise—"

"I knew the risks," he snapped. "But I've already got Tony's death on my conscience. I don't want hers."

"So what about ours?" I demanded. "Mine? Everyone else in this silo?" I gestured at the door. "Are we disposable so—"

"For fuck's sake, of course not. But you're also hunkered down, trained, and well-armed. Gianna's a civilian with *kids*."

I blew out a breath and wiped a hand over my face. I was as exhausted as I was frustrated. I needed to be on the same page with Leo and with my guys, and I had no idea how to do both. Or if it was possible. Sighing, I dropped my hand and turned to him. "The only way any of us are getting through this is if we all work together. No secret calls or texts. Nobody doing shit to compromise us."

"I know. And I know you don't, but I trust her." He set his jaw and looked me in the eye. "I trust you too, but *only* you and her. Being here..." He gestured at our surroundings. "I'm with a bunch of heavily armed battle-trained guys I don't know, and I..." He dropped his gaze.

"So you don't trust them?"

"I don't *know* them." He held my gaze, and I swore the fear in his eyes was heartbreakingly raw and childlike. "I'm scared, Rich. I'm terrified. I just... I only have you and Gianna. I'm trusting you about these guys even though it scares me to death, and all I'm asking is for you to trust me about her. I didn't tell her where to find us."

"Then who did?"

"How the fuck should I know?" He waved a hand

skyward. "Maybe talk to Redneck McDronePilot and find out what he knows."

"Smitty's talking to him right now," I growled back. "And I'm going out to call my handler and see if there's any news from the DA."

Leo straightened. "You're leaving the silo?"

"I'm sure as shit not going to call from here."

"Then I'm going with you to—"

"No. You're not."

"Rich. I'm not asking."

"And I'm not negotiating." I turned away to get my wallet off the nightstand. "You're safer here than out there."

"So you're just going to leave me with a bunch of Marines who are pissed off because they think I compromised our location?"

"They're not going to lay a finger on you, and if you really do trust me, then you know I'm right."

"But you're—"

"I'm leaving you in a secure location with heavily armed Marines who know how to protect you." I shoved my wallet into my back pocket. "If there are Grimaldis out there, I don't want them getting their hands on you."

Leo's forehead creased as his eyes widened with alarm. "What about you? You're going out there alone?"

"I'm doing my job," I said coldly. "Making sure you're safe."

"Am I, though?"

"You're safer here than you are out there. And I need to go so I can get back before it gets too late." I didn't wait for a response and headed out of our room. He didn't follow. What that meant, I had no idea, but I supposed we could finish hashing things out later.

I checked in with Sarge on my way out and got a burner phone and the keys to Dallas's truck. It occurred to me that maybe I should tell Leo my concerns that someone on the team was compromised, but...no. I had nothing but a gut feeling and paranoia to back that up, and the last thing we needed was more suspicion and distrust festering between us all.

As I drove away from the silo, I was more restless than I'd been since that shootout in Chicago a lifetime ago. I didn't know who to trust. Who to confide in. Who to be wary of. Who to rely on. On top of that, nothing between Leo and me felt resolved. I believed him about Gianna, but I was still livid that he'd gone behind my back to contact her. The least he could have done was give me a heads up or… I don't know. Something.

But I was too stressed and frayed to argue about it. I had a job to do.

First, keep him safe.

Once the danger was behind us, then we could figure out what was going on between us.

Assuming we both made it through this in one piece.

Chapter Thirteen
Leo

Watching Rich leave felt like having one of my fingernails slowly torn away. It wasn't that I couldn't handle myself without him—I could do what I had to do—but nothing would even approach the realm of comfortable for me until he came back. Even worse, Smitty and Andy were gone too.

Smitty's presence felt natural, even when he was pissed at me—I'd known him the longest, and he was the one Rich had trusted first. And Andy was a classic peacemaker, the kind of guy you could throw into the middle of a firestorm and trust to cool everyone else down. It seemed to physically pain him to watch his friends argue, and he'd been nice to me and to Gianna. It was surprising how much simple kindness could come to mean when you were under pressure.

Stockholm Syndrome. Except these guys weren't my captors, they were the people saving my ass. Rich would tell me to trust them—hell, he'd already told me that. Trust them, because he trusted them. Trust them because I trusted him.

Fat fucking chance. I didn't trust Sarge, JD, or Dallas, and I wasn't going to take anything for granted. Those three were still here, and every damn one of them was either up in that shed or keeping a lookout about a quarter-mile down the road. Apparently, Gianna and I weren't worth hanging around with if they could help it. Lucky for me, that was just going to make things easier.

The silo had a back door—a paranoid bastard like Smitty would never live in a place with only one access point, and I'd verified my hunch when he'd laid out the blueprints to the silo earlier, pointing out various defensive features to his buddies. He'd barely mentioned the door other than to say, "I'll take the traps off that, just in case we need to use it." Apparently, there was no surveillance there—it let out into the middle of the woods and was well-hidden, so why waste energy keeping an eye on it?

Why indeed. But someone needed to keep an eye on *these* guys, and that door was key to my figuring out how. I knew Papa Grimaldi's men hadn't followed Gianna here—she wasn't lying about that. So they were acting on someone else's tip. It had to be one of the Marines.

Rich didn't want to hear that, and that was understandable. That was fine. And the rest of these guys sure as hell didn't want to consider the option that one of their own was a snitch, but I lived in the real world, and I wasn't taking anything on faith.

Rich's trip would take about three or four hours, depending on how far he went out into the plains. Smitty would probably be done with his neighbor a hell of a lot faster, so if anyone was going to take this chance to do something shady, it would be before Smitty got back.

"Of course I'll cover for you," Gianna said when I told her what I was about to do. "What, you think I can't distract a bunch of hypervigilant, humorless ex-soldiers? What kind of useless *stronza* do you take me for?"

She had a point. Gianna had grown up in a mob household, but… "I don't think they're the type to be distracted by your feminine wiles."

She smiled sarcastically. "Good thing I'm an expert at pissing people off, then. Go on, go. Stop wasting time telling me how to handle myself."

I went.

The way to the backdoor was like something out of a horror movie—a narrow concrete tunnel with ancient fluorescent lights in the ceiling that would no doubt flicker ominously if I turned them on. The tunnel became a steep set of stairs that went up to a metal trapdoor. There was a camera beside it, but it appeared to be unpowered. The door was held shut by several locks, including an enormous padlock, but I'd come prepared with my lockpicks.

I *hadn't* been prepared for the difficulty of actually lifting the damn trapdoor, though. I was strong, but I wasn't a weightlifter, and it felt like a tree had fallen across this thing. If I had to get Gianna to help me, I'd never hear the end of it.

"God—damn—fucking—" I rammed my shoulder into it over and over, and eventually something on top gave way. The door cracked open, and after a brief shower of dirt, daylight peeked through.

"Jesus." I looked at myself disgustedly—soil, pine needles, and several bugs decorated my head and shoulders, but I'd worry about cleaning up later. It had already been half an hour since Rich left. I needed to get a move on.

I opened the door just enough to wriggle out—it creaked like a bitch—and found myself exactly where I'd expected, in the middle of the forest with nothing but trees in every direction. I held still for a long moment regardless—if a Grimaldi was out there, I'd know soon enough. They weren't known for being patient when it came to making their kills, excepting Dorian, and Dorian

CARI Z & L.A. WITT

wouldn't waste himself on watching anything except the main access point.

If one of the Marines saw me, well… I'd just have to hope they figured out it was me and didn't shoot first, ask questions later. Which meant I'd have to hope they didn't see me at all.

I waited another minute, until the promising lack of getting shot convinced me I was alone. I looked at the door. It was well-hidden; I had to give it that. I'd probably never find it again if I didn't have some way to mark it. After a second's consideration, I propped the door open on a chunk of wood. I left my flashlight behind for good measure but kept my Glock out. Good enough.

Time for some orienteering. Shit.

I could be dropped into a strange city bare-ass naked, dazed and confused, in the middle of winter and still orient myself. Every city I'd ever been in, no matter how dumb and illogical the layout seemed, could be cracked with just a little time. The great outdoors, however? It was the wilderness to me, literally and figuratively. The one time I'd been to New York, I managed to get lost in Central Park. This? The actual Colorado wilderness? It made me so nervous my hands were shaking, and it was still broad daylight.

I kept glancing behind me as I crept up the shallow hill toward where I figured the hut had to be, just to make sure I could still see the tree beside the trapdoor. Were mountain lions nocturnal, or did they hunt during the day? Did Colorado have wolves? Even coyotes sounded like a bad time. Raccoons… Those could get big, and they could be vicious if they were rabid. What if I ran into a rabid raccoon?

I was so worried about the local wildlife that I practically forgot about the imported beasts. The sudden *crack* of a stick up ahead of me had me darting around the nearest tree, my breath coming fast. Holy shit. What if it was a bear? They could climb trees, couldn't they? I peeked my head around the tree, and my breath caught.

It was way worse than a bear. It was a man, a man I recognized. Dorian Killoran. He was all in black and wearing a familiar scowl on his broad, pocked face. Dorian was the odd man out among the Grimaldis, an Irishman who was loyal to the Italian mob—or, more specifically, to Lorenzo Grimaldi. Dorian had been sent as a representative of a family in Boston to strike a deal with the Muranos, a now-defunct group operating out of the south side of Chicago. Things had gone badly, the meeting became a bloodbath, and the only reason Dorian had survived was because Papa Grimaldi, a friend of the Muranos and ostensibly there to help keep the peace, had personally shot a buddy through the head before the guy could kill Dorian.

He'd done it to secure territory, not out of any interest in Dorian, but Dorian had taken his salvation to heart. He was the Chicago area's most notorious hitman, after my Uncle Angelus, and he was hardest on those he deemed disloyal. I had no doubt that Gianna and I were at the top of his list.

He hadn't seen me yet. I knew that, because I was still alive. Dorian stood about fifty feet away from me, turning his balding, gray head in a slow circle. Waiting for someone—his contact among the Marines? Probably. I needed to get closer. *You can do this*, I assured myself, taking a long, slow breath. *You just need to get close enough to film them with your—*

"Meow."

I glanced down at my feet. "Oh, shit." It was Inigo. Inigo had gotten out, almost certainly through the door that I'd left open. He stared up at me, then casually licked one black and white paw.

"Mew."

"Fuuuck," I whispered. Okay, I could still do this. I just needed to grab Inigo, head back to the trapdoor and put him inside, *close* that fucker this time, then come back and—

"You took your sweet fuckin' time."

That was Dorian, speaking to—who? I risked a look around my tree again, but whoever it was wore formless camouflage and had their face covered by goggles and a tan buff.

Was it one of Dorian's guys?

"Don't tell me t'keep my voice down, who's gonna hear me in the middle of all this shit?" Dorian kicked a pile of rotting pine needles. "You said you were going t'get us inside, but here we are meetin' in the middle of the fuckin' woods."

"Meow."

"Inigo, *no*—" I grabbed for him but missed, and he slipped around the tree and started walking toward the two men.

This cat was going to get himself killed. Worse yet, he was going to give *me* away if I didn't get him. I bit my lower lip hard enough to hurt and looked one more time around the tree. Dorian and whoever it was seemed absorbed in their conversation. I could risk moving. I had to.

I left the dubious safety of the lodgepole pine and crouched down, shuffling after Inigo. My feet left long furrows in the underbrush—forget just catching a glimpse of me, if someone wanted to track me and follow me back to the trapdoor, I'd be screwed. Inigo was still moving, trotting over the terrain like a little mountain lion himself. He was going too fast for me to catch without speeding up, but if I did that I'd definitely be heard.

A grasshopper perched on a pine seedling jumped away from him, back toward me. Inigo, unable to resist, pounced after it. I lunged and grabbed him by the scruff of the neck, then rolled both of us behind a fallen log.

"*Meeeooow!*"

"What the fuck was that?"

Oh, shit. I glared at Inigo, who glared right back at me.

At least he wasn't clawing the hell out of my arms.

"Don't tell me t'calm down, you're the one sittin' pretty inside that silo while me and my lads are out here sweltering in our cars and shittin' behind the nearest tree!" There was a pause. "Don't tell me what the deal is. I *made* the deal with you. But forty-eight hours is too long! You think we want to spend the fuckin' weekend in this god-forsaken place? Get me Leotrim Nicolosi and Gianna Grimaldi before noon tomorrow, or you're lookin' at a world o' hurt, my boy."

I heard the crackle of a radio and the quiet murmur of the other man.

"Your friends will escape without bullets in their skulls for now, but the longer you delay, the itchier my boys' trigger fingers get." There was a pause. "Ah, well that's just one of the differences between us. You care whether your men live or die. Me? This is a contract, and I'm here to see it through. You don't have a lot of time. I suggest you make your move soon."

There was the rustle of leaves, the distant crunch of feet moving through the forest, and then—silence. Nothing but birdsong and the rumbling purr of Inigo, who'd apparently decided that my chest wasn't the worst place for an impromptu cuddle. I barely felt his claws as he kneaded my chest, my mind was running so fast.

Fact one: I was right. One of the Marines was a traitor.

Fact two: I didn't have any proof, which meant no one but Gianna and maybe—*maybe*—Rich would believe me.

Fact three: I knew where they wanted to get us, and loosely, when.

Fact four: I needed to get back to the silo, asap.

I started to move, then stopped as Inigo suddenly raised his head, his eyes widening a bit. He tensed, as if readying to jump down from my chest and run over to someone. I kept a firm grip on him, trying to soothe, not crush, and held perfectly still. Dorian and I might not know how to get around in the woods without causing a ruckus, but a battle-trained Marine sure as fuck did.

If I stayed where I was, I ran the risk of being found. It would be the easiest thing in the world to shoot me out here, then claim a Grimaldi had done it later. But if I got up and ran, I'd be giving myself away completely.

I did the hardest thing in the world and held still. I clenched my muscles tight against the anxious tremors that wracked me, kept my breaths shallow, and prayed that Inigo wouldn't start meowing again.

After a small eternity, the cat relaxed. I thought I heard a rustle in the bushes a little way off, but it could have just been the wind. Or fuck it, it could have been a bear and I wouldn't have cared at this point, I was so fucking relieved. Gradually, I sat up and looked around. No one.

"Jesus Christ," I muttered. Inigo looked up at me, then gently bit one of my fingers. "Yeah, you said it. Let's get the hell out of here."

I found the trapdoor, and thankfully Inigo went in without a fuss. I followed him, locked everything up behind us, and breathed a huge sigh of relief. Still alive. Now…what to do with the new information I had?

I'd start by sharing it with Gianna. I headed back down the hall, picking leaves off my clothes and pine needles out of my hair. God, the woods were a filthy place. What I wouldn't give for a—

"—for a meeting, so where is he?" That was Sarge, and he sounded pissed.

"Hasn't anyone ever told you it isn't nice to crowd a lady?" Gianna retorted. "Can't a person even use the toilet without one of you soldier boys trying to micromanage them?"

They were in the central part of the silo, their voices echoing off the pitted concrete. I kept my steps soft but hurried up, creeping through the doorway behind them and toward the nearest bathroom. I turned the light on and checked myself for more clingy bits of nature, brushing them off when I found them and throwing them into the toilet.

"If the two of you want to be kept in the loop, you'll come the first time when I announce a meeting. Otherwise, we'll happily cut you out of them."

"Oh, I don't think you're in any position to be threatening *me* with cutting," Gianna purred, and I knew that was my cue. If I let this keep going, the odds of a knife fight got dangerously high.

I flushed the toilet, washed off my hands, and exited the bathroom a second later. "My ears were burning," I said with a smirk. "You must have missed me."

Sarge scowled. "Not possible."

I affected a broken heart.

"Get to the kitchen," he grumbled. "Smitty is back."

"And hungry, I guess. Or are all of you allergic to comfort?" I gestured all around us. "Couches! Chairs! Cushions!"

Sarge turned and walked away without another word. Gianna and I followed more slowly. She raised an eyebrow at me, and I nodded—I had intel. Not everything I'd wanted to come away with, but it was better than nothing.

Now I just had to figure out what the hell to do with it.

Chapter Fourteen
Rich

I probably shouldn't have gone alone to make the call.

Partly for the obvious reasons—backup. Someone to shoot while I drove, or drive while I shot. Or one of us driving while the other tried not to bleed out in the passenger seat. It didn't matter that we were critically low on manpower back at the silo. Safety in numbers was the name of the game in combat ops.

But the less obvious reason—or at least the one that hadn't crossed my stupid, stubborn mind—was that while I was, say, two hours out into the desert with darkness closing in, my demons might decide it was a good time to show up.

Parked on the side of the highway, my tingling, sweat-slicked hands gripping the wheel painfully tight, I tried to will away the panic attack. I was on that knife's edge, one sudden sound or movement away from revisiting my past, and my heart would *not* slow down. It didn't help that I reminded myself that the fucking Grimaldis could be closing in on me, and I needed to have my shit together in case they showed up. No, that was not what a PTSD-addled brain needed to hear.

It wasn't what a PTSD-addled stomach needed to hear, either.

I fumbled with my seat belt and the car door, almost tripped when I jumped down from the cab, and somehow made it around the back of the truck before I heaved into the ditch. The force of the retching drove me to my knees, and I stayed there for a long moment, hands in the hot sand while I spat acid into the weeds.

Even after I was sure I was done getting sick, I didn't get back into the truck. I rose, staggered back, and held onto one of the bed's siderails while my knees figured out whether they were going to keep shaking or not. The rapidly fading daylight didn't help; it just made me feel more like I was blacking out.

Slowly, though, I came back into control.

I knew why I'd finally lost it. The whole way down the mountain and out into the desert, I'd let myself linger too long on our situation and how many of my friends were in danger. I'd let my thoughts wander too far into what could have happened and what had happened in the past. Truthfully, it had only been a matter of time anyway. Leo had already shaken me out of a few nightmares since we'd gone into the silo, but a waking flashback had been inevitable and I'd known it. I'd tried to hide it like I always did, but I'd known it.

And now I was out in the middle of nowhere, alone and standing here like a dumbass while a Grimaldi sniper with night vision was no doubt sighting in a rifle from half a mile away.

Fresh panic crawled up my spine, but I shrugged it away—tried to, anyway—and jogged back around to the driver's side of the truck. I got in, but I didn't put the truck in gear. I was still too shaky to drive, and God help me if I needed to elude a vehicle, but I was far enough out into the sticks to make my call.

I thumbed my handler's long memorized number into the burner phone. As the call rang on the other end, I leaned into the headrest and scanned the open, empty land in the fading daylight. There was an eighteen-wheeler about a mile in the distance. I kept an eye on it, but I wasn't too concerned.

Gaze fixed on the approaching truck, I listened to the ringing on the other end of the line.

"Vanessa Martin," she said disinterestedly.

I cleared my still burning throat. "It's Cody."

"Oh my God." She was very interested now. "Are you all right?"

"For now." I stared intently at the truck. "I can't talk long. Any word on the trial date?"

She sighed heavily. "Grimaldi's attorney keeps requesting continuances."

"Yeah, I'm pretty sure I know why."

She was quiet for a moment. "Don't tell me where you are, but are you safe?"

"Probably not." I paused to let the truck roar past, and when the noise quieted, I said, "We've got company here, and they're probably going to make their move soon."

"Christ, Cody. You need to move him to a safehouse."

"A Marshals safehouse?" I laughed dryly. "No thanks. I'll take my chances out here. Besides, if we try to leave, we'll be stepping out into the line of fire. Just leaving to make this call was risky as fuck, so I don't know when I'll be able to do it again."

Vanessa released a long breath. "Shit."

"Is anyone there making noise about us?"

"I've got some ears on the inside who say there's more than noise. Someone knows where you are."

"Uh. Yeah. No shit. I just told you—"

"No, I don't think you understand." She spoke quickly and quietly, as if she were afraid of someone eavesdropping. "Whoever they've sent your way, there's more coming. A lot more."

I gulped. "Define 'a lot'?"

"It's hard to say. There are, well, *a lot* of Grimaldi

soldiers and lieutenants missing, and a lot of vehicles missing from the family's fleet. And I don't mean missing like they've gone AWOL."

"Fuuuck."

"Gianna Grimaldi's gone missing too. There's a contract on her, and—"

"He issued a contract on his own daughter?"

"He had his son killed," she said dismissively. "Why not?"

"Jesus." Gianna and Leo had insisted her life was in danger, but the confirmation was unsettling to say the least. What the hell kind of dysfunctional family put out contracts on each other's heads? Mafia families, apparently. "Any word on where she's gone?"

"No. Her husband and kids are in protective custody, but he doesn't know where she is. No one does. I suspect the next time we hear about her, it'll be from Homicide."

I pressed my lips together. Damn. Maybe it was good that Gianna had joined us. At least now she had the safety of a missile silo and some heavily armed ex-Marines. God only knew if that would be enough.

In the rearview, a vehicle was approaching. Only its headlights were visible, but I kept an eye on it.

Especially when the car started slowing down.

My spine straightened. I started the truck's engine, then picked up my pistol from the passenger seat and pulled it into my lap. "I have to go. I'll be in touch soon. Hopefully."

"Stay safe, Cody. These guys are not fucking around."

"Neither am I." I watched the car in the rearview as it continued to slow down. "Don't worry."

I ended the call, put the phone aside, and put the truck in gear. I was tempted to hope my brain was finished with its shitfit so I could do some evasive maneuvering, but then I saw the lightbar. Heart thumping, I slid the pistol down between my legs and partway under my thigh. Accessible, but invisible from either window, especially in the dark.

The cruiser's door swung open. Sweat beaded on the back of my neck and fresh panic curdled my already raw stomach as a hefty cop stepped out and put on his hat.

He took his sweet time strolling up to the passenger side of the truck. "Everything all right, son?"

"Oh. Yeah. I just pulled over to look at a map."

He scanned the interior, and I realized I didn't actually have a map, so I just held up my phone and smiled.

"I see. Well, how about letting me have a look at your license and registration, and I'll let you be on your way?"

"Really?" I started to reach for my wallet. "Because I'm parked on the side of the road?"

He shrugged, smiling broadly, but somehow…weirdly. "It's just a formality, son."

Formality, my ass. But if I didn't play along, he'd know something was up.

In theory, I could flash him my US Marshals badge. My gut said no. And wasn't Smitty's drone-flying neighbor an ex-cop who'd worked in the area? Okay, this didn't feel right, and I couldn't be sure what I was up against.

Which meant I couldn't show him my driver's license either.

I patted my pocket, then grimaced. "Oh shit."

"Hmm?" the cop asked.

I turned to him, eyebrows up. "I forgot my wallet."

"Did you, now?" He scowled. "Do you at least have your registration?"

"Yeah." I made a slow gesture of reaching for the glove box, my pistol digging into my hamstring as I did. Fortunately, Dallas was a bit of a neat freak, and I didn't have to paw through fast food napkins or other debris to find his registration. Just my luck, there was an insurance card with it. I didn't like the idea of this cop knowing that one Jeremy Keith Dallas of Tucson, Arizona, was in the area, but under the circumstances, my options were limited.

He took the registration and insurance card and stepped away from the truck, but he didn't go back to his car. Instead, he spoke quietly into his radio. Someone responded with something I didn't understand.

A moment later, he returned to the window and handed me back the papers. "All right, Mr. Dallas. How about you make sure you have your license with you next time, yeah?"

I laughed. "Will do. Thanks, Officer."

He gave me a two-fingered salute, then headed back to his cruiser.

My heart went wild as I pulled out onto the road again. The fact that he'd let me go without so much as a ticket raised the hairs on my neck. He could have been a serious pain in the ass, and by all rights, he should have. But he hadn't. Call me paranoid, but that didn't sit right.

Halfway back to town, I pulled off on a side road and stopped. I kept the truck in gear and my foot on the brake as I took out everything the cop had touched.

And as I unfolded the registration, damn if a little black chip didn't tumble out of the crease and into my lap.

I was no technical expert, but I'd have bet a year's salary it was a tracking device. Possibly even a listening device. Whatever the fuck it was, it needed to get out of this truck before I made it back to the silo.

Question was—where to leave it? If I tossed it out the window now, he'd know I'd found it. I also didn't want to put it on another vehicle. That was a good way to have the Grimaldis descend on some innocent bystander, and that entire family was well known for shooting first and skipping the questions altogether. And if someone saw me get rid of it before I went up into the mountains, there was a possibility I wouldn't *make* it into the mountains.

I drummed my nails on the wheel. Then I put the truck back in gear and pulled onto the highway.

Hope you're ready to chase some wild geese, Officer.

I hauled ass and drove deep into the mountain back

roads, well past the winding driveway that would take me back to Smitty's silo. No one was following me so far. That was promising.

After I'd taken enough twists and turns that I was almost lost and anyone following me definitely was, I pulled into a parking area beside a trailhead. Then I worked fast because it was only a matter of time before someone caught up with me.

In the glovebox, I found a plastic bag full of receipts, emptied it, and put the tracker into the bag. Then I sealed it, jogged up the trail to a bridge, and tossed it into the river. I listened for the telltale splash to make sure it had landed in the water, then headed back to the truck.

I waited a few minutes to make sure no one arrived at the trailhead. When they didn't, it was a safe bet they were pursuing the rapidly moving tracker, and would be miles from here before long.

With my pursuers following the river instead of me, I headed for the silo.

On the way up Smitty's driveway, I had the eerie sense that I was being watched. Probably because I knew I was—someone was in the bushes somewhere, armed and camouflaged, keeping an eye out for Grimaldis. Friendly, of course, but I always hated that feeling of being watched by someone I couldn't see.

At the top of the driveway, I parked and hurried inside, ignoring the remnants of my earlier panic attack at the ends of my nerves. I was probably in for a long night tonight, maybe even some full-on flashbacks, but I had to keep it together now. This was combat. The worst possible time for a breakdown.

Just keep it together until lights out. Assuming any of us live that long.

JD and Sarge were in the middle of the silo, Sarge leaning against the railing while JD stood with a deep scowl on his face and his arms folded across his chest.

They both turned as I came down the steps.

"Well?" Sarge asked. "Any—"

"Get everyone into the rec room." I brushed past both of them and continued toward the room I shared with Leo.

"What's going on?" Sarge called after me.

"Rec room," I said over my shoulder. Whatever he said after that, I ignored.

I pushed open the door to my room.

Leo was sitting on the bed, and he was instantly on his feet. "Thank God. We need—"

"Everyone's meeting in the rec room," I said. "Get Gianna. We—"

"Rich, listen to—"

"There's no time. We have to—"

"*Rich.*" The way he growled my name gave me pause, and I met his gaze. Voice quiet and anything but calm, he said, "There's someone in the group we can't trust."

I threw up my hands. "For fuck's sake, we—"

"I saw him talking to one of Grimaldi's men."

My teeth snapped together.

Leo folded his arms and shifted restlessly. "I slipped outside. I—" He put up a hand. "Don't. Just let me finish." He glared at me, and when he was apparently satisfied I wasn't going to cut him off, he continued. "I couldn't tell who it was. He was completely camouflaged and… anyway, I couldn't see his face or hear his voice well enough to recognize him. But I *know* Dorian Killoran's face *anywhere.*"

I furrowed my brow. "Dorian Killoran?"

"Yeah. He's an Irish guy, real chummy with the

Grimaldis." Leo looked right in my eyes and swallowed hard. "And he was demanding that whoever he was talking to hand over me and Gianna by noon tomorrow, or the rest of his guys were taking out the rest of yours."

My heart dropped into my stomach. I hadn't known Leo for very long, but I'd learned a lot of his tells. I was never quite sure when he was lying, but there was no mistaking when he was scared, and right now, Leo was scared shitless.

"I don't know what to do," he said shakily. "I don't trust anyone but you, so if you've got any ideas, let's hear them. Because right now, all I know is someone out there"—he gestured at the door I'd come in through—"is planning to hand me and Gianna over to one of the most brutal hitmen in Chicago."

"Holy shit," I breathed.

"What the hell do we do now?"

I shook my head but didn't say anything.

Because I had no fucking idea.

Chapter Fifteen
Leo

"We've got to tell them."

"*Rich.*" I wanted to bang his head against the wall. I wanted to fucking kiss him and push him into bed and cover him with my body and get him to just *not*. "Stop thinking that your war-buddy honor code is a thing anymore. It *isn't*. Not for one of these guys, and it might not stop with just one."

"All the more reason that we get it out in the open."

"You're killing me here." Maybe literally, but I was less worried for myself and more worried for Rich. Gianna and I, we weren't going anywhere without a fight. That was why I'd hidden weapons, why she probably had an entire arsenal on her body that I couldn't see—I would straight-up kill one of these men before they could give me to Dorian. I knew what happened to people in the hands of a master torturer—hell, I'd learned from the best in the business. Uncle Angelus was a maestro of pain and fear, but Dorian was no slouch. And when I thought of what he'd do to *Gianna*—

No, there was no way. I'd kill myself and take her with

me first.

"They won't believe you," I said. "They definitely won't believe me."

He nodded in agreement. "I know. But if we put it all out there and agree to just run down the clock to noon tomorrow, then it'll solve itself. Whoever argues hardest for a different plan is the biggest suspect."

Okay, so that was…logical. He had me there. But… "The Grimaldis could attack before that. Then what?"

"Then we weather it, like we would if we had no idea there was a traitor here, and we see what happens next." He put a hand on my shoulder. "I don't like it either, okay? But we're not going to get any more secure until Curtis and Lucky show up."

"Oh my God, there are more of you?" I moaned. I'd completely forgotten the other two members of his unit who were on the way. "When are they supposed to get here, and how the hell are they going to get through a mafia blockade?"

"Sometime tonight, and with a lot of covering fire." His smile looked as close to relaxed as it probably could, under the circumstances. "Look on the bright side. At least you'll know neither of these guys is the traitor, since there's no way they could have taken that meeting in the woods."

"Smoker!" I heard one of the guys—Sarge, probably, with that angry tone—shout toward our room. "You called this meeting, now get your ass in here and tell us what the hell it's about!"

"Coming!" he shouted back, then looked at me. "Do you want to get Gianna?"

"Noooo," I said, pulling on the word like taffy. "Because I want to get through the next ten minutes alive, and the likelihood of her getting into a knife fight when one of your friends makes an asshole of himself is way too high." Plus, if things did get violent—and I wasn't saying they would, but if they did—I wanted to have some out-of-sight support of my own. It wasn't like the Marines wouldn't leave a guy watching the road, after all.

Only when I walked into the room, I realized that—shit—they were all here. "Whoa," I muttered. "Who's manning the front door?"

"We've got it on surveillance," Smitty said, waggling his hook at me. It had an attachment that let it hold onto his phone, where sure enough, there was a monitor of some kind pulled up. "Sarge said this was important."

"It is." Rich took a deep breath, preparing to crucify himself for me, and I couldn't let him do it. Not alone, at any rate.

"One of you is in contact with the Grimaldis," I said before he could.

Dallas was the first to react, his flat mouth widening into a grimace. "What the fuck are you talking about?"

"I'm talking about the fact that I hightailed it out the back door of this place earlier today and *saw* one of you, all covered up, talking to Dorian Killoran, their boss. Somebody here is supposed to make sure that Gianna and I get handed over by noon tomorrow, or they make a run at the silo."

"You went outside?" The toothpick JD had been chewing fell out of his mouth onto the floor. "Why the hell would you do that?"

"To see if I could get a bead on the Grimaldis."

"And why would you want to fucking do *that*?" he exclaimed. "What, you think they're just going to be out there having little chats about their plans in the middle of the goddamn woods, like idiots?"

"That's exactly what I think!" I snapped back. "Because they're not Recon Marines, they're city boys living out of their cars and undoubtedly feeling shitty about every life decision they've ever made! Jesus Christ, mafiosos are tough but they're not soldiers, not the way you people are. Not in this country, at any rate. Get them back to Chicago and yeah, they'll hunt your ass down before you know what hit you, but out here they're no better off than me, and I'm up shit creek without an oar."

"Paddle," Andy supplied quietly, looking a little shocked. "I think you mean paddle."

"Yeah, thanks."

Dallas smacked his shoulder. "Who the fuck's side are you on, Bleeder?"

"When was this?" Smitty asked. The furor of other voices died down a little. In another life, I thought, Smitty would probably have made a way better sarge than Sarge.

"It was while you were off talking to your neighbor," I said. "Right after Rich left to make his call."

"Which was also fucked up," he added, and related the story of the "cop" who'd ended up slipping a tracker onto him.

"No, no, back up, back the hell up," Dallas interjected. "We're not done with your little boyfriend's story yet. You really think one of *us* is working with the Grimaldis?" He looked from me to Rich like he didn't believe his ears. "And you believe him? Either his dick gets you higher than crack or you've gone off the deep end, Smoker."

"Do you still get the shakes?" This time the quiet voice came from Sarge. That made it all the scarier, as far as I was concerned. I could handle the guy being shouty. Quiet from him made me nervous. It clearly made Rich nervous too, if the way his shoulders tensed meant anything.

Rich shifted. "Um. Sometimes."

"Panic attacks?"

"Yeah, but not often." Rich frowned. "And this has nothing to do with—"

"Are you on any medication for them?"

"I—" After a moment, Rich shook his head. "No."

"Why not?"

"There was too big a risk of the Marshalls finding out." Every word sounded like it had been pried out of Rich with a crowbar. He couldn't lie to these men, though—not to his brothers. And now it looked like Sarge was going to try to bury him with the truth—a partial truth, but a truth nonetheless.

"You'd be deemed unreliable, probably. Maybe even mentally unfit. It would hurt your career."

"Sarge," Andy began, but Sarge held up a hand and Andy fell silent again.

"Nobody here's going to throw shade at you for having a tough time, Rich. We've all been there. You can't come back from war without bringing some of it home with you, and I know you're doing the best you can with it. But you have to see that it's made you vulnerable." He looked at me, the lines beside his mouth deepening. It wasn't quite a sneer—nothing blatant that would set Rich's protective instincts off—but it was definitely an expression of concern.

"You do the best you fucking can, and I respect that, but your need to save people has taken you above and beyond where you ever should have gone this time. You went AWOL on your last assignment, son, you abandoned your people for this…criminal." He waved a hand at me. "And I'm not saying you weren't in the right. It's hard to face up to the fact that you can't trust someone you feel you should, but I think you've carried that bad experience over to us. You couldn't trust your fellow Marshals, and now you think you can't rely on us either.

"And the whole time, you've got this guy here whispering in your ear, convincing you that he's a victim, that we're out to get him, that the whole world has it in for him and you're the only one who can stop it. But that's just not true, Rich. That's why we're here, isn't it? To help you. And *you* invited *us,* and we came because we never leave a man behind." He shook his head. "And now you really think it's more likely that one of us would sell out your charge than that Leo Nicolosi, the brains behind the Chicago mafia's money schemes, a guy who turned against his own people on a dime, is the one telling you the truth?

Richie." Sarge sighed. "Come on now. You've known all of us for years. This guy?" He pointed at me. "You've known less than a month. Who do you really think you should believe?"

For a second all I could do was stare, my mouth gaping. That was one of the most masterful displays of gaslighting that I'd ever experienced in my life. Hell, I was half-ready to believe that I *was* a liar, that all of Rich's friends were blameless and I was making things up to support my own story. Only, I knew I wasn't. And Rich knew it too.

He did, didn't he?

"Rich," I said quietly. "You know this isn't true. You know I wouldn't lie about this to you. I wouldn't. I'm *not.*"

"Oh no?" Sarge asked, sarcasm heavy in his voice. "You sayin' you always tell Smoker everything?"

"Everything important," I shot back.

"Yeah?" He limped to one of the heavy chrome lamps and leaned it over. There was my little Springfield, still taped up where I'd left it. "You tell him about your secret weapon cache too? Because I know for a fact that Smitty would never carry around a pussy gun like this."

Rich looked from the gun to me, and it wasn't my imagination that he seemed unsettled. *Goddamn son of a bitch*, I thought furiously at Sarge. "So I hid a gun." I kept my tone as bored as possible. "There's a knife under the other lamp, one that I didn't put there. And I don't believe for a second that the rest of you haven't been stowing your own little secrets all over this place."

"I'm not saying none of the rest of us are doing the same thing," Sarge said with exaggerated patience. "I'm asking if you told Rich where you kept your extra weapon. Since you share everything important and all."

I gritted my teeth. "No, I didn't."

"Then see? You—"

"I didn't tell him because I didn't want to put him immediately on the defensive when it came to you all," I continued, forcing my way back into the conversation. "He was nothing but happy to come here and see you again, and I wanted to give him—and you—the benefit of a doubt without casting shadows with my own trust issues. So yeah, I hid that gun, and no, I didn't tell Rich about it so we could all try and get things off to a good start. Maybe that was naïve. Maybe I should have 'fessed up as soon as I knew one of you was working with the Grimaldis. It doesn't matter now; that's done." And I would pay whatever price I had to for that, but it wasn't the *point*. "What's *not* done is our fight with Dorian and his people, and fuck—you don't have to believe me on this, all you have to do is *wait*. Hunker down, wait, and then see if something doesn't happen to force a confrontation by noon tomorrow. Because *that's* the deadline for turning us over, and one of you people—" I looked between all of them, even Smitty "—is going to try and make a trade by then."

Sarge shook his head again. "You lie like a cheap rug," he scoffed. "Of *course* something will happen by then. This is an armed standoff, and those men aren't going to be inclined to patience. You're just trying to give yourself cover."

The distant, slightly hollow crack of gunfire rippled down through the silo. Everyone turned their heads to look up at the distant door.

"Speaking of cover," Andy said, sounding concerned. "Weren't Curtis and Lucky supposed to show up tonight?"

Smitty glanced at his phone, then swore.

A second later, there was a fresh flurry of movement as everyone scrambled for their gear, curse words flying around as camo was recovered and guns and ammo were strapped back into place. I just stood there in the eye of the hurricane and kept my eyes on Rich, who was as freshly concerned as the rest of them. He glanced at me a few times as he geared up, and I didn't like the troubled look on his face.

I stepped up to him, holding him back while everyone else headed for the elevator. "I'm not lying to you," I said, quiet but firm. "I wouldn't ruin this for you, not without reason. I know how important family is to you." I'd learned that in the awful mess with his parents. Rich loved his family, was close to them—and it was clear he felt the same about these men, even if he didn't talk to them as often.

My family was a mine buried in the battlefield of my heart, one that I'd stepped on often enough that the thought of "family" no longer had much meaning for me. But that was my issue, not Rich's. I stared at him, willing him to understand.

"What the hell is taking the elevator so long?" JD groused, bouncing on the balls of his feet.

The door finally opened. Before the Marines could troop in, Gianna came out, an M40A5 sniper rifle held against her shoulder. Behind her were two men, one of them bleeding from the arm, both of them scowling.

"What the good goddamn is this?" the injured man shouted at them. "You all sittin' down here with your dicks in your hands while you leave a single, solitary person on watch? You're slippin', Sarge."

"You're welcome," Gianna said dryly, handing the rifle over to a dumbfounded Dallas. "Have a nice heart-to-heart chat, gentlemen?" She glanced my way and winked.

Not for the first time, I thanked my lucky stars that Gianna was on my side.

Chapter Sixteen
Rich

Smitty's missile silo hadn't been this small before, had it? As I followed the walkways ringing its main shaft—where the missile would've been had the silo still been active—I could have sworn this thing had been bigger. Wider. Taller. A team of ex-Marines had staged swordfights and paintball games in here, so there had to be room to move. Room to *breathe*.

But no. No, it was definitely small and tight. Cramped. Hot enough it had sweat sliding down the back of my neck to pool uncomfortably under my collar. And of course the sun had gone down, so the windows at the top of the silo were black, making the whole place seem more…contained. Constricting. Suffocating.

I kept my head down and stared at the metal grate at my feet, and I kept walking. I wasn't going anywhere in particular. I just needed to *move*. There was too much happening and not enough happening, and I was restless in an all-too-familiar way as my Marines argued, Curtis and

Lucky were briefed, Leo and Gianna were God knew where, and the clock was ticking down to when Dorian fucking Whatshisname would make his move. Assuming Leo wasn't wrong. Or lying.

I pushed out a ragged breath and raked a shaky hand through my hair, which was wetter than I expected. When I wiped the back of my hand across my forehead—yep. Slick. Fuck, I was sweating like crazy now. And acknowledging that meant acknowledging the accompanying jitteriness. And the fact that I couldn't draw a deep enough breath, which made me dizzier and more jittery, and—seriously, when had this place gotten so fucking small?

I needed something to do, damn it. Something to focus on. Smitty and Dallas were scanning through the day's footage to either confirm or debunk Leo's claims about Dorian. There were a number of cameras, so that was going to take time, and I couldn't do shit to help because I couldn't focus enough to watch a grainy video for someone in goddamned camouflage.

The rest of the team was in the kitchen having a very loud and pissed-off discussion about our next move. I'd handled a few minutes of that, but every time someone shouted or slammed a fist against the table, it had jolted me until I could think of nothing except how jumpy I was and who was going to make me jump next. So I'd bowed out.

Leo had gone off somewhere with Gianna, which was probably just as well, because I couldn't get my head around anything where he was concerned. *Should* I trust him? *Was* I putting too much faith in him at the expense of trusting the men who'd had my back in battle? Everything Sarge had thrown at me had made sense in the moment and made me feel like a shitty marshal, Marine, and man. Like I'd abandoned my post for a beautiful stranger because… why? He was hot? I felt sorry for him? I wanted to be a hero?

My legs were getting rubbery, so I stopped walking and just leaned on the railing, staring down into the dark core of the silo. A memory flashed through my mind of leaning against one of these very railings and losing myself in that first kiss with Leo. Smitty had seen it coming. Had known it was only a matter of time before Leo and I wound up in bed. Hell, he'd wagered fifty bucks on it, and Smitty wasn't one to make a bet if he didn't think he'd win. I'd had my doubts. Sure, Leo was hot, but screwing him hadn't been a priority.

I pushed out a breath. No, it hadn't been a priority. The only priority had been keeping him—and myself—safe after we'd nearly lost our lives in a massacre. What idiot *wouldn't* have taken cover after an ambush like that until they could be absolutely sure they knew it was safe to lift their heads? And when the ambush came from the most powerful crime family in Chicago, when they'd had the power and means to get the drop on a highly guarded and tight-lipped op to transfer a witness? Taking cover meant getting the fuck out of dodge.

Yeah. I'd done exactly what any idiot would have done in my situation. My job had been to keep the witness safe, and I had. Nearly at the expense of my own life and my goddamned parents' lives. Now I was risking my Marines' lives too, and I hated myself for that, but I was doing it because there weren't any other options. Not because I was blinded by how I felt about Leo.

You're wrong, Sarge. You're fucking wrong.

I inhaled deeply, but not deeply enough. Fuck. The jittery feeling hadn't moved. The shakiness in my knees hadn't steadied. My heart still pounded and my head still spun and *come on, Rich, now is not the time to let this shit get ahead of you.*

I gripped the railing tight, pretending not to notice how slick the metal was under my sweaty, tingly hands. Eyes closed, I held on for dear life and just breathed. And tried to talk myself down. And tried to think of anything except the past, the present, and the uncertain as fuck future. Maybe my conscience could chill now with the realization I was here for the right reasons, but I was still *here* and anyone in this building could still die before this was all over, and the sheer terror of the battlefield was closing in fast. Back then, I'd been kind of numb to it. Or at least I'd been able to handle it. Now I had all those memories to tell me why being scared wasn't optional, and I had my own private ghosts to whisper in my ear and scream in my head about dead buddies, mortars coming out of nowhere, the near-silence after an explosion temporarily killed my hearing, the—

"Rich?"

I gasped and spun around, catching myself on the slick railing when my knees gave.

Leo stepped closer, eyes wide. "Hey. You all right?"

"Yeah, I…" *Can't breathe.* "I'm…" *Freaking the fuck out.*

His hands came to rest on my shoulders. "Rich. Look at me."

I am. Except I wasn't. When had I closed my eyes? Why was I squeezing them shut so tight it made my head hurt?

I forced them open and looked in his. My vision swam. The edges were starting to narrow, closing in like the walls of the silo had been doing around me.

Okay. Fuck this. Shutting my eyes again.

That didn't help. Fresh dizziness crashed over me, and I heard myself grind out "*Fuck*" as the panic I'd been trying so hard to hold back finally broke free. "Oh God…" The platform was dropping out from under me and the silo was collapsing in, about to crash down on my head, and why the fuck was I even fighting this urge to throw up? What did it matter?

Because if I'm puking I can't breathe. Fuck, I can't breathe. I can't… How do I… Oh shit…

Strong hands grasped my shoulders, and then there were arms around me and a solid presence against me. I wanted to shrug him away because I couldn't breathe and I couldn't handle anything around me, but then I was afraid he would pull away and I didn't know if I'd stay upright if he did, and…the missile silo. What if I fell? Oh God, what if I stumbled or passed out and dropped over the railing and—

"Hey, hey," Leo whispered, stroking my hair. "I got you."

Thank Christ someone did, because I sure as fuck didn't. My heart was going too fast. My stomach was roiling. My throat was tight and burning as acid tried to come up and oxygen struggled to go down, and my head spun as the platform under my feet listed hard.

Wait, no. It wasn't under my feet.

It was under my knees.

When the fuck… How the fuck…

"Just breathe." Leo's voice was a smooth, calm sound in the middle of all the chaos.

Breathe? Easier said than done. But I focused on it. I focused hard on it because air was the only thing that mattered, and the more I thought about breathing—and about Leo's steady, reassuring mantra and constant gentle touch—the less I thought about everything my brain wanted me to see. Bombs. Bullet holes. Blood. The toughest men I'd ever known screaming in pain, anguish, or both. The bone-deep fear that came from sleeping under a sky that sometimes rained mortars.

And then everything was just…quiet.

Still too, if you didn't count my pounding heart.

My breathing slowed. My mind cleared. When I blinked my eyes open, they focused.

And Leo was still right there, kneeling in front of me and keeping me from toppling onto my face.

Cold settled in on my back and shoulders. A cool drip rolled down my temple. Another went down the back of my neck to my already soaked shirt. I felt—and probably looked—like I'd just run a marathon, but all I'd done was drop to my knees and relive the past.

Exhaling, I leaned back against the cold railing and rubbed a clammy hand over my sweat-drenched face. "Think… Think I need a shower."

"You want company?" His voice and expression told me it wasn't a come-on. A gentle promise to be there if I wasn't ready to be alone.

I nodded. "Yeah. Thanks."

Leo rose, wincing when his ankle cracked and his knee popped. How long had we been like that? He offered his arm, and I clasped my hand around it and used both his help and the railing to shakily get to my feet. I wasn't dizzy anymore, but now I was just…drained. The act of standing had taken way more work than it should have, especially with help.

Priority one—shower.

Priority two—the longest nap that has ever been napped.

I swallowed my ego and leaned on him all the way back to our room. Then we stripped out of our clothes, stepped into the bathroom, and shared the quietest, most platonic shower we'd ever had together.

That wasn't to say we didn't touch. We did. A lot. Half the time, we were wrapped up in each other, faces buried against necks and hands running up and down backs. Nobody was hard. Nobody was groping. It was just…contact. Comfort. An unspoken mutual reassurance that at the end of the day, we still had each other. He'd see me through to the end of a panic attack. I'd see him through to the end of the Grimaldis' threats. Where we went from there, God only knew, but right now we had this, and I couldn't have asked for—or offered—more.

The water started getting cool, so Leo turned off the shower and we stepped out. Once we'd dried off and put on some fresh clothes, I sat on the edge of the bed.

Leo joined me, his shoulder brushing mine as he sat down. "Feel better?"

"Yeah. I do. Thanks for, um…" I motioned in the

general direction of where I'd fallen apart on the platform.

"Of course." His brow knitted. "What set it off?"

"Fuck, I don't know. Everything?" I ran a hand through my hair, which, thankfully, was wet from the shower and not sweat this time. "And then all the shit Sarge said about me being unreliable because of this, it... I don't know. It fucked with my head, and I guess the floodgates just wouldn't hold anymore."

"He's full of shit, you know." The words came out as a growl. "He was just trying to gaslight you into questioning your own judgment, so you'd question me."

"It fucking worked too." Beat. "Making him question myself, I mean."

Leo cocked his head. "What about me? Seemed like he was getting under your skin. Convincing you I'm manipulating you."

Sighing, I leaned forward and rested my elbows on my knees. Letting my head fall forward, I kneaded the back of my neck. "I legitimately have no idea what to believe anymore. Literally the only thing I know is that I know nothing."

Leo was quiet for a long moment. He nudged my hands away and took over, rubbing the stiff, tired muscles with his strong fingers.

Finally, he said, "I don't know what to say to convince you to trust me, but I will say that I trust you." He sighed. "I don't know if that matters. But there it is."

"It does." I sat up, put my arms around him, and pulled him against me. I pressed a kiss to the top of his head and murmured into his hair, "It does."

He relaxed into my embrace, and for the longest time, we just sat there, holding onto each other in silence. There was probably still plenty left to say, and God knew this whole fiasco was far from over, but I wasn't about to pass up a moment of peace. Especially if I got to spend it with Leo. What that last part meant, I didn't have the brain cells to figure out right now, so I didn't dwell on it.

Someone pounded on the door, startling us apart.

"Smoker? You in here?" Bleeder. At least I could handle facing him.

"Yeah, yeah," I grumbled. "Hang on." I paused to steal a brief kiss, then got up, pausing again to make sure my legs would stay under me. They did, so I crossed the room and pulled open the door.

Bleeder didn't even wait before he gestured over his shoulder and quickly said, "Smitty and Dallas found something on the footage."

I stiffened. "What?"

"Fuck knows how he got on the property. He had to get past two perimeter alarms, so either they were deactivated or he knew how to breach them." He shook his head. "But the cameras caught him, and they caught him talking to someone." Eyes flicking toward Leo, he added, "Looks like Leo was right."

I glanced over my shoulder at Leo. I half expected a smug *I told you so* on his face, but he just fixed his gaze on Bleeder.

"Can they ID who was in the video?" he asked. "The guy Dorian was making contact with, I mean?"

Bleeder shook his head grimly. "Can't quite see him in the frame from either angle. Could be Smitty's hillbilly neighbor for all we can tell."

Leo scowled but didn't press.

Bleeder gestured over his shoulder again. "C'mon, though. Sarge needs you to make a positive ID on this Dorian fucker."

"I wouldn't know him on sight." I turned to Leo. "Would you?"

"I'd know that face anywhere," Leo breathed.

"Then come on." Bleeder stepped aside and motioned for us to go with him. "Let's go put a name on this asshole."

Chapter Seventeen
Leo

After a while, you got used to shit not going your way. It still sucked, but since you'd never allowed yourself the chance to hope that it would work out, it didn't hurt when everything went to hell.

There was no way to identify the man Dorian had met with. No other cameras had caught him, and there were no specific items that he was wearing to make him stand out. "It could even be one of his own guys," Dallas had helpfully interjected last night, because fuck that asshole.

"You're an idiot," I'd told him, and then Andy and JD had stepped in to keep him from wiping the floor with me.

It was a good thing the new guys were here, in a way. They helped diffuse the undeniable tension that had been building between the rest of us. Curtis was Indian American, my height, with thick dark hair and a serious face. He was another explosives expert—how many did they need in one squad of Marines? Apparently now he worked as a civil engineer.

The other guy had the most crooked face I'd ever seen—it was like God had stuck a peeled potato on top of a stick and said, "Done!" His chin leaned right, his nose leaned left, and his eyebrows met in the middle. Naturally, his nickname was Lucky. The only way it could have been more on-point was if it was Pretty Boy.

I thought the new guys would instantly flock to Sarge, since everyone seemed to want to eat out of his hand, but apparently their less-than-warm welcome had left them more inclined toward Gianna, which was awesome. Lucky brought her coffee once his arm was patched up, and Curtis asked her what she thought of Federal GMM versus LC rounds. She actually had an informed opinion on it too, which… Was there anything she couldn't figure out?

I took advantage of their fawning to go to bed and dragged Rich with me too. He'd sit and shoot the shit because it was expected, but he'd had a hell of a panic attack not long ago, and he looked like he needed the rest. He didn't fight me on it, and by the time we were in bed, curled up together despite him warning me that he was probably going to sleep badly tonight, I knew I was sunk.

Fuck me for falling for a US Marshal. God, why couldn't I have made this easier on myself? And fuck me for actually trusting the guy, too. It was like lying beneath the Sword of Damocles—one wrong move in any direction and I'd be run through.

"Stop thinking so hard," Rich muttered against my forehead.

"I'm not."

"Your shoulders are tense; you're thinking. Stop it. Go to sleep."

"*You* go to sleep," I said petulantly, and he chuckled. He took my advice, though, and once he was under, it wasn't too hard for me to follow him down.

Rich actually ended up sleeping like a baby. *I* was the one who couldn't stop tossing and turning, and by six a.m. I was tired of trying. I got out of bed, got dressed, and took off for the kitchen. Smitty was already there, looming over the coffee maker like a gargoyle to keep other people's dirty mitts off it, while Lucky relentlessly tried to bypass him.

"Just one more shot!" he begged.

"You've already had four," Smitty said flatly. "In as many minutes. Sit the hell down and give it a chance to work."

"But I want more *now!*"

"And I want to be able to jerk off with two hands, but we don't always get what we want, do we?"

Lucky threw himself back into a chair with a scowl. "Ye're such an asshole." He glanced over at me. "What's up, Jailbait?"

I rolled my eyes. "Really? That's what you're going with?"

"Better than 'Criminal,' yeah? I'd fuckin' know, man."

Oh, would he? "You do some time?"

"Yeah, 'bout a year after I got back. Got drunk, went driving—like a dumbass—and ran my truck through the mayor's prized rose garden an' right into her bedroom. She was in it at the time," he added. "Ended up breakin' her arm."

"You're lucky it wasn't worse."

"Ye're tellin' me! She was more pissed about the garden than the arm, honestly. An' it was even worse because she's my aunt."

I took the cup that Smitty handed me—mmm, the perfect latte—and took a sip to hide my smile. "Wow," I managed after a second.

"Yeah. *An'* then she told my mama, and then it became a *thing*, and then the judge threw the book at me, an' I went to lockup for six months."

"It could have been worse."

"Yeah, my mama was pushin' for a year, but the judge has a soft spot for me. He's my cousin," Lucky added.

"Where the fuck are you from?"

"Incestville, North Carolina," Smitty said dryly.

"Hey, fuck you, man, not *everybody* in that town is related to me. Maybe just…" He waggled his hand. "Fifty percent of 'em."

"Oh my god, can we not talk about Lucky and his family this early in the morning?" Dallas asked as he walked into the kitchen, rubbing his eyes blearily. "I'm not ready to bleach my brain yet."

"Aw, honey." Lucky smacked his ass as he walked by. "Still such a delicate li'l flower, huh?"

"I will knock you the fuck out, how's that for delicate?"

Lucky grinned. "The fuck do I care, honey bunny? All my teeth you can see're fake anyway!"

"Did you guys come to any decisions last night?" I asked, not because I didn't want to watch Dallas get into a fight at six in the morning, but because Smitty was starting to look like he wanted to commit murder and I preferred him on an even keel. Everyone had their breaking point, and it seemed like Lucky was pushing him toward his fast.

"Yep, sure did. We've agreed that human sacrifice is the only way to g—ouch!" Lucky rubbed his lumpy head where Smitty smacked it.

"We thought about trying to run and regroup," Smitty said calmly as he went back to leaning against his countertop. "But that gives up too many advantages, especially this late in the game. Your Chicago boys are expecting something to go down today, which means they're edgy, and we don't want to make it easy for them to try and pick us off."

Dallas sighed. "You're such a homebody. I still think we could do it."

"And end up where?"

"Scattering! Give them plenty of people to follow, give us the opportunity to find a better position—"

I could already tell what he was really thinking, though. *Give me the opportunity to get the fuck out of dodge instead of risking my neck for a mafioso.* But given how Smitty and Lucky were both ignoring him, it seemed like Dallas had been voted down.

"So, what's option number two?" I asked.

"Traps." That was from Sarge, who walked in slow, his limp obviously giving him trouble this morning. Jesus, did none of these people know how to sleep in? Gianna wouldn't be up before ten if she had her way, and after her little sharpshooting display yesterday, she probably would have whatever she wanted go her way for a while. "Whatever we can set up safely that the Grimaldis will have to walk through to get in here."

Sarge looked at me, then dismissed me just as fast. If it hadn't been courting suicide, I would have smashed my cup so hard into the side of his head it left him blind in one eye. I had no doubt, no doubt in my mind, that for Sarge, the real option number two had been handing me over to the Grimaldis with no more fuss. He had just about convinced Rich that the sky was green and the grass was blue—and that was what he did to the people he liked! Someone he was supposed to think of as a brother. I sure as fuck didn't qualify as that.

"And who gets to be the lucky guy to go outside and set those up?" I asked with all the calm I could muster.

"I was thinking I'd send Smoker," Sarge replied with equal calm. "He was pretty good at it back in the day, and he's certainly got the most invested in keeping your ass alive."

"Wow." I shook my head. "I should have anticipated that, huh? Good thing this isn't an actual battlefield where you're in charge of shit." I looked to Smitty, deliberately cutting Sarge out of the conversation. "It's your place and you guys are the experts, but I'd suggest you have a chat with Rich before you send him out to string bombs up between trees or whatever the hell it is you think booby traps are."

"Why? Did he lose it last night?" Sarge reached over

for a cup of coffee. "Saw that coming from a mile away."

"Seeing as you're the one who caused it, I fucking bet you saw it coming."

Smitty frowned, one hand firmly on the handle of the coffee pot. "Rich had a panic attack?"

It wasn't my issue to talk about—but then, it wasn't Sarge's either, and he'd made damn sure that everyone else in this bunker knew about it. "Yeah. He's okay, it just makes him a little tired the next day."

"Okay enough for combat?" Smitty pressed. "Because Sarge isn't wrong. Smoker was brilliant when it came to securing an area against attack, but there's no way we're sending him out there if his readiness is compromised."

"You gonna give up the coffee any time soon?" Sarge grumbled, waggling his empty cup in Smitty's direction.

"Not if you're going to be a shortsighted dumbass, no sir, I'm not."

"This is better than anythin' I could be watchin' on HBO," Lucky breathed, staring around raptly. "God*damn*, who needs dragons and zombies when y'all are one wrong move away from OK-Corralling it?"

Both of them turned annoyed glares on Lucky, and I felt like it was as good a time as any for me to make my exit. I'd done the most I could do, which was knock Sarge off the command pedestal he kept trying to place himself on. The question was, how to do it gracefully? The second I got up, Sarge was going to try to regroup against me. He was just that kind of vindictive shit.

My savior came in the form of JD, who stumbled into the kitchen scratching his head and looking like he was still half-asleep.

"Your cat's a thief," he informed Smitty blearily. "And a jerk."

"What'd he do?" Dallas asked.

"Stole my last damn pair of boxers and made a nest out of them." He frowned as Dallas burst out laughing. "And it's mean! It scratched me when I tried to get them back! Smitty, come move your cat, man."

Smitty sighed. "Are you serious right now? Just grab them."

"No! Look at my hand!" He held it up and, sure enough, there were three long scratches across the back of it. "I'm not going to let it have another chance to turn me into a scratching post, Leo." He turned his sad, wide eyes in my direction. "You and the cat get along, right? Help me out, man."

Any excuse to get me out of Sarge's radius was welcome. "Sure." I paused just long enough to swallow the rest of my latte before joining him at the door. "No problem."

"Looks like you're useful for something after all," Sarge said.

I rolled my eyes. "I'll refrain from making a pussy joke, because it would be a lie *and* poor taste."

"I'll make it for you!" Lucky hollered as JD and I turned away.

"Where's your room?" I asked. Aside from the glow of the bright neon lights in the kitchen, it was dim and quiet in the rest of the silo.

"Right over here." He pointed across the floor. "First room left of the hallway." We set off together, and I was almost all the way there before I realized that *none* of the rooms on the bottom floor were bedrooms. I started to turn toward JD, but the gun against my side stalled me out instantly.

"Keep quiet, or I shoot," he said softly. His eyes shone in the faint light—wet, regretful, but resolute. "Head down the hallway. Now."

It was the same hall that led to the trap door.

"There are cameras down here," I said, moving as slowly as I dared. I wanted to yell for help, but I didn't want to die, and if he was really set on shooting me and I couldn't dodge fast enough… And yep, he was taking my gun before I could even reach for it, because *fuck* me.

"They're going to see what you're doing."

"I blocked the cameras this morning. Thanks for letting me know where to look." He jabbed me in the side. "Pick up the pace, Leo."

I moved marginally faster. At least I'd thought to put shoes on—if I had to run, I wouldn't trip because I stubbed my toe.

"JD, please, you don't want to do this."

"I don't," he agreed sadly. "But I have to."

"They're going to figure out it was you. Even with the cameras off, you know it's only a matter of time before—"

Another jab silenced me. "You can't talk me out of it. I've got to do it."

"But *why?*"

He sighed. "It doesn't matter why now. All that matters is that it happens before noon. *If* Dorian gives us that long, but I think even he can't argue with getting his hands on you before dawn. And it'll keep Rich out of things, so that should make you happy."

"JD, if you just—"

"Shut up, Leo." He sounded tired but still determined. "Just shut the fuck up and walk."

Chapter Eighteen
Rich

Last night had been a long one. Though I'd slept hard, there'd been nightmares, and I still felt drained from the panic attack I'd had yesterday. I'd known for a long time that PTSD was a pain in the ass, but sometimes I forgot how utterly exhausting it could be. Not to mention inconvenient—we were, for all intents and purposes, in a warzone. This was neither the time nor the place for the past to show up uninvited and shit all over my mental readiness.

Not long after Leo had left the room, though, I was finally on my feet, dressed, and coherent enough to go hunting for coffee. Not really awake, but vaguely coherent.

The second I walked into the kitchen, though, I was awake.

All heads turned toward me, and one face in particular was missing.

"Where's Leo?" I asked.

Smitty made a vague gesture toward the door. "He went to help JD retrieve his drawers from my cat."

The rest of the guys chuckled, and usually I would have too. But I didn't. Maybe it was the nightmares and PTSD keeping me on a hair trigger, but something tightened in my gut. "He...needed Leo to get his underwear back? From the cat?"

Sarge snickered into his coffee cup. "Guess the fucker scratched the hell out of his hand when he tried to get them."

"Leo's buddy-buddy with Inigo," Smitty said, "so JD asked him to help."

That something in my gut knotted tighter. Inigo was kind of a dick, but when he'd made a nest out of one of my shirts, I'd just waited until he'd moved. After all, I had other clothes with me. And I hadn't even had time to pack like the Marines had. When the cat had tried to steal my shoe, I'd just wiggled a shoelace and he'd been distracted enough to let me take the shoe back. He was a feisty little fucker, but he wasn't exactly a dangerous animal.

I rubbed my eyes. "Okay, I haven't had coffee yet, but...am I to understand that the cat took *all* of JD's underwear? Or did JD only bring one pair?"

"What?" Sarge rolled his eyes. "Who the fuck cares about the dude's underwear?"

"I couldn't give two shits about his underwear." I turned to go and threw over my shoulder, "But I don't buy a Marine being cowed by a little cat."

The laughter behind me said no one else was as concerned as I was. Fine. Maybe I was being paranoid, and maybe Inigo had a temper I wasn't aware of. But Leo—my witness, and my... my something more than a witness— was out of my sight, and I'd take some teasing from my buddies over taking for granted that the situation was under control.

Especially when I slipped into our shared room to grab a pistol—couldn't take any chances—and saw a black-and-white tail sticking out from under the bed.

Paranoia became straight-up panic. I grabbed my

pistol and hurried out of the room. In the core of the silo, I shouted, "Leo?" My voice echoed up and down the empty cylinder. "Leo? JD?"

Nothing. Just the disorienting echo of my voice seeming to come from everywhere at once.

The rest of my Marines came rushing out of the kitchen.

"What's going on?" Sarge demanded.

"The cat's in my room," I said quickly.

Sarge's eyes widened. He apparently put the pieces together and turned to Smitty. "Get on the cameras." Sarge drew his pistol. "Bleeder, you and Dallas go out topside. "Smoker, we'll go out the back. Everyone, move fast and quiet."

Sharp nods all around.

A door opened and Curtis stepped out, looking bleary-eyed. "What's going—"

"Stay with Smitty and watch the cameras," Sarge barked. "Be ready to move."

Weapons out, Sarge and I hurried down to the silo's rarely used rear exit.

At the door, I turned to Sarge. Our eyes locked, and we both nodded. Then, as carefully and quietly as I could, I opened the latch on the door and started to ease it open.

Abruptly, Sarge seized my arm. "Don't move."

"Huh?"

He pointed at his eyes, then up ahead and down. I looked, puzzled for a moment, but then I saw it—a wire. One that definitely hadn't been here before. Whether it was rigged to an explosive or a noisemaker to give away our position, I couldn't say, but I wasn't going to take chances. I eased the door shut again and released the latch. We exchanged looks, then hurried back up the way we'd come.

The rest of the guys might've had a chance to grab radios on the way out, but Sarge and I hadn't. And now that we'd already hit one dead end, we had even less time to stop. Incommunicado wasn't ideal, but neither was letting JD and Leo get any farther down whatever the fuck path they were headed down. So help me, if they were just outside having a smoke, or—

Then they wouldn't have booby-trapped the goddamned door.

Or made up the bullshit about the cat.

No, something was wrong. Very, very wrong, and I was just glad I'd put on my shoes before I'd gone into the kitchen, or else I'd be running out into the crisp morning barefoot. I would have, too. Because Leo. Because *where the fuck was Leo?*

The silo's main entrance hadn't been tampered with. When we came out topside, Curtis and Lucky were on our heels, and Bleeder and Dallas were nowhere in sight.

"Shit," I whispered, my breath coming out in a thin cloud as I scanned our surroundings for a sign of someone. *Anyone.* "Where the—"

A radio crackled, spinning me around, and right then, I could've kissed Lucky. Sarge and I had been in too much of a hurry, but Lucky had grabbed a radio.

"I've got movement east of the driveway," Smitty said over the radio. "Lot of tree cover, but it—yep, there's Leo. That's gotta be JD with them."

"Where are they headed?" I asked.

Lucky held the radio close his mouth. "Where are—"

"Down the mountain. Parallel to the driveway." Smitty paused. "Looks like about twenty yards east of the drive, fifty yards from the bottom."

"Any visible weapons?" Lucky asked.

"JD's got a pistol at... Jesus. He's got Leo at gunpoint."

My stomach dropped into my sneakers. My Marines and I exchanged looks. Sarge actually paled a little, and in any other situation, I might've indulged in a smug "*don't you feel stupid?*" look, but that could wait until we were all alive at the other end of this. I turned to Lucky, mouth open to ask if he could see anything else, but Smitty spoke first.

"We've got vehicle movement." Pause. "Two—no, three." He whistled. "These mafia fuckers don't ride subtle, do they?"

Ice replaced my blood. "Dorian. It has to be Dorian." I started toward the driveway. "We have to get down there before they hand off Leo."

Sarge grabbed my arm, damn near hauling me off my feet. "Don't be an idiot, Smoker."

I whirled around and was about to deck him for holding me back, but he gestured sharply at Dallas's truck.

"There's no time to move quiet," he said. "We need to move fast."

I nodded. "Keys? Do we have—"

Something shiny flew through the air, and Sarge caught them, the keys crunching in his closing fist.

"We'll be right behind you," Dallas said. "Lucky, have Smitty bring up his keys."

Sarge and I didn't wait. I jumped into the bed of the truck while Sarge got into the cab. Lucky joined him, still barking into the radio to get Smitty up here with his keys.

The engine roared to life, and my heart sped up. In this quiet forest, there was no way JD and Leo—probably even Dorian—hadn't heard the engine, and my neck prickled with the certainty that I'd hear a gunshot at any moment as we started down the driveway.

The driveway was steep and winding, and Sarge drove so fast and took the curves so hard, the truck almost lost its ass a couple of times. I kept a white-knuckled grip on the siderails to keep from being flung out into the bushes, and my teeth chattered with that old familiar surge of adrenaline that came from charging headlong into battle.

Near the bottom of the driveway, Sarge braked so hard the truck fishtailed on the loose gravel. I lost my grip on the siderail and slammed shoulder-first into the cab. The impact stunned me for a second. On my side in the truck bed, I started to push myself up but froze.

"JD. Think about what you're doing." That was the voice Sarge used when he was trying to defuse a situation. A boot crunched on gravel. Then another. "Put the gun down and let him go, JD."

My throat constricted.

One cab door shut. Then the other. Craning my neck, I saw both Lucky and Sarge outside the truck, hands raised in surrender.

"Come on, JD." Sarge sounded calm, but worried. "Think about what you're doing. You're—"

"I don't have a choice." JD was...the opposite of calm. He sounded fucking terrified, and that scared the shit out of me. The only thing more dangerous than being held hostage was being held hostage by someone who was more scared than you were.

God, how do I get Leo out of this?

"You have a choice," Sarge insisted. "Let him go, and let's all get back up to—"

"Damn it, I *can't*. Get out of here, Sarge, and let me do this. It's gonna happen, and I don't want any of you getting killed in the process."

Blood pounded in my ears. I scanned what little I could see from here, trying to assess my surroundings. The truck had slid almost completely off the road on the driver's side, the bed pushing up against some low branches. It wouldn't take much for me to climb over the side rail and disappear into the foliage. Only problem was, the forest was too quiet. JD would hear me, and he'd likely see the movement behind Sarge.

Unless he were distracted.

Moving as silently as I could, I got on my hands and knees. Lucky was still by the passenger side of the truck, hands up.

"Lucky, don't look at me," I whispered. He didn't take his eyes off—I assumed—JD and Leo, but he tensed enough I could tell he was listening. While Sarge continued trying to talk down the increasingly agitated JD, I said,

"Tell Sarge to back down. Get loud and animated. Get *him* loud. I'll use the noise for cover."

The faintest nod acknowledged what I'd said.

Oblivious to our conversation, Sarge was saying, "What's going to stop them from killing you, JD? They're mafia fuckers."

"And they've got me by the balls," JD said. "If I don't give them this asshole, I'm dead anyway. This is my only chance to—"

"He's right, Sarge," Lucky said. "Let him take the fucker to those goons and—"

"What?" Sarge boomed just like I'd hoped he would. "Are you out of your—"

"I came here to keep my Marines alive!" Lucky threw back, flailing his arm. "Not take a bullet for this—"

And just like that, Lucky and Sarge were shouting over the top of each other, same as they had during our combat days. The noise was the perfect cover for me to slide over to the driver's side of the truck bed. Lucky started gesturing wildly, waving his arms as he tore into Sarge for putting this mafia punk over the lives of his boys, and my feet barely made a sound as they touched down on soft undergrowth.

I crouched low behind a tree and looked through the branches, craning my neck to try to see past Sarge.

JD was about ten yards in front of the truck, one arm keeping Leo in a tight headlock while the other hand pressed a pistol into his temple. My stomach somersaulted. JD was scared shitless. His eyes were frenzied, darting back and forth between Sarge and Lucky, and his fingers were tense and twitchy—especially the one curled dangerously tight around the trigger.

The shrill sound of a cell phone ringing broke through the noise.

JD swore. Then he kicked Leo's knee out from under him, and Leo dropped to the ground with a grunt. Gun still trained on Leo's head, JD snarled, "Don't move," as he fished around in his jacket pocket.

I took advantage of the distraction and carefully moved a few paces closer.

Unaware that I was there, JD put his phone to his ear. "Yeah?" His eyes lost focus and his brow furrowed. Then they sharpened, fixating on Sarge and Lucky. "Yeah. I've got him and we're on our way down. Just had to take care of something, but we're on our way."

I took another step. Leo's eyes flicked toward me, and my chest hurt with fear and guilt and helplessness.

I'm supposed to be keeping you safe. Now I can't even get to you.

Leo pulled his gaze away and stared at the ground, breathing hard like he was close to panicking.

"We'll be there in a minute." JD stuffed the phone back into his pocket, then jerked Leo to his feet. He swung the gun toward Lucky and Sarge. "You two. Radio the others to stand down, then get over there." He waved the weapon toward the woods where I was hiding. "Go. Now. And leave the keys."

My heart stopped. Oh no. No, no, no. Shit, why didn't I stay in the truck?

Lucky and Sarge started to move, but another sound broke the silence—an engine. Coming from up the hill.

JD grabbed Leo's arm and hauled him toward the truck. "Move! Move!" he shouted at Lucky and Sarge.

They did. What choice did they have?

JD shoved Leo into the cab, then got into the driver's seat. The tires spun, spraying gravel everywhere, and the truck continued down the driveway, taking Leo out of my reach and straight toward the goons who would either kill him or take him back to the Grimaldis, who would torture and *then* kill him.

I wasn't about to assume they were going to keep him alive any longer than they had to, so I broke into a run.

"Smoker!" Sarge called after me, but I didn't stop. I couldn't.

Staying low, I moved fast through the brush. Ideally, I'd have camouflage on. Maybe even a ghillie suit. There hadn't been time, though, and my jeans and black Under Armour shirt would stand out like a bright red flag.

Funny—we had all the gear we could possibly need, from body armor to weapons, but when the shit actually hit the fan, we'd all been drinking coffee in our civvies. There'd only been time to grab what we could on the way out, which meant I was running down a hostage exchange with sneakers and a pistol with only one magazine.

But I didn't have to take them all down. I just needed to grind things to a halt and buy time for my Marines to catch up with the good firepower. Smitty wasn't far behind. I wouldn't need much time.

I'd been through these woods enough times in the last few days to have a solid grasp on the topography, and I did have one advantage here—the driveway swept east before doubling back west and letting out on the main road. The hairpin and the grade would force JD to slow down unless he wanted to roll the truck.

Meanwhile, going through the woods, if I continued straight and moved fast enough, I could gain some serious ground before he could reached the end of the drive. The hill sloped sharply downward out here, and I had to be careful in a few places—a broken ankle wouldn't do Leo any good—but I still managed to move fast.

And it paid off. By the time I reached the bottom, the truck was just emerging from the trees.

All I had to do now was—

The sound of a pump action shotgun stopped me dead in my tracks.

"You know, for a US Marshal," an icy, Irish-accented voice said, "you're rubbish at protecting witnesses."

I gritted my teeth. That had to be him. Dorian fucking Killoran. Oh…shit.

The truck rolled to a stop, and I met Leo's gaze through the windshield. The door swung open. JD got out, and he dragged Leo with him, hauling him flailing and stumbling out of the cab.

"All right. I've got Leotrim." JD gestured at me. "What are you gonna do with him?"

"Kill him," Dorian said coolly.

Someone grabbed my arm and pulled me back a step. As I stumbled and regained my balance, I turned and found myself face to face with Dorian Killoran. He was still a good twenty feet away with a pistol in his hand, flanked by a pair of heavily armed goons, but yep. That was him.

He gestured at me and motioned toward the road. "Take him someplace they won't find him any time soon."

"Wait!" JD said. "Hold on, man. He's not part of our deal."

Dorian snorted. "I don't give three shits about that. He's a witness now. He's gotta go."

The man tried to pull me another step, but I jerked my arm away. JD glanced back and forth between all of us. Then he inhaled deeply and pushed his shoulders back.

"Let him go, or you don't get Leotrim."

Dorian inclined his head, an eyebrow arched as if to ask *the fuck did you just say?*

JD set his jaw. "He's one of my Marines. Let him go, or you're not getting Leotrim." He paused, and the sound of an approaching engine swelled in the distance. Narrowing his eyes, JD added, "I've got more Marines on their way. They don't give a shit about this fucker"—he jerked his chin at Leo—"but they'll put you in the ground over him." He nodded at me.

Dorian considered him for a moment. He glanced at me. Back at JD. At Leo.

Then, moving so fast I didn't have time to react, he leveled his pistol at JD and pulled the trigger.

In a heartbeat, the gun moved again.

The muzzle flashed.

Twice.

And I was on my way to the ground before it fully registered that I'd been hit.

Twice.

Chapter Nineteen
Leo

Time had never slowed down for me before the way it did when Dorian fired his gun. I thought he was going to shoot me where I stood, like a dumb fucking steer at the front of a cattle chute. I expected it, almost anticipated it. All my hairs stood on end, my mouth went dry, my lungs knotted up in my chest—but that was normal for a man who was about to die.

What *wasn't* normal was the way JD's arm around my neck suddenly jerked to the side, wet heat staining my skin. Blood—not mine, though. Before I could really register what was going on behind me, I saw Dorian turn and shoot Rich.

Now time slowed down. *Now* my brain decided to step up its frame-rates and register everything in Technicolor, so I could watch Rich stagger under the weight of his own body, pressing his hands to his stomach with a gasp even as his knees buckled and he went down. I heard the tiny crunch of the dried leaves beneath him, saw the look on his face as it changed, the tightly-controlled fury giving way to shock as the pain set in. I saw it happen and felt it happen, and the only thing I could do was drop my jaw in the beginnings of a scream, because I knew that the next bullet Dorian fired, if he was smart, would be for me.

"Son of a *bitch!*" The honey-slow moment broke when JD shoved me hard right between the shoulder blades, knocking me to the ground as he fired back at Dorian and the guys who'd just been flanking Rich. I had to hand it to him, he was a quick shot. "Fucking move!" he shouted at me before diving for the truck.

I glanced frantically around the road looking for more cover. Apart from the truck there wasn't much—trees, but those were too far away to do me any good. I heard the roar of more engines in the distance—Marines or mafia, I didn't know who and at the moment I didn't care. None of it really mattered. What mattered was lying on the ground fifteen feet away from me. I got into a crouch, resting on the balls of my feet, and got ready to run for him.

A hard hand on the back of my neck jerked me onto my ass before I could take a step, hauling me around the far side of the truck before I could do more than shout. "What the—"

"You trying to get yourself killed now?" JD demanded, lifting his head over the edge of the bed just long enough to fire two more rounds. He was missing about half of the shell of his right ear, which had leaked a bloody mess all over his neck and shoulder. You wouldn't know he was hurting by how he moved, though.

"Fuck off!" I yelled in his face. I was maybe a *little* less controlled than I would have liked, but screw it—I had plenty of reasons. "I need to get Rich!"

JD grimaced and shook his head. "He's too close to the enemy position. We have to wait for backup."

Oh, hell no. "What if—" A bullet smashed through the windshield, spraying glass everywhere. "What if their backup comes first?" I finished.

"It won't! Sarge and the rest of the boys are right behind us. They'll be here in—"

"You stole their motherfucking truck!" I slapped the metal we hunkered behind with my palm. "You think Sarge is going to be able to run after us as fast as Rich did? *Fuck* you, give me back the gun you took off me."

"We don't have time to—"

"Give me my goddamn gun!" What, did he think I would take the time to shoot him? No way—not until Rich was safe. After that, all bets were off.

"Fine," he said at last, reaching to the small of his back and pulling out my Glock. "Stay here and cover me, and I'll—*Leo!*"

I was running the second the pistol hit my palm, darting out from behind the truck and racing toward Rich as fast as I could. The gravel road seemed weirdly slippery, and I stumbled twice before I made it across and into the tree line where Rich had managed to roll over onto his side. He stared at me as I skidded in beside him, like he couldn't quite believe what I was doing.

Yeah, me neither.

"Hi," I said breathlessly, followed by a quick, "Oh, fuck—"

Shotgun-man had just edged out from around a tree, weapon aimed at us. I fired twice, but both shots went wide. At least it made the guy retreat for a second.

"We've gotta move."

"I tried." Rich was gritting his teeth—his red, stained teeth. "It...didn't go so well for me."

"Shit." *Shit shit shit.* Had one of the bullets hit his spine?

"I took a round to the thigh," Rich clarified. "My leg's all screwed up now."

"Okay." I nodded, looking from his thigh to his bloody stomach and back again. "Okay, okay. We...uh. Um—"

"Get a fuckin' move on if you're goin'!" JD yelled at

CARI Z & L.A. WITT

us, taking potshots at the mafiosos' protective trees. I heard Dorian swear in Irish, and I didn't even stop to think, just threw my arms around Rich and rolled both of us to the side. Bullets followed us, but I didn't stop going until we hit something too big to get over—a spiky gray-green bush of some kind. JD was still shooting, holding Dorian and his guys back, but it wouldn't last.

I pushed to my knees, jammed my hands under Rich's armpits and dragged him around the bush and back behind the nearest tree. It was shitty cover for two guys who couldn't stand up—pine trees were too skinny to be much use—but it was better than nothing, and the bush helped to obscure exactly where we were.

"God damn it," I swore as I pulled off my t-shirt and pressed it to Rich's stomach. He made a sound somewhere between a grunt and a whimper, and I felt like an absolute shit for making him hurt worse, but blood was still seeping out between his fingers. I ripped a strip off the cheap cloth and turned it into an awkward binding to help hold the pad there. "We need to do your leg next."

"*You* need to get out of here."

I stopped and glared at Rich, who had the audacity to look completely calm. "Whatever you're thinking, stop it."

"You're a federal witness—"

"Rich, I swear to God—"

"—*my* federal witness—"

"—if you don't shut the hell up—"

"—in the biggest mafia case the federal government has pursued in decades, and—"

"—I will stuff the next wad of cloth in your mouth."

"—you'll hate yourself if you don't testify to put the Grimaldis away after what they did to Tony." Rich's face was pale but resolute. "If you get injured, or the trial is called off because of this bullshit, or God fucking forbid you have to go on the run again. You'll hate yourself, Leo, and you'll hate me too."

I barely heard the gunfire in the background, growing

louder and more numerous. A shot hit close to us—the tree sent a shower of splinters off to the right. I didn't even flinch.

"Don't bring him into this now," I said after a second. "This isn't about Tony."

Rich grimaced. "This whole thing is about Tony. We wouldn't have a case if there was no Tony, because you wouldn't have started down this road in the first place. You need to be around to finish it, so I want you to grab your gun and run low, toward that boulder over there, so you can loop back around to JD."

"JD is the guy who put us here in the first place!" I whisper-shouted. "And you want me to trust him now? Are you insane? He'll shoot me in the face if I show up without you!"

Rich reached up and wrapped a red-stained hand around the back of my neck, hauling me in close. Blood coated the edges of his lips now, the stain spreading. "The others will be here any minute," he said quietly. "They'll make sure you stay alive. Please, Leo, if you feel anything for me like…" He blinked and swallowed. "Just go. *Go*, for fuck's sake. I've got a gun of my own, and none of those guys really give a shit about me. I'll be all right until backup gets here, but you can't take the risk."

His breath came in warm, shuddery bursts. I felt it against my cheek, my nose, my lips. Just the thought of it stopping made prickles of panic rise in my mind, tiny spires of misery like needles in my brain. I couldn't look at Rich—if I looked him in the face right now, I would definitely lose it. I squeezed my eyes shut and prayed for a second of calm to pull myself together. I could do it. I'd come up with a plan. I *always* came up with a plan…

The shots dwindled off.

"Leotrim Nicolosi!" Dorian called out, his voice like someone had scraped an Irish accent together out of metal filings and cigarette smoke. "I have over twenty men in these woods, spread out and coming at you from every direction, and the road is blocked off! You want your company to survive the next few minutes, you'll walk out where I can see you with your hands up and let me take you away from this."

I opened my mouth to reply, but surprisingly, JD got there before I did.

"Fuck you!" he hollered. "You had your chance to take him and run! You screwed up when you got greedy, motherfucker."

Dorian chuckled. "I think you're the one that ruined any chance of that, Mr. Daimler. Who would have thought simple sentiment would be enough to sway a man who was willing to walk Mr. Nicolosi down here to die?" I could picture his smile in my head, teeth like sagging tombstones in his mouth. "It isn't too late to save yourself, though. Just get in the truck and drive away. My people will let you through without harm."

That was the second most bald-faced lie I'd heard all day. Fortunately, JD wasn't taking the bait. "Not happening, Killoran."

"Then you'll just have to wait to die with the snitch and the marshal, I suppose. Not for too long, though." Dorian whistled sharply, and a second later I heard JD shout, surprise turning to pain at the same time a gun went off. Then there was a second shot, and then…nothing.

Rich's jaw clenched as he banged his head against the tree trunk. "Fuck," he whispered. "James. *Fuck.*"

I tried not to give a shit that the guy who'd forced me into this at gunpoint had just been murdered, but he was also the guy who everybody in the unit loved, the cracky squirrel who shook my hand when we first met without a qualm. Of course, he'd already been planning to betray me then, but the fact that he was gone, and especially that his death hurt Rich, sucked.

It also sucked that we were down to just us and two guns, and Rich was bleeding bad enough from his gut wound that it had soaked through the top of his pants.

"Think that's that then, gentlemen. Wherever your boyos are, they're not going to get here in time to save you." I heard the sound of Dorian flicking his lighter. "But I'll cut you a deal, eh? Lorenzo wants Leo to die slow, in the old fashion. I have all sorts of tools laid out in my car just waiting for you, lad. But if the two of you come out now, together, I give you my word to simply shoot you both in the head. You can die with your dick still attached, Leo, and your marshal can die with you instead of lingering on listening while I torture you to death. What do you say, then? It don't come fairer than that, I think."

Fuck, I had nothing. I had *nothing*. It didn't matter how I racked my brain, I couldn't come up with any way out of this. We were dead; it was just a matter of how and when. It was my fault, too—I had done this to Rich. His family had gone through hell already because of his association with me, and now I was going to drive the last nail into the coffin—almost literally—by getting their son killed. The world blurred, and it took me a moment to figure out it was because I was crying.

"You can still run," Rich whispered, his lips brushing my jaw. "My guys are coming, Leo, I know they are. They'll find you."

I shook my head. "Nah, can't do that." I turned my head and kissed his lips, gently. They tasted like blood, but I savored it anyway. "Never leave a man behind, right?"

"Leo…" He sounded helpless, just the way I felt. But at least we were together.

"Five seconds, boys, and then my whistle gets you two dragged down into the dark with me," Dorian warned. "Five…four…three…" I tightened my grip on JD's gun and lifted my eyes, looking for movement. It was hard to see, and my hand shook like a leaf. "Two…one." He whistled, and a second later I saw Shotgun-man round a tree just ten feet away from us, his weapon raised menacingly.

"Drop the—"

He didn't get a chance to finish his threat. A hole blew through his head sideways, and he followed it, falling into his own scattered brains. Another shot sounded, then another, and suddenly it was pandemonium again, only this time we weren't the ones trying to outrun bullets. Out of the chaos stepped Gianna, back in her black leather jacket, but this time wearing a bulletproof vest underneath it. She lowered her pistol as soon as she saw us. "Jesus Christ, Leo." She reached for a radio at her hip even as she ran to us. "Get Andy over to my position, *now*. I've got both of them, they're injured—"

"I'm not," I gasped, interrupting her but needing to set the record straight. "I'm not, I'm fine, it's Rich, he needs help."

"Help is coming," Gianna assured me. "The guys are mopping up Dorian's crew as we speak. There were a lot of them, but they couldn't move silently for shit. I've never seen anything like it."

"You were watching?" Rich managed around a grunt as Gianna helped me lay him on his back. "Waiting to move in?"

"Yeah. It was your sergeant's idea." She shook her head. "I have to hand it to him, he knows how to plan an ambush. I didn't want to wait, but he insisted." She frowned, staring at Rich's abdomen. "This doesn't look good."

"Well, it feels great," Rich joked weakly.

"God, shut up." I slumped onto the ground next to Rich and let the frozen air leave my lungs. "Just shut up and let her keep you from *dying* on me, you..." God, why the hell did I still feel like crying? I hadn't been this tangled up inside since Tony's death.

Oh. *Oh.*

Thankfully Andy arrived before I broke down into a ball of pure misery.

"Hey kids!" he said brightly, emerging from the trees like some sort of camouflage phantom with a gun in one hand and a small medkit in the other. "Looks like you got yourself shot, Smoker. What'd I tell you about jumping in front of bullets?" He spoke with perfect calm even as his hands worked fast, opening compartments and pulling gauze, bandages, a syringe that I hoped had a painkiller in it, and—tampons?

Rich saw them too. "Aw, come on, man," he slurred. "Seriously?"

"You know where the rest of my gear is, buddy? Up in Smitty's bunker. I can't carry QuikClot and tourniquets and all the rest of it everywhere I go, but this fits in my pocket kit. This'll get you as far as the nearest hospital. Don't worry, the doctors will still think you're plenty manly."

I didn't watch him pull back Rich's shirt to inspect the wound. I didn't want to see it. I stared straight ahead instead.

"Did you find JD?" I asked dully.

"Sure did. Safe and sound, except for that shit with his ear."

Wait a second. "No...he was killed. One of Dorian's guys shot him."

"Nah, Dallas came in on his side. He had time to get into position and take out the shooter before he could get to JD. The rest was just improv."

"...Improv." I'd thought a mafia goon was killing JD, the only cover Rich and I had, the guy who'd tried to give me up only to change his mind at the last minute to try and save the man I lo—and it had been fake?

I dropped the gun and pressed my thumbs hard against my eye sockets, staring into the colored stars that floated across my vision. Maybe if I pushed hard enough, I'd stop seeing Rich covered in his own blood, telling me to run away and leave him. Fuck, he was *right here*, and he had Andy and he was going to be okay—he *had* to be okay—but I still felt like I was on the edge of a cliff, like I had when I thought we were going to have to go down shooting. I'd sooner have shot *myself* than let Dorian take me, and now...

"Easy, Leo." Gianna gently pulled my hands away from my face. I blinked at her. Wait... Where had Rich gone? "Andy and Curtis took him away already," she said when she noticed my confusion. "He was unconscious and you were out of it yourself, so I'm not surprised you didn't notice."

"Where's Dorian?"

"Tied up in the back of Sarge's truck, I believe. Along with the three surviving men who came on this little adventure. There are a lot of bodies in these woods." She sighed, but it was a sigh of pure satisfaction. "Would you like to go and look?"

"No." That was pretty much the last thing I wanted to do right now. "I just want to... Can we just get the fuck out of here?"

"Yeah, honey." Gianna put her arm around me and helped me to my feet. "We can do that."

Chapter Twenty
Rich

Bullet holes could eat shit and die. Seriously. I'd fucked myself up in plenty of ways in combat, and I'd spent my downtime licking plenty of wounds, but this? This could go straight to hell.

And was the hospital staffed with military docs or something? What the hell was this painkiller button giving me? Motrin? Because it sure as shit wasn't the good stuff. Maybe the button wasn't working. Was it broken? It had to be broken. Only explanation.

I felt around for the button to call the nurse. That was easier said than done—whatever the bullet and surgeons had done to my midsection, every-fucking-thing hurt. I found it, though, and pressed it.

Then I closed my eyes and waited.

I vaguely remembered a doctor coming in...this morning? Yesterday? Whenever the fuck it was. She'd given me a rundown on my injuries, emphasizing how fortunate I was that the bullet to my midsection had missed my spine and only nicked a few organs on its way through, and how lucky I was that the one in my thigh had just taken off a piece of my femur rather than actually snapping the bone. I was also lucky as fuck I'd made it to the hospital in time. The tampons Bleeder had shoved into the bullet holes, plus the QuikClot sponges he'd added once someone had brought him his kit, had kept me from bleeding out, but I'd still lost a lot of blood. Enough that I'd coded twice on the table, which would make a nice addition to the library of nightmares my psyche chose from whenever I tried to sleep.

She'd given me more gory details, but I'd pretty much stopped processing it after the part where I'd coded. Bullet holes sucked, blood loss sucked harder, and I kinda didn't want to know how many times they'd had to hit me with the paddles before I'd come back. Kinda? Scratch that. Did not want to know. Ever.

A nurse walked into my room, and she offered a smile that was familiar, so I must have seen her before. "What do you need, hon?"

I made a weak gesture of holding up the hand with the pain pump taped to it. "This thing isn't working."

She came closer and gave my arm a gentle pat. "Still in pain?"

"You think?"

Her expression was sympathetic, but she didn't do anything to unfuck the button. "I know you're uncomfortable. There's only so much the medication can do, unfortunately."

I groaned with both pain and frustration. "This is bullshit."

Her eyes were full of what seemed like genuine sympathy as she said, "If we give you a higher dose than this, you're going to get sick again."

That gave me pause. My memory of the last few days or hours or whatever was pretty foggy, but there was a bright flash of begging someone to kill me after I'd puked.

Foggy as it was, there had definitely been some clarity in there about how puking was a million times worse with your midsection sewn, stapled, or duct-taped back together, and how the words *we're going to give you something for the nausea* had almost instantly turned me heterosexual and made me fall in love with the nurse.

So…fine. Fine. I'd just have to suck it up and deal with the pain for a while.

I licked my dry lips. "How long have I been here?"

She pulled up her sleeve and checked her watch. "Almost seventy-two hours."

I blinked. "Seriously?"

Grimacing a little, she nodded. "Between the blood loss, surgery, and sedatives, you've mostly been asleep."

"I don't suppose I can get more sedatives?"

"I'll have to check with the doctor. In the meantime, do you feel up for a visitor?" She gestured over her shoulder with her pen. "Because there's someone who's been waiting to see you."

I instinctively tried to sit up, but very quickly decided against it. Settling back against the pillows, I said, "Who is it?" *Leo? Is Leo here? Is he okay? Tell me Leo's okay.*

"I… didn't catch her name, but—" She stopped, cocking her head as I deflated. "Would you rather I didn't send her in?"

"No. No, you can." I sighed. "I was just hoping it was someone else."

She studied me like she wasn't sure what to make of that, but then left the room to bring in my visitor. I wasn't actually sure who to expect—my mom? my handler?—but it wasn't Leo. It wasn't one of my Marines. It wasn't *Leo*, damn it.

The sharp thunk of heels on a hard floor told me who it was even before Vanessa came into the room. I hadn't been a deputy marshal for long, but I knew that no-nonsense, I-have-a-place-to-be gait anywhere.

No surprise at all, Vanessa strode into the room, and

as soon as she saw me, she sighed with obvious relief. "Oh my God, you look like shit."

I flipped her off, and was inordinately proud of my ability to lift my hand long enough to do that.

She laughed and stopped beside the bed. "You had us all worried, kid." She squeezed my forearm. "The doctors weren't sure you were going to make it."

A chill went through me, and if I hadn't been in so much pain, I'd have shivered. I must have tuned that part out when the doctor was briefing me, and I was thankful for it. My own mortality was a fleeting thought, though, and the more important one came out instead: "Where's Leo?"

She blinked. "Leo?"

"The witness. Nicolosi." I swallowed, my throat dry and sore. "Where is he? Is he all right?"

She cocked her head but then shook herself. "He's at a safehouse. Under Marshal protection until Grimaldi's trial."

My battered stomach dropped. "How can you be sure he's safe? The Marshals were compromised, and—I mean, that's how he and I ended up in this situation in the first—"

"Cody." She squeezed my arm again. "He's well out of Grimaldi reach. I hand-picked the marshals in charge of his protection right now and made sure he's far out of state."

Out of state. Out of Grimaldi reach. Out of *my* reach.

I closed my eyes. At least he was safe and alive, but for how long? The Grimaldi crime family had infiltrated the Marshals once—who was to say they couldn't and wouldn't do it again? They were highly motivated to shut Leo up for good, and nothing that had gone down in recent weeks would have tempered that.

"Rich," she said softly, using my first name for once. "He's safe. He's in good hands now. I promise."

"I need to see him." I looked up at her. "Or just…talk

to him. Something."

"That's not possible right now." She shook her head. "If we bring him out of the safehouse, then his safety is compromised. And look at you." She gestured at me and all the various tubes, wires, and monitors attached to me. "You're not in any condition to leave this room, never mind travel to another state to see him." A gentle smile formed on her usually hard features. "You did your job. The witness is safe, and now he's in good hands. All you need to do now is concentrate on recovering from your injuries." The smile broadened a bit. "And maybe ironing your uniform, because you'll probably wind up with an award for going above and beyond to keep this witness safe."

I winced. This witness. God, how long had it been since I'd thought of Leo as my witness? Keeping him safe had stopped being the reason I got a paycheck and started being my sole purpose. Keeping him out of harm's way had become a single-minded obsession the way keeping my fellow Marines safe in the field had been—not a professional obligation, but a reason to keep going.

"Your work is done," she said. "Just focus on getting—"

"You don't understand," I whispered. "I... I need to see with my own eyes that he's all right. Or talk to him. I need..." I swallowed hard. "Just let me talk to him."

Her brow furrowed. It was entirely possible she saw right through me, that I was wearing more on my sleeve than I should have because I was raw and in pain and irrationally—or maybe rationally—terrified that Leo wasn't okay after all. Vanessa might have been able to see in my eyes and hear in my voice all the reasons she could have the Marshals take away my badge and show me to the door.

I didn't care. The only thing I cared about right then was Leo. "My entire world has revolved around keeping him safe. I just need to see for myself that he is."

She watched me uncertainly, but after a moment, she gave a curt nod. "I'll see what I can do about getting him on the phone. It may take some time."

"Thanks." I managed to both smile and hide the deep, bone-shaking relief. "I don't think I'm going anywhere." I paused. "How did they find us? I mean…not just JD, but…" I exhaled. God, talking was exhausting. "The cop that pulled me over. That asshole neighbor of Smitty's."

Vanessa scowled. "Your friend, the one who sold you out—he put trackers on your other friend's vehicles. That's how they zeroed in on where you were. By the time you left to contact me, someone from Killoran's team had convinced the sheriff's department that there was some possible terrorist activity going on." She sighed. "That's how they got the neighbor to start nosing around too—convinced them all it was in the interest of national security."

"I'm surprised they didn't shoot any of us."

"They weren't interested in you or your Marine friends. They wanted Nicolosi."

I shuddered, which hurt like hell. "So that's why the cop just put another tracker on me."

She nodded. "Killoran didn't need two trackers on one vehicle, but that way they could be sure the cop had made contact and wasn't fucking around."

I grimaced. "Anything happen to him after I ditched the tracker?"

"Fortunately, no, but we've got people keeping an eye on him and the neighbor just in case the Grimaldis try to go scorched earth."

"Good." My eyelids were starting to get heavy. That must've meant the painkillers were kicking in, though it wasn't doing a damn thing for, like, the *pain*.

Vanessa gave my arm a squeeze. "Get some rest, okay? Everything's under control."

I nodded. For once, I actually believed things *were* under control.

Wasn't much I could do if they weren't.

Visitors came and went. My dad was still recovering from his own bullet holes, so he couldn't make the trek to Colorado, but we talked on the phone and commiserated about much it sucked getting shot. My mom came, though. The second day I was awake, my Marines showed up. They had to fight a bit to see me in the ICU because of that whole "family only" policy, but my mom rattled some cages and made herself a pain in everyone's ass until they backed down.

They only allowed two visitors at a time, though. I wasn't at all surprised that Bleeder was one of the first two, but I was admittedly startled to see Sarge. They greeted me with careful hugs and got the rundown on my battle scars-in-progress.

Then Sarge sighed and leaned against the windowsill. "Man, we should've listened to you. And to your boy. You guys saw something we didn't, and everyone damn near got killed because of it."

"I don't think anyone wanted to believe it," I said. "Even Leo didn't. He just had to be paranoid because in his situation…"

"Yeah." Sarge nodded. "I get that. I just… JD. Fuck."

"What the hell happened, anyway?" I asked. "I mean, why was he even working for Dorian?"

Bleeder grimaced. "Money. Fucker was up to his balls in debt. His ex was killing him for alimony, and he made some bad investments, and…" He waved a hand. "Anyway. He was desperate, and the Grimaldis probably just had to go down the list of people you're close to." He gestured at himself and Sarge. "I'm sure we were on the list too. All us assholes they interviewed about you before you got your clearance."

I winced. I'd let myself believe Leo was the weak link, but it was me and my personnel file—either at the Marshals office or the Marine Corps—that had provided them a list of people to use against us. Who else would I have called in a situation like this but my old trusted war buddies? All the goons had had to do was go down the list and find leverage on *one* of them. Hell, they'd probably started digging into my history and looking for weak spots the moment I'd gone on the run with Leo in the first place.

Sarge went on, "JD said he told the cops that the day before he got to town to help us out, he got a call from someone. Guy had loads of dirt on him, stuff that would cost him his clearance and any shot he had at a government contract, which is what he was trying to get so he could get his head above water again. They used that to get is attention, but what reeled him in for real was how much shit they knew about his kids. Where they go to school. Their class and extracurricular schedules. Even where their friends live. They weren't specific about what they would do with that information—what they might do to his kids—but once they played that card, it was all over."

I shuddered as much as my various wounds allowed. "They used his *kids* to threaten him?"

"Ain't much of a surprise, is it?" Bleeder asked.

"Nah, I guess not." And it really wasn't. Not in a crime family run by a man who'd taken out hits on two of his own three kids.

"JD's good people," Sarge said. "We know he is. As soon as I realized he'd turned, I knew they *had* to have used his kids against him somehow. I can't think of anything else that would have made him turn on us."

I nodded slowly. It made sense. As much as I wanted

to kick the fuck out of JD for what he'd done to Leo, to me, to all of us, I *knew* him. People did crazy shit to protect their families, especially their kids. We'd seen that in combat zones. One of our boys had been killed by a young woman who thought we'd come to take or kill her kids. Why would one of our own be any different?

"Where is he now?" I asked.

Sarge gestured toward the hallway. "On a psych hold right now. He tried to hang himself in his holding cell, so the cops brought him here."

Bleeder nodded, grimacing. "Dude's a mess, and I don't mean physically. They had him sedated for a while, and every time he's even a little bit lucid, he starts crying and wanting to know why Dallas didn't just shoot him and be done with it."

"Fuck," I whispered. Then I said, "I want to see him."

"What?" Sarge shook his head. "Smoker. Dude. You need to rest and—"

"I *need* to see him," I pushed back. "And I think he needs to see me. He probably thinks I hate him right now."

Bleeder and Sarge both fixed skeptical looks on me, their eyes clearly asking if JD was right.

"He was protecting his kids," I said. "Yeah I'm fucking pissed, but… What am I supposed to tell him? That in the name of staying loyal to us, he should've let a mob assassin torture his kids in front of him?"

They glanced at each other, uncertainty written all over their faces.

"Listen," Sarge said. "We'll talk to his doc on the other floor. No promises, though."

"You focus on getting some rest." Bleeder gave my arm a gentle nudge. "Just take some Motrin and walk it off, wuss."

I laughed, which hurt. "Shut up, Captain Kotex."

Sarge barked a laugh and elbowed Bleeder. "And he has a new nickname."

"The hell I do!" Bleeder shook his head. "No way."

"Sorry, brother." I flashed him a toothy grin. "You're stuck with it."

Bleeder groaned and buried his face in his hands.

"You earned it." Sarge put an arm around Bleeder's shoulders. "Now let's let Smoker get some sleep. C'mon, Captain Kotex."

"Motherfucker…"

"Mr. Cody?" A nurse tapped her knuckle on the doorframe. "Are you up for another visitor?"

My heart sped up. There was no way they could have gotten Leo here that fast, but hope sprang eternal. Every time a visitor came, I had that short-lived surge of excitement that maybe this time it was him. "Yeah. Sure."

Not surprisingly, my visitor wasn't Leo, but my breath still hitched when he walked in.

Pale and exhausted, flanked by Bleeder and an armed guard, JD shuffled into my room. I held my breath. Christ, he looked like a walking, talking representation of how I felt. Like he was barely holding himself up. Like it hurt to breathe. The hospital gown and slippers were all wrong on him, but they seemed too heavy for the broad shoulders that had carried packs, weapons, and even wounded Marines across rugged terrain. The guard walking behind him was probably half his size, but I had no doubt he could have broken what was left of JD with little more than a glare and a half-hearted shove.

Holy shit, this was not the bouncy, squirrelly guy we'd all joked about needing horse tranquilizers just to sit still. He was always vibrating with energy and life. Today, he was just…broken.

"Smoker," he whispered as he came closer, moving like he'd taken more bullets than I had. "Jesus…" As he stopped beside the bed, he covered his face with his hand, and his voice came out as a ragged sob. "I'm so sorry, Smoker. Fuck, I am so…"

"Don't, man. I get it. They used your kids against you."

"Still. I turned…" He dropped his hand onto the rail and pushed out a breath. "I turned on my fucking *Marines*. I… Fuck, I almost got you and all the guys killed." With a grimace, he added, "And Leo. I… I fucking handed him over to—"

"JD." I shook my head. "Don't. Look, I'm not happy about it, but they threatened your kids. I wish you'd said something to us, let us help you out somehow, but man, you were protecting your kids. I… I get it." I didn't want to. I really didn't. I wanted to hate him and vow to put the motherfucker in the ground if it was the last thing I did. He'd nearly gotten me, Leo, and all of our buddies *killed*. He'd *turned* on us. Semper Fi, my ass.

But I couldn't, and it wasn't even because I was too weak and doped up to dig up some rage for him. Would I have been able to live with myself if something had happened to JD's kids because he was helping me protect Leo? That shit just wasn't as black and white as it should've been. If JD's body language were to be believed, his betrayal had hurt him more than it had any of the rest of us. *Combined.*

"I know you, JD," I said. "I forgive you, okay?"

He lifted his head and looked in my eyes. "I never would have done it. Not on my own. Not for the money. But… My kids…"

"I know." It took some work, but I gave his fingers a weak squeeze. "These are mobsters. They get shit done by any means necessary, and when they back you into a corner…"

Bleeder squeezed JD's shoulder, and more tears welled up in our broke buddy's eyes.

"I could've..." JD exhaled hard. "I could've grabbed my kids and brought them with me to Smitty's place. Hidden them with us."

"Dorian would've found us one way or another. You know damn well he and his boys wouldn't have stopped until they'd taken out your kids, and they would've made sure *you* survived."

He shuddered hard. "Just wish... Man, I panicked. I'm sorry."

"I know." I let my hand slide off his just because I couldn't keep it up there any longer. "We're good, okay? I just wanted you to know that."

He searched my eyes, and a few tears slid down his unshaven face. His chin quivered, and he looked away as his jaw worked and he clearly tried to pull himself together.

"Mr. Daimler," the security guard said quietly. "We need to let Mr. Cody get some rest."

JD nodded. He turned to me. "You're gonna be okay, right?"

"Yeah." I chanced a playful grin. "Gonna have way cooler scars than yours now."

He managed to laugh, but it was mixed with a sob, and he shakily wiped his eyes. Then he patted my arm and, without a word, turned to leave. Leaning heavily on Bleeder, he shuffled out of the room with the nurse and security guard on their heels.

I watched until they'd disappeared into the hall. JD didn't look back.

Alone in my room, I closed my eyes and released a long breath. What happened to JD from here wasn't up to me. I'd be asked to make a statement at some point, and I'd present the objective facts as I understood them, but his fate was in the hands of the cops, the DA, and likely a jury of his peers. From there it would depend on how much they believed his show of remorse—and I couldn't see how anyone wouldn't believe he was truly broken by what he'd done—and whether they sympathized with an ex-Marine who'd been blackmailed with not just his financial security but quite possibly with the lives of his children. I'd taken two bullets and nearly lost Leo because of him, and even I couldn't make myself hate JD.

I just hoped a jury felt the same.

Each passing day felt worse than the one before it. My body was healing slowly but surely, and the doctors and physical therapists reassured me at every turn that even if it was frustrating now, I would be able to walk...*almost* normally. The muscles in my thigh had to heal, not to mention those in my core, and it would just take time. I had a cane for now and I'd probably always have somewhat of a limp, and the kind of running I'd done daily since boot camp was behind me now, but I'd walk.

I was pretty sure I now held the record for the shortest career in the history of the US Marshals. They'd saved me the trouble of quitting—my injuries meant I was no use in the field. Even if the physical problems hadn't left me permanently benched, there was no hiding the PTSD anymore. Not after a few flashback episodes in the ICU, two of which were witnessed by my handler. Whether I liked it or not—and quite frankly I liked it just fine—my days as a deputy marshal were over.

My Marines had all gone back to their respective homes, scattering to the wind like we'd all done after we'd been discharged. They'd be called back to testify, but for the moment, they were returning to their normal lives.

Two weeks after the shootout by Smitty's silo, I was

still in the hospital thanks to a follow-up surgery and subsequent infection, but they finally transferred me back to Chicago so I was within easy reach of the DA and anyone else with questions. I spent a week in the hospital in Chicago with armed guards outside my room 24/7. When I was discharged, I was taken to a safehouse to await the various trials. The deputy marshal-turned-witness in Marshal custody. How fucking poetic.

My days were spent sleeping, answering questions, being ferried to and from grueling physical therapy, and waiting, waiting, waiting for the trials that would end all this bullshit.

I was numb to all of that, though. It was impossible to feel anything about my job or my future because Leo's absence throbbed like the exposed nerve of a broken tooth. Physical pain sometimes drove me to the brink of tears, especially during physical therapy, but it was when I tried to sleep alone that I actually let them come. Falling asleep with nothing but covers and empty space, waking up from nightmares without that comforting voice and gentle but firm touch, opening my eyes in the daylight and knowing he hadn't just gotten up to go get coffee—it hurt every time, and it wasn't getting any easier. I hadn't even known Leo existed until a handful of weeks ago, and now I felt his absence as acutely as I felt my inability to walk without a cane—like something that had always been there, and now it was gone.

On day... I don't know, 7,031? Vanessa showed up at the safehouse. I hadn't seen heads or tails of her since I'd been in the ICU. Now she was here, and from her expression, she was pissed about something. That was...unnerving.

"We need to talk," she said as she stepped into the apartment I was "living" in.

"Um. Okay." I motioned for her to follow me, and the other marshals made themselves scarce. I was moving better now, aided by the cane that my physical therapist insisted I wouldn't need forever, though she didn't always sound as convincing as she probably meant to. At least I was getting around.

I hobbled over to the couch and, with some swearing because *fuck* I still hurt all over, I sat down. I leaned the cane against the armrest so I could still reach it and did my level best to get as comfortable as my battered body was capable of.

Vanessa sat primly in a chair beside the couch, and she didn't waste any time. Inclining her head, she glared across the small space between us. "I need to know the nature of your relationship with Leotrim Nicolosi."

I raised my eyebrows. "Huh?"

Her expression didn't change. "I believe I was clear enough."

"The Marshals assigned me to protect him." I swallowed. "What more is there to tell?"

She stared at me. I stared at her. My heart was thumping because there was no telling how much she knew or how much she thought she knew. I doubted Leo had told her the truth about us. He'd been born into organized crime. "*Omertà*" had probably been his first word. If Vanessa believed there was something between Leo and me that shouldn't have been there—which of course there was—it hadn't come from him.

Apparently fed up with the staring contest, my handler took and released a long breath. "Cut the crap, Cody. Is your relationship with Mr. Nicolosi the professional relationship as spelled out in your assignment?" Her eyes narrowed *just* slightly. "Or is there something more that I should know about?"

"Such as…?"

"You tell me."

"You asked. I assume there's some reason."

Vanessa pushed out an impatient breath. "Well, in the hospital, you were all but pleading with me to see him. Now Nicolosi has ceased cooperating with the DA, the

Marshals—essentially, everyone. He refuses to speak to anyone until two things have occurred." She ticked them off on her fingers. "One, that he has confirmation that Gianna Grimaldi is safe. Two..." She glared at me. "That he sees you. Not talks to you on the phone. Not gets a recorded message. Sees you. In person."

My heart fluttered. It took all the control I had to keep my expression neutral, but deep down, I was freaking out with excitement and relief. He hadn't forgotten me. He still wanted to see me. Hell, he was taking a huge risk and *demanding* to see me. With my tone as even as I'd hopefully kept my expression, I said, "So, what's the problem?"

Vanessa folded her hands in her lap again. "Why is he so fixated on you?"

"He trusts me." I shrugged tightly. "That happens when you've—"

"Is that all there is to it?"

Again, we stared at each other. I weighed my answers. It was possible she didn't know. It was possible she *did*. At this point, she couldn't exactly have me fired, but I couldn't be positive that the revelation wouldn't have some effect on my long-term disability claim. Since my misconduct predated my injury, and I didn't exactly have the HR handbook in front of me to confirm all the pertinent policies, it wasn't a risk I could afford to take. Not with the sheer volume of medical bills I was almost certainly racking up thanks to Dorian's bullets.

No, I had to keep my relationship with Leo quiet. Especially since I didn't even know how to define it.

So I looked in my handler's eyes and said, "Have you ever been to combat?"

Her brow furrowed. "What?"

"Have you or haven't you?"

"No, I haven't."

"So you don't know what it's like to be out in the field somewhere, surrounded by enemies who could take you out at any time and from any direction, do you?"

"I'm not sure how this—"

"You don't know what being in that situation with someone does to your relationship with them."

She blinked.

I shifted, wincing at the pain in my gut and my leg. "It changes you. It has to, or else people get killed. Those boys who were at the silo with us? They've been in combat with me. We've walked through fire together. We've *taken* fire together. That's…" I swallowed gingerly. "That's a bond no one understands unless they've had it with someone."

She huffed, impatience radiating off her. "Yet one of those men betrayed your team and—"

"And sobbed on my shoulder afterward because the only thing that could make him betray his Marines like that was someone threatening his kids."

"I fail to see what this has to do with your relationship with Nicolosi."

"Have you read my statement about everything that went down after that massacre in Chicago?"

"Of course I have."

"Okay?" I raised my eyebrows. "And you still can't put the pieces together?"

Her lips thinned. "I'm questioning whether this is as simple as brothers-in-arms."

"If you think there's anything simple about that, then I don't even know where to start. There have been occasions over the last few weeks where he could have easily let me die while he slipped away and vice versa. But we didn't. Right now, Leo doesn't have a lot of people left he can trust, and God knows he's had plenty of justification not to trust the Marshals." I set my jaw and returned her glare. "So if he wants to see me now, and he's jeopardizing his own freedom and safety to force your hand, then maybe you should be making calls to get him and me in the same place instead of wasting your time trying to conjure up some bullshit relationship between me and him."

Vanessa blinked, drawing back slightly.

"How unsafe does he have to feel right now?" I went on. "He knows what's at stake if he pisses off the DA or the Marshals. He was also nearly killed multiple times while in marshal custody. If he's digging his heels in and demanding to see me…" *Then God, please, give him what he wants, because I need to see him too.* "Then he's worried, and he's scared. So how about we quit playing games with trying to see something that isn't there and give the man what he wants before he blows this entire case?"

She set her jaw and glared at me. My heart pounded because I was sure she could see right through my tirade and all the way to the parts that physically ached from this long and growing separation from Leo.

Finally, she sighed, shoulders dropping with what I hoped was defeat. "Fine. I'll see what I can do to arrange a visit between the two of you." She stabbed a finger at me. "But the two of you had damn well better cooperate with the DA, or Nicolosi might find himself—"

"What? Out on his own and at the mercy of the people the DA is trying to put behind bars but can't without his help?"

She pursed her lips. Then she rose. "I'll be in touch."

As she stalked out of the room, I exhaled, sagging back against the couch.

And I silently begged anyone who was listening to let me see Leo soon.

Chapter Twenty-One
Leo

One of the maxims I'd modeled my life around was not to get powerful women mad at you. Powerful men were by and large predictable, especially in the mafia. They'd rage and roar and pull a gun or set somebody on you, and you'd either fight it out or you'd come to terms. Women, though... I had never met one that I could predict like that. Not my mother, not Gianna, not the capos' wives. Women were too good at hiding their edges for me to ever think I saw all there was to see with them, and the powerful ones would cut you as soon as look at you.

Which is why it was pretty dumb of me to be blatantly manipulating not one, but two powerful women with significant control over my life, but it wasn't the first time I'd done something dumb for Rich's sake. Hell, at this point it probably wasn't even the hundredth time.

"Threatening to derail *months'* worth of work just because you haven't seen your babysitter in a few weeks?

225

Leo, are you insane?" my lawyer demanded, standing over me with her hands on her hips. In her power suit and heels, Dawn St. James could have been a corporate dominatrix. "If this stonewalling gets back to the judge, I can't guarantee the deal we've worked out for you will stand."

"I don't care about the deal."

Dawn narrowed her eyes and huffed. "Well, you should care about it, seeing as it's going to ensure you don't get hunted down and murdered once you're done with this fiasco. Look, Vanessa is fine with us setting up a phone call—"

"That's not good enough." I hadn't seen Rich since he'd been bleeding out in front of me on the forest floor. I should have insisted I go with him, should have done *something* to make sure he was all right, but I'd frozen. It would have worried me if I had a more active future stretching out ahead of me, but as it was, WITSEC wanted to set me up as a forensic accountant in a specialty firm somewhere. Hiiiiilarious. "I already told you that this was nonnegotiable."

Dawn made a *pfft* noise. "Nothing is nonnegotiable."

"This is."

Another fifteen minutes of fighting led to her stalking out with a vague promise to "see what I can do while keeping you out of prison." Gianna laughed quietly at me from the wingback chair in the corner of the room. I couldn't believe that seeing *her* had been easier than getting a meeting with Rich. Femme fatale whose family is going on trial? Sure! Your former marshal, who you last saw barely breathing? No way in hell.

"It's a shame you weren't born into the family," she told me, a little wistful. "You would have made a fascinating capo."

"Nah," I said, picking at the bedspread with a fingernail. The cloth wasn't polyester, at least, although the brown color didn't do it any favors. This whole fucking room was brown, or shades of beige and tan with weird salmon and periwinkle accents. Gianna stood out like a Titian surrounded by a bunch of kitschy Kincaid prints, in a dark red dress that rode high on her thighs and black leather boots. "They'd have gone after me even faster if I'd been a made man. I'm kind of amazed Tony was able to survive as long as he did. I can't have been his first guy."

"You were the only one he was ever serious about."

"And look where that got him." I rubbed my hand down my face. "Fuck, maybe I should just let Rich get on with his life. I've almost gotten him killed so many times since we met... Maybe he's sick of me, maybe—ow!" I rubbed my shoulder, which throbbed from the paperback she'd swiped off the table and chucked at me hit. "Jesus, what was that for?"

"That was to stop you from making more of an idiot of yourself." She pointed a sharp-nailed finger at me. "Rich has gone to extraordinary lengths for you. It's absolutely impossible that he doesn't want to see you right now. Maybe things between you will change, but that's not a decision you should make on your own. Besides." She sat back and crossed her legs. "You just made a stand. If you take it back now, Dawn will walk all over you."

"Good point." She was right; I couldn't back down now. I was banking hard on the feds needing me to help deliver their prosecution of the Grimaldis. I was their ace in the hole. I was the whole reason they had a case to begin with, never mind all the evidence to back it up. While I wasn't their star witness anymore—that was Matteo Grimaldi—I was still a key player. As long as they needed me, I had leverage to get what I wanted. And I wanted Rich.

I glanced at Gianna. "As long as I'm annoying people, do you need anything from these guys?"

She smiled slowly at me. "Now that you mention it..."

It took five days of arguing, cajoling, and generally being a pain in the ass, but eventually I ended up sitting alone in the empty chambers of a judge—not the one who was presiding over the Grimaldi trial, of course—in the George N. Leighton Courthouse, in a suit that was too big for me, waiting for Rich to show up. I was literally going to start testifying in an *hour*, but Dawn had briskly told me that it was impossible to see Rich any sooner, that I should be grateful for any time I got, and that at the very least, here I could be assured that nobody was going to be listening in. I wasn't so sure—this was Chicago, after all, and stranger things had happened in the courts of law than a listening device in a judge's chambers—but it didn't matter. Nothing mattered until I saw Rich.

Gianna had already left, benefiting from the wheeling and dealing I'd done to get her released without any charges or any need to testify as long as I crucified myself on the stand for long enough. Getting her out of this fiasco was good, not to mention necessary. She needed to get back to her kids, to prove to her ex and his lawyer that she wasn't going to drag them into her family drama, and that she could distance herself from everything Grimaldi. I was glad she'd come to me when we both needed help but happier she was gone now.

I paced the chamber irritably, looking at the clock on my phone over and over again. 12:01. 12:02. They were supposed to get Rich here at noon on the dot, and I was supposed to take the stand at one, right after the lunch break. The courthouse was filled with reporters, the families of victims, with looky-loos and lawyers and probably more than one hitman. It wasn't a safe place for Rich, but then—where was safe anymore?

The door cracked open for a moment, letting the hubbub of the action outside filter in. I whirled and stared at it, but for a long moment no one entered. I was getting ready to grab the brass statue of Lady Justice off the desk before the door opened a little farther and Rich slipped through.

It had been almost a month since I'd last seen him. He

looked tired, the lines around his eyes and mouth deeper than I remembered. The suit he wore was too big on him as well, although it was probably because he'd been losing weight in the hospital, not because he was borrowing one like I was. His hair was shorn short, almost too short to make out the color of it, and he made grudging use of the cane in his left hand.

He was alone. He was standing. He was *alive*. He looked like the best thing I'd ever seen in my fucking life.

"Wire?" I whispered as I stepped toward him.

Rich shook his head. "No. You?"

"No." I moved closer but clenched my hands at my sides. I wanted to grab him and reel him in tight to me, but... "Shit, shouldn't you be in a wheelchair or something? Are you missing a kidney? Gallbladder? Half your liver?"

"The shot was the wrong side for the liver," Rich said, pointing to just under his left ribcage. "The bullet went in over here."

Oh right, I remembered now. The blood had seeped through his clothes so fast, pinpointing the location of the shot had been a challenge. "Ah."

"Leo." He shifted his weight a little, then held his free hand out to me. I took it, and all of a sudden it was like being there again—in the woods, surrounded by gunmen, Dorian shouting at us to give up, give in, there was no point and we were only going to be tortured to death if we made it any worse... "*Leo.*"

Both his hands were on my shoulders a second later, his cane forgotten as he gripped me tight enough to bruise.

"Leo, deep breaths, okay? In with me, come on." He put my hand on his chest so I could feel the rise and fall of his ribcage. "And out. In...and out. It's okay."

After a few more seconds I could breathe again, and then I felt really stupid.

"Christ, stop it," I muttered, brushing a hand over my wet eyes and using the other one to support his side—the side that hadn't been shot—and assist him over to a seat. "Stop helping me. I'm supposed to be helping you."

"I think at this point we're even on that particular score." He sat down with a little groan, then startled when I sat in front of him, right there the floor. Fuck keeping this goddamn suit tidy—my legs literally wouldn't support me any longer, and I wasn't going to crawl across the room and grab the judge's rolling chair just to keep us at an even level.

"I never knew it was possible to be this happy and also this freaked out at the same time," I confessed. "I'm not... I don't know why I'm acting like this."

"Well, the last time you saw me was a little stressful," Rich pointed out. "Your body is just still working through what your mind already knows." He shrugged. "Or at least that's how somebody who actually went to therapy for his PTSD put it to me once, I don't know." His hand moved to the back of my neck, squeezing gently. "It's good to see you."

I choked out a laugh, and the tension inside my chest unknotted. All crappy circumstances aside, it was really fucking good to see him again. "You too. Even though you look like shit."

"Blame my physical therapist. She's a menace."

"Are you kidding me? You're up and walking after being shot twice not so long ago; I want to send her a bouquet." I sighed and leaned my head back, looking Rich in the eyes. "Not that I can, since I technically don't have access to any of my accounts, but..."

"Technically?"

I smirked. "You could call it a technicality, actually. I'm not allowed to do anything that makes my keepers nervous until the trial is over, and that includes fiddling around with computers. They won't even let me have a cellphone."

Rich frowned. "That sucks."

"Yeah. They were really unhappy that I wanted to

meet with you."

"Same here." His frown lines deepened. "My handler in particular was pretty opinionated about it."

Of course, now *these assholes can be bothered with proper conduct and propriety, after we cleaned house for them.* "I bet. I got to listen to an entire spiel about how once the trial is over, my life as I know it is too, and how I have to say goodbye to everyone and everything, including you. *Especially* you."

Rich, already sitting pretty gingerly, went still. "I—I understand that. I've… Do you…"

Oh please, he couldn't be thinking what I thought he was thinking. "You don't actually believe I bought any of that, right? There's no way in hell I'm giving you up now, not unless you pry me off your leg with a goddamn crowbar and beat me unconscious with it."

Rich grimaced. "I wouldn't blame you if you wanted a fresh start. Everything about the two of us has been pretty intense. We've gone from crisis to crisis, over and over again, with no break."

"I don't care about any of that," I insisted. "You think I was living an easy life with Tony? It was nothing but hiding and dodging and stealing a minute together here and there. I wouldn't even know how to have a normal relationship, and I don't want one either. Nobody out there—" I waved vaguely at the door. "—is gonna understand me, and I'm not gonna be able to trust them." My stupid eyes were watering again; I scowled as I swiped my thumb over my cheeks. "I don't want to be alone," I said frankly. "And the only person I know I want to be with is you. But if you're going back to the Marshals, I understand if you want to make this our goodbye." It might kill me, but I'd understand it.

"Leo, get up here." I let him turn me until I was upright, on my knees between his legs. He bent over to lean his forehead against mine, a little flash of pain sparking across his face at the bend in his abdomen before he settled again. "I'll never be a marshal again," he said,

231

and this time there was no pain in his face, none of the regret I expected to see. "For a lot of reasons, not just the bullet wounds. I don't feel right about going back, not without treating the panic attacks, and even if I did that, I'm not sure if I'd ever completely have faith in the people I work with again. I'm out. After the trial, I'm going to go home for a while, stay with my parents and heal up the rest of the way. And after that…I'm open to starting something new."

"Really?"

Rich ran his thumbs over my cheekbones. "Yeah. Jesus, Leo, you get that I love you, right?"

He said it first. I shivered like the air had just turned ten degrees cooler when inside I felt like a furnace had been lit underneath my skin.

"I love you too," I whispered, taking his hands in mine, then leaning in and kissing him softly. One kiss turned into two, into more, and it wasn't until the insistent knocking at the door broke through the reverie that I realized my knees were aching and my neck was sore. We had been at this for a while.

"Leo!" It was my lawyer. "Two-minute warning. We need to go over your testimony again before you take the stand."

Of course we did. We'd only practiced it ten times in the twenty-four hours.

"Got it," I shouted toward the door. I looked back at Rich. "You're going to your folks' house?"

"Yeah," he said, his voice a little rough.

I remembered the code he and his dad had, the one that clued them into each other's status using sports metaphors.

"They might get a weird message once the trial is over. It might be about the Seattle Seahawks or the Denver Broncos or the Atlanta Braves. You should tell your dad not to delete it until you've listened to it."

"Their number isn't listed."

"I've watched you dial it," I said dryly. "That's enough of a listing."

Rich smiled. Really smiled, a wide, boyish smile that made him look ten years younger. "Just don't make it the Detroit Lions, okay? I can't take rooting for a team that sucks so bad."

"You lived and worked out of Chicago for years. You don't get to talk about bad teams," I replied.

The door rattled on its hinges again. "One minute, Leo!"

"She should work for NASA," I muttered. "Look, I don't know how long the trial will take. Don't stick around for it, okay?" Dawn and Vanessa had gotten Rich out of testifying due to his injuries, and I was all about that. The fewer of us that had to be dragged through the mud, the better.

"I can't. It's part of my deal with Vanessa."

"Good, then she's not a moron." I kissed him again. "I love you," I said, and it came easier this time. Maybe one day I'd be able to say it without feeling like my heart was going to burst out of my chest. "Go home, get better."

"I will." He framed my face with his hands and looked at me intently. "Don't chicken out on me, Leo. I'm gonna be waiting to hear about the Saints."

"Ha! We're not *that* lucky." I joked, but in truth I felt reassured. "I promise," I said, and I meant it with every cell in my body.

"Good."

The trial of Lorenzo Grimaldi was long and terrible and involved reliving a lot of awful things and telling a lot

233

of horrible truths. It lasted for a full two weeks, and over the course of it, there was one more clumsy attempt to kill me and a lot of other people via a pipe bomb in a backpack, but the cops found it and the idiot trying to smuggle it into the courthouse before it became a problem. My official questioning took place over the course of three days, and after that it was Matteo's show, but I still had to be there for all of it. Apparently, the whole thing was an internet sensation—but for once I didn't want to steal someone's phone and check the news. I was happy to let the interest and furor pass me by.

Papa Grimaldi was found guilty on multiple counts of murder, assault, racketeering, conspiracy to commit fraud, and a dozen other charges. His sentencing wouldn't happen for a while yet, but I didn't have to stick around for that, and the marshals didn't want me to. My part was finally done. I had justice for Tony and for a lot of other people I'd never met. The Grimaldi family was out of the game in Chicago.

It should have felt like an accomplishment, but mostly I was just tired. Before meeting Rich, I'd known what I'd do at this point—I had money, and I was good at evasion. I was going to get to Florida, take a boat to Cuba, and fly from there to whatever tropical beach I wanted to spend the next part of my life on. Sticking around to play nice with the marshals hadn't been in the cards, but now it was my gateway to reconnecting with Rich. I needed to play nice, so I didn't even smirk when Vanessa took over my preparations, working fast to get me as far from her agency as possible.

Less than a week after the trial wrapped, I was given a new identification, a job, and a place to live somewhere I'd never even heard of before, much less been to. The marshals were as eager to get rid of me as I was to go. No more people up my ass telling me what to wear, when to eat, or how long I got to spend in the bathroom. Heaven.

Honestly, the worst part about relocating? Realizing

that Maine had no professional sports teams. I had to leave Rich a message about the fucking New England Patriots.

Epilogue
Rich

A few months later

That had to be the twelfth Moose Crossing sign I'd seen since crossing the state line. I was definitely not in Chicago anymore. Or Boston, for that matter.

As far as anyone who mattered knew, former Deputy Marshal Richard Cody absolutely *was* still in Chicago or at least a suburb. Somewhere in Illinois, anyway. Only a handful of people were aware that Jason Matthews had flown into Logan International three nights ago and left Boston this morning in a newly leased Toyota. On Monday, he'd start a new job teaching history to middle school kids in Bar Harbor, a small tourist town on the coast of Maine.

My handler was not happy. The lawyers, the Marshals, and basically anyone who'd been involved in this were not happy. I wasn't on the Grimaldis' shit list, so I didn't need to be hidden away while law enforcement finished off the family and its remaining devotees. They were very sorry that I'd grown close to my witness and wanted to be with him, but policy was policy, and putting us together was very much against that policy.

Now, normally I wasn't one to use nepotism to get what I wanted, but quite frankly, the Marshals owed me one, and my dad agreed. So he'd made calls and used every connection he had to call in an entire career's worth of favors, and despite lots of grumbling and bitching, he'd gotten his way. I suspected the surrender had ultimately been to get me and my father to shut the fuck up, but I didn't really care as long as I got what I wanted.

Starting today, I'd have what I wanted, and I only had about eighty miles to go.

Around Bangor, the signs started mentioning Bar Harbor, and each time I passed one, my heart went wild. I was vibrating with excitement, but also sick with nerves.

Thing was, Leo didn't know I was coming.

I had a feeling it was bullshit, but the Marshals had insisted that every time they made contact with someone in witness protection, it increased the risk of their cover being compromised. As my handler had put it, "We're not going to put him at risk by contacting him to let him know you're coming."

Fine. Whatever. They'd given me his location (which totally *was* against Marshals policy, but I didn't complain), issued me my new identity, and wished me the best of luck. I just had to hope that when I got there, all that earnestness in Leo's eyes before the trial hadn't faded during the months we'd been apart. For that matter, I had to hope he hadn't vanished into the wind—as it was, the marshals in charge of keeping track of him were making bets on how soon he ran.

Don't run yet, Leo. At least wait for me.

I gripped the wheel tighter and drove faster. He'd made contact when he'd reached his new location—a brief phone call that included a cryptic comment about the New

England Patriots—and that had been almost three months ago. I'd hoped to come sooner, but my recovery had had some setbacks, and I hadn't been able to contact him.

The moment of truth was happening today. Leo would either be there or he wouldn't. He'd either want me to stay with him or he wouldn't. If he didn't... Well, then I supposed Jason Matthews wouldn't show up to work on Monday, and Rich Cody would suddenly start looking for a job in Chicago.

It was so simple. Make or break. Heads or tails. Yes or no.

I couldn't say this was the *most* I'd ever had on the line—not after multiple combat tours and the number of times Leo and I had narrowly escaped Grimaldi bullets—but there was a lot riding on this. My entire future hinged on whether Leo opened the door or closed it. Had months apart been long enough for him to realize that our brief and harrowing time together wasn't enough to bank on this thing working out? Had he already moved on, met someone, and started a new life that had no room for me?

The highway took me through forests, wilderness, and small towns. Every mile was closer to Leo and deeper into a place that wasn't familiar at all. Some part of me thought I should stop being an idiot, turn around, and go back to my life as Rich Cody. Was I really giving up everything for a man I barely knew?

In my mind's eye, I saw his face right before he walked away for the last time. No one had ever looked at me like that. Like he was utterly terrified we'd never see each other again. Like I was staring straight into a mirror of my own deepest fears.

We've been through hell together. All I want is a chance to love you when the sun's out.

I crossed a bridge to Mount Desert Island. The highway split. Going left would take me toward Bar Harbor and Acadia National Forest. Going right... Well, it didn't really matter right now since I wasn't going that way, so with my heart in my throat, I followed the road to the left. Not far to go now.

The last several miles seemed to stretch on forever, but then when I turned down the driveway of the address I'd been looking for, the last few hundred miles may as well have been six inches. I was here already? Oh fuck.

Heart pounding, I followed the driveway to a light gray two-story house. There was a black Honda parked out front, and a bumper sticker read *Bad Cop, No Donut.* I swear, I almost cried. If that wasn't Leo's car, then I was the fucking Pope.

I shifted into park and shut off the engine. Now I could really hear my own heart, and I swallowed hard to keep myself from throwing up out of sheer nerves.

Okay. Here we go. Moment of truth.

I took another deep breath, then collected my keys and got out of the car. My leg was stiff after my flights and the long drive, and the muscles were still weak, so I grabbed my cane too. I was used to using it now; I'd made peace with the idea that it was either lean on the damn cane or pick myself up off the ground. Bruised ego versus bruised ass. Easy choice.

I carefully made my way up the concrete walk, and just as I took the first step onto the porch, a deadbolt clicked. Then another. A third lock disengaged, and as I cleared the top step, the door opened.

And there he was.

We both froze, staring wide-eyed at each other through the storm door.

Then he pushed the storm door open and took a cautious step out onto the porch. "Rich?"

I laughed because I was this close to breaking down. "Well, Jason according to my driver's license."

He blinked. "You're... You've got..."

I hobbled a bit closer. "Identity. Job." I gestured over my shoulder. "Car."

He glanced past me, lips parted. Then he met my eyes

again. "Are you serious?"

"I'm here, aren't I?"

Leo pushed out a ragged breath. He gave me the longest, slowest down-up, and when he reached my eyes, he whispered, "I can't believe you're here."

"I am." I swallowed. "Question is, do you want me to be?"

That seemed to break whatever spell had kept him still, and he laughed as he crossed the last bit of distance between us and threw his arms around me.

"Are you kidding?" He hugged me so tight I could barely breathe. "I've been losing my mind without you."

I squeezed my eyes shut and buried my face against his neck. I really was going to cry. I was so relieved to see him, and even more relieved that he wanted me here, and… I sniffled and stroked his hair. "I missed you so much."

Leo drew back a little, and there were tears clinging to his long lashes as he said, "You're not crying, are you?"

"Shut up." I cupped his face in my free hand and kissed him, and good God, I was home. Standing there on Leo's front porch in the middle of a place I'd never been, holding on to a man I'd only had for a short, violent time before I'd had to let him go, I was absolutely home. Every question I'd had on the way here, every doubt, every moment I'd second-guessed this insane plan to join him in witness protection—gone. Immediately. It would still take time to work out the kinks in our relationship and figure out how to live together without bullets flying, but I had never in my life been surer of anything.

He touched his forehead to mine. "Do you, um, have a place to stay?"

"Not yet." I licked my lips. "I only got as many ducks in a row as I needed to get here and be with you. Figured I'd sort out the rest once I was here."

He looked in my eyes. "You're giving up everything? I mean, they're not going to let you stay in contact with people. You know that, right?"

I nodded, smoothing his hair. "I know. It's temporary, though. The marshals and the feds are cleaning house, and they're doing it fast. My handler doesn't think we'll need to be here for more than a couple of years."

"Still," he whispered. "That's a couple of years away from—"

I kissed him again, and he melted against me.

"There are channels I can use to stay in contact," I said. "It's not going to be easy, but with as shitty as I've felt without you the past few months, I'm willing to do whatever it takes to be with you."

He stared at me, some of that disbelief from when I'd arrived returning to his expression. "For me? Rich, I'm just a two-bit hacker who had to turn state's witness to stay alive. I'm nothing special."

I shrugged. "And I'm just an ex-Marine who got in over his head as a rookie deputy marshal and wound up falling in love with his witness."

Leo held my gaze, then laughed and pulled me close to him again. Resting his head on my shoulder, he exhaled. "I'm just… I am so glad you're here."

And you have no idea what a relief it is to hear that.

"Me too."

He lifted his head and started to speak, but a high-pitched meow cut him off. He looked over his shoulder, and I craned my neck.

Inside the storm door, an orange tabby stood on its hind legs and just managed to get its chin high enough to look through the screen. "Meow!"

"You have a cat?" I asked.

Blushing, Leo turned a sheepish smile on me. "The house was kind of empty when it was just me. And I missed Inigo. So…" He gestured at the cat.

I laughed, shaking my head. "Are you going to at least introduce me to your cat? Or are we just going to hang out on the porch?"

He chuckled. "Okay, okay." He started for the door,

but paused. "Do you have stuff with you? Luggage?"

"Yeah, I…" I gestured at the car. "I figured I'd find a room somewhere and—"

"Rich." He rolled his eyes. "Shut up and bring your crap in the house."

"You… I mean, do you really want—"

"I've been going out of my mind without you." He put a hand over mine on top of my cane and kissed me lightly. "You'll be lucky if I let you out of bed long enough to go find a job."

"Well, I already kind of have a job, so—"

"Doing what?" He smirked. "Don't tell me you're taking people on those guided puffin-watching tours or something."

"No, I'm teaching at the middle school."

Leo blinked. "Seriously?"

"Yep. History."

He grinned, and it was that wicked grin that had made my toes curl during those precious quiet moments when we'd been able to fool around. "I might have to play out some of those student-teacher fantasies and—"

"Oh my God." I gave his hand a playful swat. "Just introduce me to your cat already, and we can talk about your dirty fantasies later."

He laughed for real, and holy shit, it was good to see him smile like that again. Then he gestured for me to come inside, and I hobbled into the house—into *our* house— with him, and his cat, and this uncertain but perfect future that lay ahead of us.

And for the first time since that massacre in a hotel hallway had turned my life on its head, I could truly breathe again.

The End.

About the Authors

Cari Z. is a Colorado girl who loves snow and sunshine. She writes award-winning LGBTQ fiction featuring aliens, supervillains, soothsayers, and even normal people sometimes

Cari has published short stories, novellas and novels with numerous print and e-presses, and she also offers up a tremendous amount of free content on Literotica.com, under the name Carizabeth. Follow her blog to read her serial stories, with new chapters posting every week.

Want to follow along or get in touch? No problem!

Website: http://cari-z.net
Email: carizabeth@hotmail.com
Twitter: @author_cariz

L.A. Witt is an abnormal M/M romance writer who has finally been released from the purgatorial corn maze of Omaha, Nebraska, and now spends her time on the southwestern coast of Spain. In between wondering how she didn't lose her mind in Omaha, she explores the country with her husband, several clairvoyant hamsters, and an ever-growing herd of rabid plot bunnies. She also has substantially more time on her hands these days, as she has recruited a small army of mercenaries to search South America for her nemesis, romance author Lauren Gallagher, but don't tell Lauren. And definitely don't tell Lori A. Witt or Ann Gallagher. Neither of those twits can keep their mouths shut…

Website: www.gallagherwitt.com
Email: gallagherwitt@gmail.com
Twitter: @GallagherWitt

CPSIA information can be obtained
at www.ICGtesting.com
Printed in the USA
LVHW101524260722
724458LV00016B/114